# Lady Mary's Revenge

Another Luke Tremayne Adventure
Deaths on the Medway England 1657

Geoff Quaife

Order this book online at www.trafford.com
or email orders@trafford.com

Most Trafford titles are also available at major online book retailers.



Print information available on the last page.

ISBN: 978-1-4907-7336-0 (sc)
ISBN: 978-1-4907-7335-3 (hc)
ISBN: 978-1-4907-7337-7 (e)

Library of Congress Control Number: 2016907494



*Trafford rev. 05/10/2016*

www.trafford.com

**North America & international**
toll-free: 1 888 232 4444 (USA & Canada)
fax: 812 355 4082

# THE LUKE TREMAYNE ADVENTURES

(In chronological order)

1648–49 *The Irish Fiasco*
*Stolen Silver in Seventeenth-Century Ireland*
(Trafford, 2008)

1650 *Chesapeake Chaos*
*Malevolence and Betrayal in Colonial Maryland*
(Trafford, 2009)

1651 *The Black Thistle*
*A Scottish Conspiracy 1651*
(Trafford 2010)

1652 *The Angelic Assassin*
*Criminals and Conspirators London 1652*
(Trafford 2011)

1653 *The Frown of Fortune*
*A French Affair 1653*
(Trafford, 2013)

1654-5 *The Spanish Relation*
*Murder in Cromwellian*
*England*
(Trafford 2007)

1656 *The Dark Corners*
*Malice and Fanaticism*
*Wales 1656*
(Trafford 2014)

1657 The Garden of Deceit
*A Daughter Sacrificed*
*England Early 1657*
(Trafford 2016)

1657 *Lady Mary's Revenge*
*Deaths on the Medway*
*England 1657*
(Trafford 2016)

# MAJOR CHARACTERS

## *Cromwell's Men*

| | |
|---|---|
| Luke Tremayne (colonel) | Cromwell's special agent |
| Sir Evan Williams (captain) | Luke's deputy |
| John Martin (lieutenant) | Luke's third in command |
| Bevan Stradling [Strad] | Luke's senior sergeant |

## *The Medway Garrisons*

| | |
|---|---|
| Thomas Digges (captain) | Commandant, Dockyard |
| Harry Proctor (lieutenant) | Infantry commander, Dockyard |
| Alexander Dewhurst (major) | Governor, Upnor Castle |
| Matthew Hatch (captain) | Deputy governor, Upnor |
| William Neville | Ordnance officer, Upnor Castle |
| John Neville [Red] (lieutenant) | Frigate commander |
| Michael Scot (lieutenant) | Dragoon officer, Dockyard |

## *Holt House*

| | |
|---|---|
| Prudence, Lady Holt | Wealthy and powerful widow |
| Richard Holt | Brother-in-law of Prudence |
| Roger Linton | Secretary to Prudence |
| Mercy, Lady Bartram | Daughter of Edward and Katherine |
| Sir Giles Bartram | Husband of Mercy |
| Elizabeth Bartram | Daughter of Giles and Mercy |
| Frances Bartram | Daughter of Giles and Mercy |
| Alicia Bartram | Daughter of Giles and Mercy |

| | |
|---|---|
| John Headley | Lawyer, Prudence's steward |
| Caroline Headley | John's wife |
| Charles Franklin | Prudence's bailiff |
| Barnaby Partridge | Vicar, and brother of Lady Mary |

## *Other Medway Inhabitants and Visitors*

| | |
|---|---|
| Billy Pratt | Medway fisherman |
| Tommy Pratt | Billy's brother |
| Sir Nicholas Lynne | Magistrate, former Royalist |
| Matilda, Lady Lynne | Nicholas's wife |
| David Harvey | Magistrate, former Royalist |
| Ralph Croft | Queensborough harbormaster |
| Simon, Lord Stokey | Leading Catholic peer |
| Simon Cobb (major general) | Commander, Flanders army |
| William Acton | Thurloe's deputy |
| Basil Miller | Dockyard corporal |
| Betsy Miller | Wife of Basil |

## *Key Persons Referred to, but now Deceased*

| | |
|---|---|
| Sir Arthur Holt | Prudence's late husband |
| Sir Edward Holt | Father of Arthur, Richard and Mercy |
| Katherine, Lady Holt | First wife of Edward, mother of Mercy |
| Mary, Lady Holt | Second Wife of Edward, mother of Arthur and Richard |

## ***Real Historical Personages***

| | |
|---|---|
| Oliver Cromwell | Lord Protector |
| John Thurloe | Cromwell's intelligence head |
| John Desborough | Leading general |
| Charles Stuart | Claimed English throne |

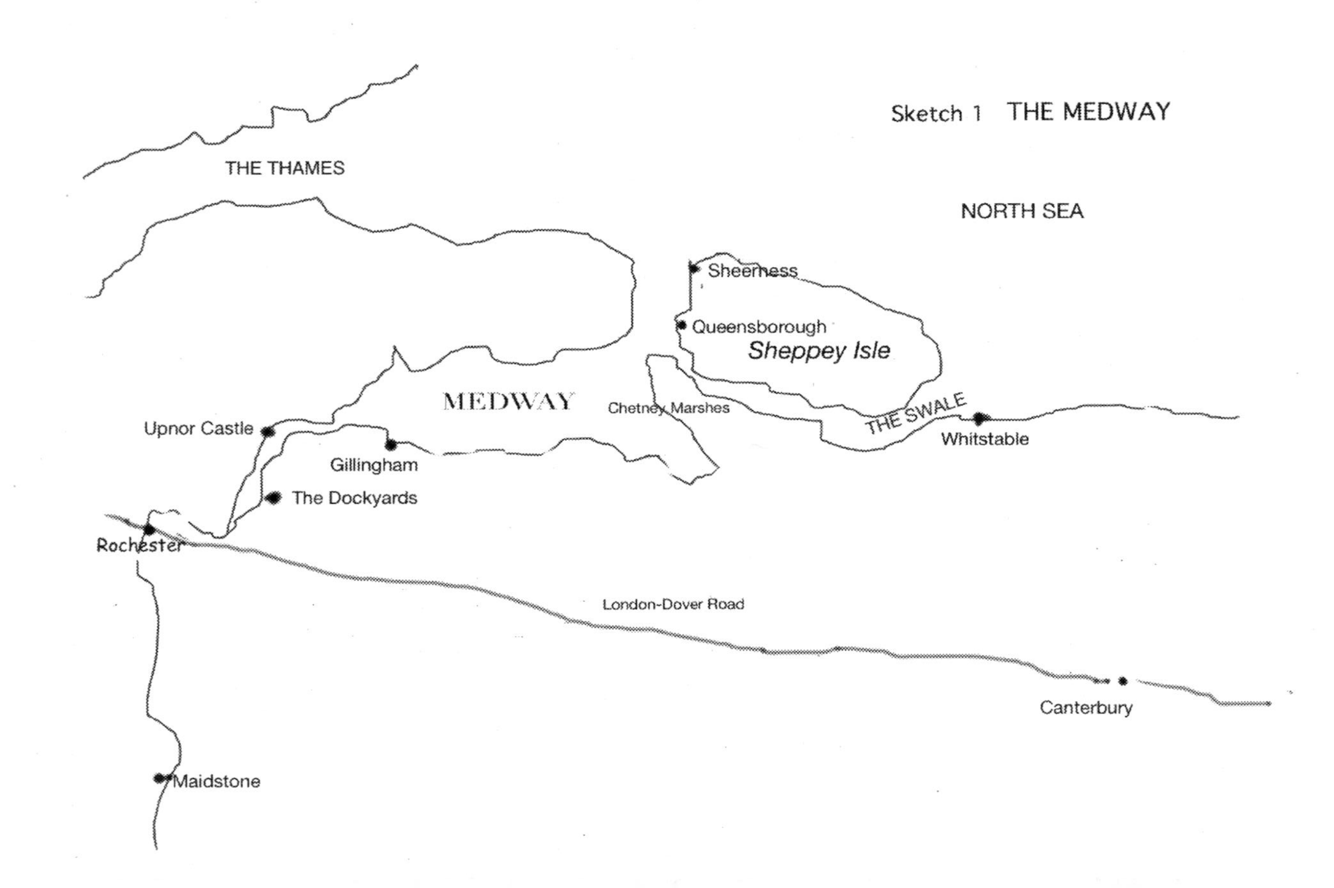

Sketch 1 THE MEDWAY
THE THAMES
NORTH SEA
Sheerness
Queensborough
Sheppey Isle
MEDWAY
Chetney Marshes
THE SWALE
Whitstable
Upnor Castle
Gillingham
The Dockyards
Rochester
London-Dover Road
Canterbury
Maidstone

# Prologue

In 1657, conspiracies were detected among Royalists, religious radicals, and disaffected senior officers of the army. Discontent was fueled by parliament's decision to offer Oliver Cromwell the Crown, remove the rule of the major generals, and increase taxation to continue the unpopular war with Spain. Royalists prepared for an invasion, awaiting only Spanish money and troops to launch the attack and an English port to accommodate the invasion fleet. Radicals saw the attempted recreation of monarchy as a betrayal of the principles that had driven them to remove Charles I. Senior army officers resented their potential loss of power in the increasingly civilian-dominated Cromwellian regime.

A military revolt on the Medway by maverick Royalist amateurs was so easily quashed that Cromwell was convinced that this episode was simply to test his government's responses and was a prelude to a serious foreign invasion supported by local gentry.

This gave government agents two simple and related tasks—stop the invasion and uncover the local gentry who would lead the Royalist uprising. This task was made more difficult as suspected public plots, and the countermeasures adopted to thwart them were often a cover for personal vendettas and dynastic feuds.

A personal friend of Oliver Cromwell reported the possible disappearance of a senior army officer in the sensitive strategic location of the Medway.

Luke Tremayne is sent to talk to this informant to assess the validity of the concern.

# 1

Luke Tremayne, Cromwell's top agent, sat uneasily in the parish church of St. Margaret, which was adjacent to the Chatham Dockyard—a vital location for repairing the warships of the English government.

His assignment was unusual.

He was to meet *a friend of the government* in this church at ten o'clock.

This *friend* would reveal the details of his new mission.

Luke despised self-proclaimed *friends of the government*.

He expressed such views to his companion, his sergeant Bevan Stradling, known to all as Strad.

"These creatures are vicious little people who manipulate the political situation to destroy their enemies by concocting fantastic tales of subversion and murder, allegedly aimed at bringing down the government. With luck, we will hear the drivel purporting to reveal an antigovernment plot, assess its total uselessness, and be back at Whitehall by nightfall."

As Luke waited, his anger increased.

Why send him on a mission of low priority, and of a personal nature, when the country was overwhelmed with serious conspiracies?

Several recent assassination attempts against the Protector had been foiled, and a dangerous insurrection in the army, very close to Chatham, had been suppressed only two weeks earlier.

The government viewed this failed Royalist conspiracy as a trial run by Cromwell's opponents for an imminent, more serious invasion and uprising.

Luke felt he could be better employed at this critical time.

The door of the church opened and three people entered.

Their features were initially obscured by the bright external light that streamed through the entrance. As they progressed down the aisle, Luke identified the first man as an elderly cleric. The next figure surprised him—a well-dressed woman of the upper classes. The third was a man more typical of an informant—a wiry person with sun-tanned skin, straggly hair, narrow eyes almost concealed by bushy eyebrows, and an unkempt beard. He wore a leather apron and emitted the nauseating odor of rotting fish.

Luke greeted them.

The vicar ignored him and turned to the woman. "My Lady, will I stay?"

"Leave, Mr. Partridge! I will speak to this gentleman alone."

She waved the fisherman to the back of the church and, with a look, suggested that Luke do the same with Strad.

She then moved into the most prominent pew and beckoned Luke to join her.

"Colonel, I am familiar with your record and I'm pleasantly surprised that Oliver reacted so quickly, and sent a man of your quality to investigate what might prove to be little more than gossip and prejudice. I am Prudence, Lady Holt, widow of Sir Arthur Holt, who was killed in suspicious circumstances when the Royalists rose in revolt in 1648. He was a passionate supporter of the army."

"As are you!" commented Luke, beginning to take an interest in the speaker, if not her information.

"A little more covertly, especially since Oliver became Protector. I have concealed my personal relationship with him, and even more so with the attempt to make him king. In such times, even the loyalties of your closest friends might change."

"And this special relationship with the Lord Protector?"

"My father and Oliver went to school together. He is my godfather, and he attended my wedding. Although I am a little older, I remain close to his eldest daughter."

"And why precisely am I here?"

"That's the problem, I'm not sure," replied Prudence.

Luke's mood, which had begun to mellow, now regressed to barely concealed irritation.

"You must have some reason for bothering Cromwell, and he ordering me here, when I could be hunting real conspirators in the alleys of London, or in the ranks of the army."

"It is within the army on the Medway that your most dangerous conspirators may lurk."

"Elaborate!"

"For the last five years, I have regularly informed Matthew Hatch, the deputy governor of Upnor Castle, on the political activities and loyalties of my neighbors. He has suddenly disappeared, and no one at the castle knows where he is. Billy Pratt, the fisherman here with me today, also reports strange events on the Medway."

"Lady Holt, do these events endanger national security, or the life of Oliver Cromwell?"

"The Medway is a mighty river estuary the control of which would bring any enemy army within striking distance of London. With its many islands and creeks, it provides an environment where such an army could be hidden until ready to strike."

"Who would make up this mythical army?" asked a now-acidic Luke.

"Troops that are at the moment outwardly loyal to the government. Admittedly it would take conspirators time to organize such subversion because the military and political situation in this area is complex and confusing."

"How complex?"

"There are government garrison troops manning Upnor Castle. This is simply a poorly defended artillery battery with its cannons pointed in one direction—to blast enemy vessels that might dare to venture down the main channel of the Medway. A clever navigator could keep his ship out of their range, and still attack the dockyard."

"Surely the dockyard has its own defense?"

"There is a company of infantry, and another of recently arrived dragoons to protect its infrastructure."

"This is a naval facility. Doesn't the navy contribute anything?"

"Informally! Ships under repair have their cannons removed, which are temporarily relocated on the main wharf of the dockyard. A group of naval gunners man these weapons. In times of panic, ships of the line are stationed off or in the estuary."

"There is no overall military control of such a strategic area?"

"Correct, there is none, but a civilian, the mayor of Rochester, has administrative control of the river as admiral of the Medway. He also has an army of law enforcement people such as water bailiffs, and a troop of local militia. Local magistrates call on his militia to enforce law and order."

"What a mess! The Medway is too close to London to allow it to become a center of antigovernment activity. It is also the destination of a rumored foreign invasion. If the Dutch or Spaniards land troops here, it would be a disaster. I am not sure if the latest local military development will improve the situation."

"What would that be?" asked an alert Prudence.

"The relocation of several regiments of newly recruited troops from the Chetney Marshes to just out of Chatham. They are to join the French against Spain in the Netherlands. A rogue general misled them a week or two ago to march against the government. They are relocated near here for further training until embarkation for Flanders."

Luke was surprised at Prudence's comment.

"I know. I own both the former and new location. I initially offered Oliver my Chetney estate, Austin Friars, for a training ground. He has since requested the more suitable Medway Court.

Perhaps the situation here warrants your attention after all. I must leave. Question Billy! He will direct you to my home, Holt House. Be my guest for as long as it takes! No need for false names, but I will introduce you as my cousin stationed at Whitehall, and leave the locals to guess the rest."

Lady Holt signaled for Billy to come forward and left the church by a side door.

Billy was in his mid-to-late twenties. He accepted Prudence's story that Luke was her cousin. He tugged at his forelock as he approached.

Luke asked him to sit beside him in the pew.

Billy was appalled at this breach of manners.

"No, sir! This is her ladyship's pew. I will stand at its gate."

Luke asked Strad to join them.

He then questioned Billy, "What's happening in the Medway that might concern me?"

"Six weeks ago, my brother and I were fishing late at night near the mouth of the river. We showed no lights. We were fishing in the wrong place at the wrong time. If caught we would be expelled from the Guild of Fishers and Dredgers, and our living taken from us. That is why I told her ladyship, and not the water bailiff or the mayor."

"Why Lady Holt in particular?"

"It was never intended by our father that my brother Tommy and I would be fishermen. Our two elder brothers were apprenticed for that role, and we went into service with the Holts as very young boys. When the Royalists revolted in 1648, both our elder brothers were killed defending Sir Arthur, and father, to maintain the family business, apprenticed us as fishermen in their place. We have only just been admitted to the guild."

"What are your rights and duties as guild members?"

"Protect the fish and crustaceans of the river, and inform the mayor or his officers of any developments that may be against the interest of the navy."

"You ignore your first obligation, but take the second seriously! What has worried you?" asked Luke.

"While fishing recently, a longboat of the type used on the warships, some of which lie moored to the wharf just a few yards from here, nearly collided with us. What surprised us was that it also showed no lights and was making its way towards the mouth of the Medway at such a late hour."

"Did you hear or see anything that would help you identify the boat or its crew?"

"Not that time, but a fortnight later, we were trawling nearer the mouth of the river. The same thing happened. A longboat just missed us. One of its crew protested that they had nearly hit another boat. Another voice shouted, 'Keep rowing! We have no time to stop.' Several hours later, we heard a boat returning which Tommy swears was the same vessel. It was much lower in the water than when it travelled downstream."

"As if it were laden with goods?" asked Luke.

"Or people?" added Strad.

"Anything else?" Luke continued.

"Four nights ago, we were near the east bank of the river itself when we were nearly run down by a large longboat. There were shouts of abuse from its crew, and then without warning, three or four shots were fired at us. One just missed Tommy, who was so incensed that he rowed after them. They easily outpaced us, but before they were out of earshot, we both heard a loud splash. Something large had been thrown overboard."

"Man or contraband?" asked Luke.

"Next day at low tide we rowed to the vicinity hoping to find something stranded on the mudflats. Nothing."

"Smuggling and the unauthorized movement of people are both illegal! Thanks, Billy."

"I'll show you to Holt House," he replied.

The three men left the church.

They walked to the riverbank where Luke and Strad had hitched their horses to a bollard on the wharf.

As they mounted, two shots rang out.

Billy, who was standing beside them, fell to the ground.

Luke and Strad dismounted and threw themselves lengthways behind a bollard.

Two more shots hit the iron bollards.

Considerable shouting erupted all along the wharf.

Dozens of men appeared.

Within minutes, three ship's cannon that had sat idly on the wharf were manned.

A naval officer ordered them to bombard the source of the musket fire on the other side of the river.

Much later, a troop of horsemen arrived and surrounded the would-be victims.

An officer dismounted and ordered Luke, Strad, and Billy to stand.

Strad replied, "No, sir, not until your men fire several volleys into the opposite bank. I will not stand up to be shot down."

"Enough of that impertinence. I am Lieutenant Michael Scot of the dockyard's dragoons. You are a stranger here, and will answer to my captain for your presence in this area, your provocation of that gunfire from across the river, and your refusal to obey my simple order."

Luke, still prone, spoke. "And *you,* Lieutenant, will obey my orders. I am a colonel of dragoons. Get some fire into the opposite bank, or you will answer to your captain and to a higher authority—me."

"If you are a colonel of dragoons, then I am the Lord Protector himself. Get up! Or I will have my men roll you into the river mud until you come to your senses. There is no need for my men to fire. Unless you are deaf as well as stupid, the naval gunners have already shelled the source of the gunfire."

The lieutenant ordered his men to dismount and to toss the recalcitrants into the rapidly emerging mud.

Just as Scot dismounted to oversee his order, two more shots were fired, one hitting the padded shoulders of his coat.

The naval bombardment resumed with three more salvos.

Luke moved across to examine Billy's inert body.

# 2

Luke knelt down to ascertain if Billy was still breathing.

Billy opened his eyes and winked at him. "Have they stopped firing? I learnt as a boy during the 1648 insurrection to fall to the ground and lie inert, whenever a shot was fired. I am unharmed."

Billy got to his feet just as the lieutenant changed his mind.

The three would-be victims were marched to his commanding officer.

Billy complained, "I am a fisherman of this river and I have just left my church. To prevent any member of our guild access to their place of worship is illegal. You have no authority over me, a licensed dredger of this river."

"You are consorting with strangers in an area that is sensitive to the government. Until your companions are identified, and cleared of possible subversion, you will come with them."

The three suspects were herded towards a brick building and pushed into the room where Scot reported to an officer seated behind a tiny desk.

"Sir, I have detained these three men on suspicion of subversion. The tall man claims to be a colonel of dragoons."

The captain rose from his seat.

He grinned broadly and berated his lieutenant. "You fool Scot! This is not any colonel of dragoons but the most senior colonel in all of England. If it were not for his own reluctance, he would be one of our leading generals. This is Colonel Luke Tremayne, who commands a special unit answerable only to the Lord Protector."

The senior officer gave Luke an exaggerated acknowledgement and shook his hand. "I am sorry, Colonel, for my subordinate's rudeness. I am Captain Thomas Digges. Until a few months ago, I commanded a dragoon company at Chepstow Castle, where you were also based for most of last year. I saw little of you as you were away most of the time uncovering plots and fighting Welsh rebels, but I was well aware of your status as the most senior officer in the castle. I was also present, as were you, at General Berry's council of war to save Hereford and Worcester from those insurgents."

Digges's demeanor suddenly changed.

His joviality was replaced by an anxious intensity.

"While my lieutenant's behavior is unforgivable, your very presence here, giving your particular talents, is worrying. What is so wrong on the Medway that the Lord Protector has sent you here?"

"As you are aware of my special role, you will appreciate my reluctance to say more than I am here to investigate developments that may threaten the security of the state."

"Someone must be aware of your mission to attack you so early in your assignment. You must have been the intended victim."

"No, I don't think so. Nobody in the area, except my cousin Lady Holt, knows my identity, and she would have no knowledge of my specific instructions," said Luke, lying to minimize the significance of the attack.

"The shots were aimed at the local fisherman here," said Strad.

"I know Billy," Digges commented. "Why would anyone be firing at you, my man?"

"There are many disputes among fishermen, Captain. It may even be a family matter. I will sort it."

Luke was impressed at Billy's presence of mind in directing attention away from security concerns.

"Excuse me a moment, Colonel. The government's dockyard has been fired upon and my officer has done nothing except arrest you. Scot, take a troop upstream to the bridge and then ride down the opposite bank to where the shots came from! Search the area well! Tell Proctor, if you can find him, that I want him to send three boatloads of his infantry across the river to assist you."

A chastened Scot withdrew.

Luke asked, "What is your relationship with the infantry?"

"The infantry have been here for four or five years. They were stationed at the dockyard during the Dutch wars, as it was feared that the Hollanders might destroy it. A reasonable assumption! A few months ago, my dragoons were dispatched here to patrol the larger area up and down the river for any signs of trouble. We were also to assist the county and town magistrates to maintain order should the local militia prove insufficient. I was made commandant of the dockyard garrison with Lieutenant Harry Proctor, the infantry commander, as my deputy. Normally our roles do not overlap. The infantry defends the physical precinct of the dockyard, the dragoons gather intelligence and maintain order in the surrounding countryside."

"Where is the infantry now? Those shots could have been the beginning of a full-scale attack. I have not seen a single foot soldier," observed an alarmed Luke.

"You ordered the absent infantry to cross the river. Do they possess many boats?" asked Strad.

"Yes and no. There is one former fishing boat located permanently within our precinct, but there are at times up to ten longboats from the ships undergoing repair that are available. They are used by soldiers and sailors alike to move across river or to the ships anchored along the Medway."

"Does anyone control their use?" asked Luke.

"Not really. If they belong to ships anchored in the river, then the ship's captain has sole authority. If they belong to ships that have been dry-docked or otherwise undergoing extensive repairs, the master shipwright under the authority of the commissioners of the navy has control. In practice, the naval gunners who man the cannons that have been temporarily removed from ships under repair, keep an eye on them. Why do you ask?"

"The illegal use of longboats in the middle of the night has been brought to my attention."

"I wouldn't waste time on that. Such excursions are innocent. At times sailors, musketeers, or even dragoons take a boat, load it with alcohol, and drift down the river."

"You condone such behavior?" asked a moralistic Luke.

"Yes! Garrison duty is boring. Drunken men aboard a boat at night can do less damage than if they were in the towns of the area, or on base."

"Surely there must be complaints?" asked Luke.

"The mayor of Rochester as admiral of the Medway complains that such behavior interferes with the fishing, and is a danger to shipping as almost invariably the boats show no lights, but he has taken no action to stop it."

"So stories that these nocturnal journeys involve the smuggling of goods or people in and out of the country using foreign vessels moored somewhere in the Medway, the Swale, or off Sheppey Island are false?"

"Most likely. I have not been in the area long enough to have any firm evidence. The water bailiffs have fast little skiffs patrolling the river to monitor such activity, and the watch at Upnor and Sheerness castles further down the river have similar responsibilities."

"Upnor Castle is outside your control?"

"Yes, the castle was seized by the Royalist rebels in 1648 and largely destroyed. When parliament had it rebuilt, it was given few defenses. It is little more than an artillery battery with large cannons pointed downriver. They cannot be used to defend the dockyard itself as they are imbedded in concrete, and cannot be turned more than a few degrees. It has no defenses on the landward side from which it would take only a small force to disable the guns, and then signal a fleet to proceed up river with impunity."

"Who controls Upnor Castle?"

"Its governor is Major Alexander Dewhurst, a very old artillery officer responsible to the master of ordnance in London. I have only met him once, and he seemed in a bit of a daze. The effective officer in the castle is his deputy, Matthew Hatch. The castle also serves as a prison for dangerous Royalist officers who are kept in shocking conditions. They are Kentish cavaliers who committed atrocities during the 1648 uprising, and whose lives were spared only because of their local position and influence."

"What about your deputy, Proctor?"

"A disgrace! Local gentry rather than professional soldier. He spends most of his time at home on the estate of a wealthy friend whose family brought him up after the early demise of his parents. He rarely visits his company. It suits me because if we should ever come under attack, Proctor would be a liability. He would surrender or run. His men despise him."

"He still receives his army pay?" probed Luke.

"Yes, but it is supplemented by a large allowance he receives from Lady Prudence Holt, his benefactor."

Proctor, and the military situation in general, began to interest Luke.

He summarized the complicated situation. "You command dragoons and infantry at the dockyard, there are sailors and their ships on the river or here within the dockyard, and we have an ordnance company downstream at Upnor Castle."

"This structure, or rather lack of structure, should help you unearth conspiracies. It is unlikely that all these groups could unite against Cromwell at the same time. Is that why you are here—to assess the loyalty of the army and naval units along the Medway?"

"Maybe—and the situation has become even more complicated. Half the army that the Protector is creating to fight alongside the French in Flanders against the Spaniards was raised around London, and was being trained in the eastern Medway where two weeks ago they were tricked into marching against the government. Those who have been retained are now in barracks not far from here at Medway Court."

"I am well aware of that crisis. We were put on alert and ready to resist, but a cavalry company from London stopped the insurgents without calling on our assistance. Were you involved?" asked Digges.

"Yes. The government now sees that pathetic effort as a deliberate and expendable trial by the Royalists to test our responses. We expect a more professional attempt at any time."

"You have brought the problem much closer to us. Medway Court is only half an hour away. It is typical of the creeks, mud plains, and higher grazing lands of the Medway estuary."

Tom changed the subject and asked, "Do you and your man need accommodation?"

"No, thanks, Tom, Billy will show us the way to Holt House."

"You are important! Holt House is the hub of the county elite—the political power base of the Medway. Our friend Proctor lives there. Be careful, Luke, they may not all be the loyal supporters of the government that they pretend to be."

The door burst open, and a redheaded man of immense proportions entered the room. "What is going on, Digges? The dockyard is fired on and all your men can do is to gallop up and down the wharf and arrest the men who were fired upon. Why arrest the victims? My sailors had several salvos away within minutes and I sent a few men across river in a fishing boat. I see that idiot Scot has just galloped off to Rochester. By the time he reaches the site of the attack, it will be Christmas."

"And good morning to you, John! Colonel Luke Tremayne, commander of a special unit, meet Naval Lieutenant John Neville, known to most around here as Red Nev."

"Welcome, Colonel. Did you provoke the attack, or was it discontented fishermen who know we favor the Pratts? Thanks, Billy, for that last meal of oysters. Delicious!"

"Luke could not be the target. No one, not even I, know his exact mission. He was just unlucky being with Billy when a few rivals tried to frighten him. If they were serious at that range, all three would be dead," commented Tom.

"Agreed. A marksman could not miss at that distance, but a fisherman is a different animal," commented Red Nev.

Red turned to Luke and Strad. "Do you fish? When you have a spare moment, join me and trawl for a decent meal."

"Isn't that illegal? Only members of the Fishers and Dredgers Guild can fish," said Luke with tongue in cheek.

"True, and that is why I always go out with Billy or his brother. In return for this help, the dockyard buys all of its fish from the Pratts."

"When out fishing in recent weeks, have you noticed anything unusual?" asked Luke.

"Plenty" was the unexpected reply.

# 3

Red had second thoughts. He knew nothing of this colonel from Whitehall. Discretion was called for. He changed the subject.

"Time to eat! Let me show you a tavern with the best roast lamb and ale in the county. Billy, return to your fishing! I will show these gentlemen the way to Holt House. Tom, will you join us?"

Digges declined.

Billy disappeared.

Red walked with Strad and Luke as they led their horses across the marshy hinterland of the dockyard onto the higher ground on which the village of Gillingham was located.

The three men were soon settled beside a blazing fire in The Black Eel.

Reacting to a signal from Red, the buxom barmaid brought pint mugs of the lightest ale Luke had seen.

Red asked what else she had to offer. She giggled at his deliberate innuendo but suggested a choice of bread, cheese and chutney, roasted portions of lamb, or the tavern's specialty, eel stew.

Strad ordered the stew.

His senior companions preferred the lamb.

Luke asked, "What did you see, and why did you not want to discuss it in front of Digges?"

"Nothing against Digges. He is a marked improvement on most of the army officers in the region, but he is new. His predecessor as commandant was the outrageous Proctor who still draws his pay for doing nothing, except plot and scheme his own advancement. If there is something amiss on the Medway, start with Proctor!"

"What's amiss?"

Red was still suspicious of this inquisitive stranger—safer to outline some relevant local history and avoid the direct question.

"I am a Medway man, born just out of Rochester to a strong parliamentary family. My uncle, a bitter opponent of Charles I, was in the Long parliament. I was sent to sea as the youngest son in my family, and have served much of it with my younger neighbor Richard Holt, the only brother of the late Sir Arthur. When our ship suffered damage during a recent encounter off the coast of the Azores, we returned home for repairs. During this period, the captain retired, and the crew were stood down. I used my local influence to obtain my current position in the dockyard awaiting the repair and refitting of our ship, *The Valiant*. I am its new commander, with Holt as my deputy."

"Congratulations! You have an excellent social, political, and naval pedigree, so what is it in the current situation here that worries you?"

"Changes of mood. Since I have been ashore, I have attended several social occasions among the solidly anti-Royalist gentry. There is growing disillusionment with the Lord Protector among the more radical of the group, especially with his attempt at reconciliation with our Royalist opponents. The latest list of magistrates removed many of our people and replaced them with former Royalists. Loyalty to the government as is is one thing. Loyalty to a new monarchy under King Oliver is another—a dangerous unknown. Would you, a devoted supporter of the Lord Protector, continue to serve Oliver if he accepted the Crown?"

"I hope I will never face that problem. The army is exerting all its influence to persuade Cromwell not to take such a step. It is bad enough isolating his current enemies. If his closest friends move into that camp, the intelligence officers of the government, including myself, will be placed in an impossible position."

"I have a second worry. The military in this area, apart from the new fellow Digges, are incompetents, has-beens, or former Royalists. Hatch at Upnor Castle seems capable and outwardly loyal, but I have heard he is too friendly with the Royalist prisoners. Apart from doubts about their basic loyalty, even if these officers stayed with the government, they would be incapable of defeating local insurgents, let alone foreign invaders."

"I'm here to assess the strength of any threat to the government, the effect on loyalty should Cromwell accept the Crown, and how effectively government forces would respond to a crisis. In the last month, the government received a fright with the defection of the general responsible for the training of new troops. The attempted insurrection was so badly handled by our enemies that it was probably a trial run to test our responses, and that the real invasion is imminent, and will be much better organized."

"The specific event that alerted me to possible problems occurred while fishing with Billy Pratt a week or so back. Just before first light we heard the rhythm of well-trained oarsmen sweeping down towards us. A boat full of people passed our position just as daylight broke, heading for the mouth of the estuary."

"A boatload of drunken soldiers or locals enjoying a ride on the river?" queried Strad.

"It could be—except for two things. The oarsmen were professionals, and the boat was not local."

"How could you tell in such poor light?"

"Apart from the time spent at sea, I have spent all my life here. I know the shape of every boat on the Medway, and within our naval service. This boat had a square stern."

"It was Dutch?" asked Luke.

"Yes."

"Doesn't mean much," said Strad, dividing his time between ogling the promiscuous barmaid and swallowing a disgusting-looking plate of stewed eel.

"Why is that so?" asked a somewhat annoyed Red.

"During the Dutch conflict a few years back, we captured several Dutch warships and many smaller boats. This could be one of those captured at that time," Strad replied.

"If it is, it has come from outside the Medway," Red riposted.

"Several of the Dutch boats, which were confiscated then, are used up and down the Thames. This could have been a group of people returning up the Thames to London, and the expertise of the oarsmen could reflect that rowing passengers about is their occupation," Luke countered.

"Well, I have never seen Dutch boats in the Medway before," repeated Red, somewhat annoyed that his information was being belittled.

Luke called for a second helping.

Serious discussion ceased with the arrival of more food.

After completing their enormous meal, and several tankards of beer, Red led them in the direction of Holt House.

He whispered to Luke, "Holt House is full of unsolved mysteries. It is known locally as Petticoat Palace."

"Because of Lady Holt's dominance?"

"Both the current Lady Holt, and her recently deceased mother-in-law were, and are the real powers within the Holt family. Lady Mary dominated during the minority of her eldest son, Arthur, following the incarceration of her lunatic husband, Sir Edward. Following Arthur's short marriage to Lady Prudence the two ladies combined to run a very efficient conglomeration of estates. Sir Arthur was killed nine years ago. Lady Mary became a recluse for the last five years of her life, allowing Lady Prudence complete control. Mary died two years ago."

"How do you know so much?"

"My shipmate and longtime friend is Richard Holt, Lady Mary's younger son. There is nothing like long lonely sea voyages aided by gallons of West Indies rum to make us all talkative."

"What are the mysteries you mention?"

"There has been gossip since I was a child that there have been unexplained deaths and disappearances—horrific stories of young children wandering off into the mudflats never to be seen again. Two years ago, just before Lady Mary died, her lawyer, allegedly carrying a casket of family jewels, was lost in the mud. His body has never been found and the local fishermen are still eagerly looking for the cache."

Red, Luke and Strad left the flat lands, and with the two soldiers leading their horses, they started to climb into the North Downs.

Eventually, Red pointed out a large manor house across an extensive field on which hundreds of sheep were grazing.

"I will leave you here. Take a shortcut across this field! Give my regards to young Richard, who is staying with his sister-in-law until we return to sea."

"Before you leave, something you said puzzles me. If Richard is the childless Sir Arthur's surviving brother, why has he not inherited the title and the lands of his brother? The law is very clear that in matters of succession the nearest surviving male inherits."

"Not when it is overridden by a special act of parliament. The Long Parliament, at the prodding of the late Lady Mary on the death of her eldest son Arthur, passed an act that all of the property should stay with Lady Prudence until her death or remarriage."

"Richard must have been livid," commented Luke.

"He has never shown it, and is devoted to his sister-in-law, even when recently she made things even more difficult for him."

"What worse could she do?"

"She used her influence with Oliver Cromwell to have the first parliament of the Protectorate alter the succession even further. On her death Richard will not necessarily inherit the land or title. It will be disposed of according to the terms of her will."

"Highly unusual!" said Luke.

"And reversible by a less favorable parliament," commented Red.

"But for the present, technically legal?" queried Luke.

Red nodded positively.

"Thanks, Red. I will need your help in the future."

The sailor turned and walked briskly back towards Gillingham.

Luke and Strad mounted their horses, ignored Red's advice regarding the shortcut, and began the gradual ascent on a winding chalk path towards Holt House.

It was a magnificent late-Elizabethan mansion of four levels, built largely of bricks manufactured in the area from the local clay.

Luke and Strad were admitted into a large entrance hall where Strad was immediately led away by a footman, while a liveried valet steered Luke up a majestic winding staircase to the second level.

He was asked to wait outside an ornate double door on which the valet knocked.

It opened and the valet announced, "Colonel Luke Tremayne, your ladyship!"

Luke was dazzled by the opulence.

His admiration of the surroundings was curtailed by his appreciation of the striking beauty of the statuesque woman who rose from behind a large flat-topped desk.

The semidarkened church and her elaborate clothing had concealed her features at their meeting earlier in the day.

"Welcome, Luke. I trust Billy convinced you that this visit to your cousin Prudence is not a waste of time?"

"To be shot at after leaving the church was enough convincing I needed," replied Luke diplomatically.

"I heard the gunfire while I was having a drink in the vicarage. I assumed it was an exercise. Was anybody hurt?"

"No, but it did lead me to meet Lieutenant Neville, a naval gunnery officer, who more than confirmed much of what you suggested."

"Neville's a fine fellow. He has been immensely protective of my brother-in-law Richard."

Luke noticed a flaxen-haired, chubby-cheeked, blue-eyed youth sitting at a smaller desk in the corner of the room.

Prudence saw his distraction.

"Luke, my secretary, Roger Linton."

Linton rose and nodded deferentially in Luke's direction as Prudence explained his visit. "Luke is a distant cousin, but more importantly, he is a top agent and personal friend of the Lord Protector. He has been invaluable in our cause."

Luke was not sure in what particular cause he had proved invaluable.

He was intrigued that Prudence had as her secretary such a youthful and handsome man. His background would need probing, as he was obviously a confidant of her ladyship. The womanizer in Luke wondered if there was more to their relationship.

Prudence brought the meeting to a sudden end, curtly informing Luke that supper was at nine, when he would be introduced to the current members of the household and assorted guests.

His presence *was* required.

Luke turned to leave when a very tall young man with an erect bearing, relatively long brown hair, and a well-manicured beard entered the room.

"I'm sorry, Prue, I did not know you had company."

"Richard, this is my cousin Luke."

They shook hands and Luke commented, "I have heard much good about you from your new commander, Lieutenant Neville."

"A brilliant gunnery officer. He will be wasted as commander," replied Richard.

"Luke, I will see you at supper," interposed Prudence, making it clear that he should leave.

A valet immediately appeared and led Luke to his living quarters. Prudence, Richard, and Roger remained closeted in the room.

Already Luke's mind was racing as he conjectured plots, hidden loyalties, and personal conflicts between the parties he had met on his first day in the western Medway.

After Luke had inspected his large bedroom, and two adjacent smaller antechambers allotted to him, he went in search of Strad, who had been classed as a servant.

Luke found him in the stables supervising a groom brushing their black Friesian horses.

Strad had warm comfortable quarters above the stables and would eat with the senior servants.

Luke asked him to discover the servants' views about all members of the family and household.

In a few days, Strad would move into one of the antechambers off Luke's bedroom and act as his personal valet, replacing Prudence's servant whom Luke suspected was a spy for his mistress.

Luke returned to the main house by a detour through the extensive gardens.

He moved through an elaborate gate, into a wilder, more natural part of the landscape.

Just ahead of him, two men were arguing.

Raised voices escalated into mutual fisticuffs.

Then they realized they were being observed.

They separated and disappeared into the wilderness—in opposite directions.

# 4

Supper was taken in a spacious, brightly lit dining hall, which was larger than many a farmhouse. The room oozed opulence, but given that two austere Puritan women, Lady Mary and Lady Prudence, had controlled it for thirty years, it was not ostentatious.

One half of an extensive side table already groaned with platters of cold collations ready for consumption. The other half had space for the hot dishes whose appetizing aromas had preceded their arrival.

A long central table was prepared for about twenty diners.

A servant intercepted Luke and led him to a position beside the head of the table.

When all were seated the same servant announced the arrival of Prudence, Lady Holt, at which point the assembled group rose to their feet. After she had taken her seat, the other diners sat.

The ritual had not finished.

There was no move to eat, although the inviting smell of many of the cooked dishes now wafted along the table.

Luke was hungry, despite his massive midday meal at The Black Eel.

Prudence spoke. "Seated on my left tonight is my cousin and the Protector's special representative, Colonel Luke Tremayne. He will be staying here for the next few months. Luke, I will not attempt to introduce all of your fellow diners at once. On your immediate left is my brother-in-law, Richard, whom you have already met. Opposite you are his half sister, my sister-in-law, Lady Mercy Bartram, and her husband, Sir Giles."

Luke guessed that Mercy was at least fifteen to twenty years older than Prudence.

At last food and drink arrived in an avalanche of plates, platters, and jugs propelled around the table by an army of minions.

As Luke looked around the table, the relative status of the diners was apparent.

Closest to Prudence were her immediate family; furthest away were her senior servants. Among the latter, he recognized Roger Linton, the vicar Partridge, and the two men he had seen fighting.

Between family and servants sat local dignitaries, and three attractive young women, two of whom were identical twins.

Richard integrated Luke into the conversations of the nearest diners.

The woman next to Luke was Lady Matilda Lynne, wife of Sir Nicholas, the new magistrate for the area, who was seated on her other side.

Matilda was of a tradition alien to Holt House. She wore her hair in long ringlets controlled by an array of bright orange ribbons, and her low-cut bodice must have affronted Mercy and Prudence.

Luke was immediately attracted to her—and she seemed to reciprocate.

The moment of mutual attraction was shattered when her husband leaned in front of her and addressed Luke directly. "Colonel, I understand that the two fine black Friesian stallions in the stable belong to you and your man. Before our civil wars, I fought for the Spaniards in the Netherlands and well remember my first major defeat at the hands of the Dutch cavalry, all riding Friesians. They were stronger and faster than any of our steeds."

"I started my career when little more than a lad with the Dutch cavalry riding Friesians. We may have opposed each other on that very day," replied Luke.

"You must love defeat," interposed Richard. "First, the Spaniards, then the king. Thank God you have seen the light."

Prudence glared at her brother-in-law.

"Richard, we are now all united in maintaining the current government. The past must be forgotten, if not forgiven."

Sir Nicholas ignored the Holts and explained to Luke, "I was a Royalist until very recently, but with young Charles gallivanting around the continent, and various radical groups attempting to subvert the current administration, I thought it time to support order against anarchy—and your Lord Protector is the best guarantee of that."

Luke's response surprised the gathering.

"I have met Charles Stuart on two of my missions. He is not the weak, bad lad that my colleague Mr. Thurloe makes out."

All conversation ceased.

Prudence looked at Luke incredulously, while Matilda, conversely, gave the impression she would kiss him.

Luke struggled to recover from this faux pas at the dinner table of the most anti-Royalist family in the southeast.

"But that in no way altered my loyalty to Oliver Cromwell," he quickly added.

Richard changed the conversation.

"Across the table, next to Sir Giles is his eldest daughter Elizabeth, and next to her is David Harvey, esquire, who is the second magistrate for this area. He has special responsibility for the estuary of the Medway, Sheppey Island, and the coast as far as Whitstable. Next to him is Giles's eldest twin Frances."

Both young ladies nodded to Luke, smiled, and then looked intently into their wine glasses.

Luke addressed Harvey, "You must have an extremely difficult job. The people of the Medway and the Swale are subject to so many competing jurisdictions. The military must usurp many duties of a normal county magistrate?"

"Yes, that is one of the reasons why I made myself available to serve this government. I am an unreserved protagonist for Oliver Cromwell accepting the Crown. Pardon me saying it in your presence, and that of Richard, but England has had its fill of military rule. If Cromwell becomes king, he will return us to the rule of law, exercised by local magistrates and parliamentarians. The threat of anarchy posed by potentially rebellious troops, and religious fanatics will be gone for good."

"Many on the council of state would agree with you," commented Luke.

Prudence intervened, "Luke, you have served Oliver well as personal bodyguard and secret agent for years. Will he accept the Crown?"

"Dear cousin, part of my visit here is to provide the Lord Protector with evidence that will help his decision. Accepting the Crown may have the positive effects that David has suggested, or it could spark rebellion in the army and among the more extreme Puritan congregations across the land, creating even greater anarchy."

Luke whispered to Richard, "It is impossible to talk with those further down the table, but I would like to know who they are."

"Next to my niece Frances is the good-for-nothing, incompetent excuse for a soldier and gentleman Lieutenant Harry Proctor. Prue puts up with him because my mother took him in on the death of his parents. He was educated as if a brother to Arthur and myself. After Mother died, I tried to persuade Prue to get rid of him."

"Why hasn't she?"

"She made a solemn promise to Mother that she would look after him. Next to Harry is the man who for decades has run the estates, the steward, John Headley. He has been around since Grandfather's day and was very close to father. In the last years of father's illness Headley was the only member of the household allowed to visit him. Since mother's death Prue has taken away much of John's authority and responsibility and distributed it to others."

"Is he resentful?"

"No, he is getting old and is very unwell. He coughs up blood and has trouble breathing. He enjoys the lighter workload. The nasty side of estate management—dealing with recalcitrant tenants and laborers—is now undertaken by the bailiff, and the boring paperwork by the boy secretary."

"And who is that alluring woman next to the steward?"

"Headley's much younger wife, Caroline, whom I advise you to avoid."

"What have you against her? Have you been a naughty boy?" teased Luke.

Richard blushed and seemed genuinely revolted by the suggestion.

"No! Mother, from an early age, and more recently Prue advised me to keep clear of her. Even though she is free with her favors, their ladyships emphasized that she is a married woman, and even though we Puritans do not accept marriage as a sacrament, it is still a legally binding contract that every true gentleman should respect."

It was Luke's turn to feel uncomfortable as he thought of his own womanizing ways.

He changed the topic.

"I saw Proctor fighting the man who is sitting at the far end of the table on our side."

"That is Charles Franklin, Prue's bailiff, a nasty piece of work, according to the tenants, but I quite like him. He is direct and honest. What you see is what you get."

"What does an estate bailiff do on lands of this size, already overseen by so many agencies?"

"He terrifies the tenants and workers. Along the estuary sections of the many estates he liaises with the water bailiff. Everywhere he is very ready to hand over malcontents to the parish constable, which is often himself. In this role he presents serious cases to the magistrates."

"Why fight Proctor?"

"Caroline Headley! The rest of our mutual diners are the two clerics, Barnaby Partridge and Roger Linton, and the third of my nieces, the garrulous, inquisitive, irritating Alicia."

"Linton is a cleric? That is unusual nowadays for a secretary. They are almost always lawyers or experts in accounts."

"Linton is a mystery. I was at sea when the former secretary died. Prue overlooked the obvious replacements, went to Cambridge, and returned with Linton. His only claim to fame was that he was a brilliant theology student who sat at the feet of the great Puritan divines of the last few decades."

"Hardly relevant as secretary to Prudence? Is he being groomed to replace Barnaby Partridge as vicar at St. Margaret's?"

"St. Margaret's is not a living controlled by the Holts. Prue appoints to a dozen or so other parishes in Kent, but not St. Margaret's. That is in the keep of the Guild of Fishers and Dredgers."

"Then why is Partridge here?"

"Two reasons—he is Prue's private chaplain, and he is family. He is my uncle—Mother, Lady Mary, was a Partridge."

Next morning, Luke came down for an early meal and found the three Bartram girls and Roger Linton in a smaller room off the great hall.

One of the twins confronted him. "Colonel, I am Alicia. I hope Uncle Richard did not fill your head with silly stories about us."

Luke did not want to deflate the ego of this girl, who imagined that his whispered conversation with the young naval officer the previous evening must be about her.

He replied diplomatically. "I am sure whatever your uncle told me cannot do justice to your real achievements."

The eldest sister Elizabeth asked seriously, "Did you really meet Charles Stuart?"

"Twice," replied Luke.

Frances changed the subject. "Aunt Prue says you have been to the Americas, and fought against the savages."

"I fought both with and against the Native Indians of Maryland. They are, like the English, divided into rival groups."

Alicia interrupted again. "Did Aunt Prue bring you here to investigate us?"

Luke thought that this was indeed an irritating young woman and replied impatiently. "Of course—if you are a threat to the government."

Roger turned on Alicia. "Stop annoying the colonel with your silly questions!"

Alicia glared at Roger and blurted out, "I know things."

And then ran from the room.

Luke looked at Roger, who explained, "Alicia has a vivid imagination combined with a staggering ignorance and naivety of the real world. Her father spoils her beyond reason."

Harry Proctor entered the room, flirted with Elizabeth and Frances, and commented, "What's wrong with Alicia? She just passed me sobbing very loudly."

"I reprimanded her for wasting the colonel's time with petty household gossip. He has more important work to do," replied Roger.

Luke asked Harry, "Any further developments at the dockyard following yesterday's attack?"

Harry replied testily. "How would I know? I am having a week's break from that boring routine. This new man Digges is a pain. He sent a horseman here yesterday afternoon informing me of the trouble and requesting my immediate return to duty. The man's incorrigible."

Luke was about to explode.

Instead, he shocked Proctor with his proposal or, more accurately, *order*.

"As you are a paid officer in the national army, I will, as of now, second you to my personal service. I will let Digges know you are, for a day or two, helping me. Have plenty to eat! It will be a long day. Report to me at the stables in one hour! You will give me a detailed tour of the nearer Holt properties."

Harry was trapped. He could not disobey a direct order of a superior officer.

Frances and Elizabeth giggled and gave Luke a knowing smile.

Roger grinned.

# 5

---

A reluctant and seething Harry led Luke and Strad on an inspection of the Holt estates that could be reached and returned from within the day.

Luke was determined to inspect as many Holt properties that could be seen within that time.

Harry was incandescent.

He was informed before they left Holt House that there were no servants to carry food and drink.

Luke made clear that apart from their water bottles, there would be no refreshments.

This was a military exercise.

Harry took Luke and Strad along the ridge of the Downs pointing out the numerous estates that the Holts had accumulated over nearly a hundred years. Those to the south were adjacent to the main London-Dover road, while most of those to the north ran down into the Medway estuary or the Swale.

Harry indicated that Lady Prudence also owned many urban properties in Rochester, Chatham, and Gillingham that gave her great influence within each town.

The mayor of Rochester, the admiral of Medway, was her nominee.

Luke was alarmed at the number of large outbuildings, patches of dense woodland, and navigable creeks than ran further inland than he had imagined—the ideal country to hide invading troops and illicit arms.

Arriving back at Holt House after dusk, an utterly exhausted and starving Harry ordered the first servant he came across to bring him food and drink immediately.

Luke and Strad went over the day's events.

"Thank God her ladyship is on our side. If a Royalist controlled her estates, the government would be in serious trouble. Troops could be landed up any of the several creeks and hidden in the multitude of buildings and forests that cover her land. They would be in a perfect position to take the dockyard, sever the London-Dover road, and be within hours of attacking London itself. If any of our troops in the area were to be subverted, and rose against the government, such an uprising with local support would most likely succeed."

"Most unlikely," countered Strad. "Our opponents are amateurs—and hopelessly divided. If they had acted in unison, we would not have suppressed the Welsh insurrection last year, or the local mutiny a week or so ago."

"That mutiny did not have local support. Those Royalists were all outsiders. If the local gentry had supported them, the result would have been very different. Ride to Whitehall in the morning and report my concerns to Thurloe, and have our company of dragoons relocated here immediately. At the moment, I do not trust any government officers at the dockyard or the castle, except for Digges and the sailor Neville. Suggest to Thurloe that the recruits training for battle for Flanders should be sent to a less strategic location."

Supper was held in the smaller dining room. Prudence presided with Lady Mercy and her daughters close to her at the top of the table. Sir Giles, Richard, and the magistrates of the previous evening were absent. The senior servants—Headley and his wife,

Linton, Partridge, and Franklin—occupied the middle. At the far end was an array of military men—Alexander Dewhurst, the governor of Upnor Castle, Harry Proctor, Thomas Digges from the dockyard garrison, and John Neville, commander in waiting of the frigate *Valiant,* currently being refitted.

Luke, at Prudence's request, sat opposite her at the far end of the table, close to his military comrades.

"Luke, whatever did you do to Harry? I had to refuse his request to miss supper. He was so exhausted that he wanted to retire immediately." Luke replied, smiling at the highly embarrassed Harry, "My Lady, by the time I have finished with him, he will much prefer to be at his post at the dockyard than assisting me. Do not encourage him to desert his post for the comforts of Holt House!"

Prudence glared at Luke, shocked by his impertinence.

He responded aggressively. "Cousin, you forget that we are at war. The Dutch threatened to sail up the Medway and sink our ships and take London. The Spaniards may actually do it. We must all be alert—and at our posts."

"They don't have the appropriate landing craft," commented Tom. "Quite right, but at this very moment, the Royalists are negotiating with the Dutch to provide landing craft for the army that the Spaniards have promised to provide. Charles Stuart will invade once his supporters have secured an effective haven to receive such troops. The Medway is ideal."

"My gunners will put an end to any such stupidity," said Dewhurst.

"But what if your gunners went over to the enemy?" Luke asked.

There was absolute quiet.

The possibility shocked the listeners.

John Headley broke the silence, changing the subject. "Why are you here, Colonel?"

"By now most are aware that I am here to ascertain if the Medway poses a threat to national security as a base for a Royalist insurrection fueled by foreign invasion, or the subversion of existing government forces on the ground."

"A tall order for two men!" commented Charles Franklin.

"Agreed, sir, but in the next day or two my full company of dragoons who only recently won plaudits on the battlefield against the rebellious Welsh, and in the last few weeks contained the army mutiny further along the Medway, will arrive."

Luke continued. "I must visit you, Mr. Franklin, in the morning for advice regarding the various creeks and inlets, and Mr. Headley, I need your help regarding the current use of the buildings under your control."

"Before we move away from military matters and enjoy our meal, you have overlooked a pressing matter," Prudence advised Luke.

He was momentarily confused until Prudence inclined her head in the direction of Major Dewhurst.

Luke got the message.

"Major, I will visit Upnor Castle tomorrow afternoon to investigate the disappearance of your deputy, Captain Hatch."

"Not much to examine. He has deserted. Probably gone over to the Royalists. He was too friendly with the prisoners. Not a good look—gaolers and prisoners being close!"

"Nevertheless, I must talk to you and your men," Luke declared.

The meal continued with a high degree of amiable chitchat.

Prudence ended the repast by leaving with her female relatives, followed by John Headley and his wife.

The remaining men moved into the long gallery at the far end of which was a billiard table. Digges and Dewhurst challenged each other to a game. The two clergy Linton and Partridge called on a servant to produce a chessboard, while Luke signaled for Charles Franklin, John Neville, and Harry Proctor to join him on a comfortable bench close to a small but effective fire. Servants brought them mugs of mulled wine.

Charles Franklin was a strongly built man whose physical presence would cower most opponents. He wielded a club in his law enforcement role to allegedly fatal effect. If Luke's arrival had not stopped the earlier fight, Harry would have been severely beaten.

Luke discovered during his tour with Harry that the bailiff lived on an island surrounded by the mudflats and tidal movements of the Medway estuary. He enjoyed the water and visited many of his victims by a small rowing boat, which his strong physique propelled through the water at great speed. He knew the estuarine lands of the Holt estates better than anyone—expertise that would be invaluable to any invading force.

Luke was anxious to tap and if necessary control this knowledge.

Luke asked him, "In recent months have you noticed strangers or unexpected movements on the creeks of the estuary?"

Charles's demeanor suddenly changed.

He eyed Luke with some apprehension and replied, "You trouble me, Colonel. Are you really here on matters of national security? Or has her ladyship employed you to investigate her officers, and the level of illicit trading activity that pervades our waters?"

"Petty crime and estate maladministration do not concern me unless they relate to the survival of the government," Luke replied.

"Meet me at the little jetty on Gillies Creek tomorrow at nine, and I will take you on a tour of our waterways, and show you the dangers they may hold. If you want answers to any malaise that pervades the estates, speak to the steward," advised Charles.

"You don't like Headley?"

"We have our personal differences. John has been in the position too long. When Lady Mary died, Lady Prudence should have replaced him, but our antagonism has nothing to do with national or estate issues. It is a private matter."

"Caroline Headley?" whispered Luke.

Harry Proctor giggled—and could not conceal a provocative smirk.

Charles moved as if to smash Proctor in the face.

The bailiff regained his composure and withdrew his fist.

"Colonel, do not believe the false rumors put about by others to damage me! As bailiff and constable, I discover unfavorable information about most people, gentlemen and commoners alike. I am not popular, and there are many out to destroy me."

"Such knowledge must give you power. You would be in a position to blackmail a lot of people."

"Indeed, I would, but Lady Prudence would dismiss me immediately she was made aware of it. My potential victims would not provide me with a decent living. I have to leave. See you in the morning!"

As Charles bid his farewells, Luke considered him a possible clandestine Royalist.

He knew the waterways, and he knew many local secrets.

Luke turned to Harry. "Your fight with Franklin was over Caroline Headley?"

"Most conflicts between gentlemen on the Medway involve Caroline. She may be John's wife, but many men claim her as their mistress."

"Such behavior one might expect within a Royalist household, but this is overtly an extreme Puritan establishment. Why does Lady Prudence permit Caroline to remain on the estate, let alone grace her table?"

"That has always puzzled me," commented Red. "It is not something new. Caroline's behavior and her continued residence here has been a constant for a decade or more."

"Before Sir Arthur's death?" asked Luke.

"Yes," replied Red. "In fact, there were rumors at the time that Arthur and Caroline were close, which forced Mary to marry him in haste to Prudence, who was much older—and more readily compliant to Mary's influence."

The billiard players finished their game and joined the others around the fire.

"All we need now is a pipe of tobacco," commented Tom.

"Her ladyship condones such behavior?" asked Alex.

"Yes, Richard and Giles are regular smokers. A servant will bring us some pipes and tobacco," answered Harry.

"Can they bring us some plugs? I prefer to chew my tobacco," commented the sailor, Red.

The military men settled down to serious drinking and smoking, except for Harry, whose unexpected physical exertions of the day had suddenly induced a deep sleep punctuated by bursts of porcinelike snoring.

The smoking gradually created a bluish haze that quickly enveloped the end of the gallery.

The chess players were not amused by this thickening smog but continued their game until a bout of coughing by Partridge forced Linton to carefully carry their half-completed game to the other end of the long room.

Red tried to lob a small cushion at the retreating clerics and just missed the board.

He laughed.

Linton gave him a menacing look.

"Those godly parasites can't take a joke," the sailor commented in response to looks of disapproval.

The night drew on and eventually as one by one the candles burnt out, servants led the guests to their bedrooms.

Some had imbibed so much wine that it took two servants to half-carry their charges to the relevant room.

Finally, only the elderly Alexander Dewhurst remained.

He had dozed off a little after Red lobbed the pillow at the clergy and their chess set.

A servant tried to gently shake him awake.

There was no response.

The servant ran after Luke, who was just climbing the main staircase to his bedchamber.

"What is it?" asked Luke.

"I cannot awaken Major Dewhurst. Please come!"

It did not take Luke and Red, who had overheard the servant's request, long to assess the situation.

The major was dead.

Luke instructed all that no one must enter that end of the long gallery, and he would inform Lady Holt first thing in the morning.

Luke turned to Red.

"I need another drink after this. There is some excellent Irish whiskey in my room."

The two men drank in silence for some time.

Eventually Luke asked, "Why are you so glum, Red. You were not close to Dewhurst?"

"No! It's only a trivial matter. All night I was on the edge of asking him what was going on at the fort."

"Why?"

"Earlier today barge loads of men, equipment, and materials were unloaded in the area of the gun emplacements. My men sailing past claim that the voices they heard were not English."

"Spanish or French?"

"Neither. They swear it was German or Dutch or maybe Swedish, although I doubt that my men would have any real knowledge of what language it was. But they were absolutely sure it was not English. Surely Cromwell is not opening up a key defensive castle to foreigners at such a crucial stage in our war with Spain, and before an imminent Royalist invasion?"

"Tomorrow, you and I will visit the fort, overtly to inform them of the tragic death of their commanding officer—and investigate these matters. Then I will meet Franklin for a tour of the waterways."

Red looked Luke in the eyes and asked, "Was Dewhurst murdered?"

"I can't see how. We were all with him for hours. Prudence will send for a physician in the morning. He may be able to tell us something about the cause of death," Luke replied.

"Not likely. Give me an apothecary or surgeon any day if you need that sort of knowledge," replied an agitated Red.

"I agree. Is there either close at hand?"

"There is an apothecary in Rochester. We have a naval surgeon based at the dockyard, but he is currently in London."

# 6

Luke informed Prudence of Dewhurst's death while she was still abed. She immediately sent for the family physician.

At Luke's insistence, she also reluctantly sought an apothecary from Rochester.

David Harvey, the nearest local magistrate, was notified, but Luke insisted that this was an army matter, and he would conduct the initial enquiry.

Luke then sent a message to Charles Franklin delaying their meeting until eleven.

Immediately after breakfast, Luke, Red, and Tom went to the dockyard, from where Red had his men row them downriver to Upnor Castle.

As they approached the castle, the activity that Red had described was visible. The forecourt was a hive of activity with guns having been moved out of position, and the area littered with piles of clay and stacks of bricks. Several large holes were being excavated.

A perfect time for an enemy warship to sail up the Medway unimpeded!

There was not a single soldier to be seen.

The sentries, who usually flanked the forecourt and defended the guns, were missing.

Luke asked one of the workmen who was the overseer.

The laborer pointed in the direction of a man standing on a low wall, and shouting orders in Dutch, the only foreign language in which Luke was fluent.

After a few minutes of conversation with him, Luke signaled his comrades to join him.

They entered the fort and eventually found a soldier standing before a closed double door.

"Take us to your commanding officer," ordered Luke.

"He is not here. He is at Holt House."

"Then can we speak to his deputy?"

"Whom shall I say wishes to see him?" asked the orderly.

"Colonel Luke Tremayne and two officers from the dockyard," answered Luke.

The officers waited—and waited.

Luke used the time to inform his comrades of his talk with the overseer.

"He is a Dutchman. Claims to be an engineer experienced in the building of artillery batteries. But I don't believe him."

"How can you tell in such a short time?" asked the skeptical Tom.

"He has been an intelligence officer for too long," joked Red.

"The Dutchman said he had been born and educated at Leiden. I asked him whether the rebuilding of the local church on the waterfront had been completed. He told me it had. It has not. I was in the battle in which the Spaniards broke through our lines and burnt the church to the ground. It was not rebuilt in such a vulnerable location. He should have known that the site of the original church is now a small fort."

The soldier returned and informed Luke that the deputy commandant, Captain Matthew Hatch, would receive them.

Luke and his companions were shocked.

According to Prudence, Hatch had disappeared some weeks earlier and had not been seen since—a perception reinforced less than twelve hours earlier by his own commanding officer.

A small man, whose face was so heavily bandaged that only his eyes could be seen, received Luke, Red, and Tom.

His left arm was in a sling and he hobbled forward to greet his visitors. He had trouble walking.

He was so well disguised with bandages that Luke thought it could be anyone pretending to be Hatch.

The bandaged man spoke. "Please forgive my appearance. Ordnance officers occasionally meet with accidents. I was almost blown apart several weeks ago. What can I do for you gentlemen?"

Luke's initial suspicion dissipated as Hatch continued.

"How are you, Red? Your ship still in dock? Richard and you must be anxious to return to sea. Captain Digges, I heard you had taken over from that idiot, Proctor. Welcome to the Medway. And why, Colonel, has the Protector placed a man of your eminence among us?"

"Before we attempt to answer your questions, I have to inform you that your commandant, Major Alexander Dewhurst, died last evening while visiting your friend Lady Holt," stated Luke.

"Murdered?"

Matthew's response surprised everyone.

"Why ask such a question?" asked Luke.

"Alexander and I have experienced a number of so-called accidents over recent months. My injuries were the latest, until Alex's unexpected death."

"How did your injuries occur?" asked Tom.

"I inspected the gun emplacements about to be completed at Sheerness. I received what I thought was a direct request from the garrison there to assist them with the final installation. When I arrived, the commandant told me he had made no such request. Nevertheless, as I was on the spot, he would use my expertise. A few days later, I was in a cellar with a soldier checking a box of mortars. They combusted, and as other ammunition exploded, it created an inferno that smoldered for days. My assistant was killed, and most thought I was dead. An apothecary on the island patched me up and the locals took me by barge up river to London where I was nursed back to health by relatives. I was unconscious for weeks, and when I did come to, for some time thereafter, I could not remember what had happened, or who I was."

"I know the feeling. I had a similar experience a few years ago," commented Luke.

"Consequently, I could not inform Dewhurst or her ladyship. I thought Sheerness might have. Now, Colonel, tell me why are you here!"

"Because your friend Lady Prudence informed the Protector that you had disappeared."

"I'm sorry I have caused you so much trouble. I did not recall anything until two days ago. I returned here as soon as I realized who I was and arrived yesterday about noon."

Luke looked at Red and Tom with a quizzical glance and addressed Matthew.

"I am glad to see you alive, but the death of Dewhurst and your own accident give weight to the suspicions of several, that something is amiss on the Medway. The armed forces of the Protector may be the target of as yet an unknown evil. Why is a Dutch engineer and foreign workmen removing your gun emplacements? At the moment you are defenseless."

"I know. Just before he left for Holt House last night, Dewhurst accused me of engaging these men without his knowledge. I assume that he did this to cover his own tracks. He *must* have engaged them. I did not."

"So you returned here before Dewhurst left for Holt House. He was well aware of what had happened to you?" asked Red.

"Yes, why do you ask?"

"When I told Dewhurst I would come to Upnor Castle and ask a few questions regarding you, he said you had deserted. He gave no indication that you had returned," answered Luke.

"I am not surprised. Dewhurst seemed elsewhere when I spoke to him. He probably did not recognize me with all these bandages. Increasingly I have wondered whether his mind functioned normally. He forgot almost everything he was told. Old age befuddled his brain. I do not want to speak ill of the dead, but Alex was losing his mind."

Matthew asked about the details of Dewhurst's death and accepted the invitation to be present at two that afternoon when the medical men were to examine the body.

As Luke left the castle, he asked the Dutch engineer the precise nature of his work.

It was simple.

He was to build a low thick wall in front of the new emplacements to protect the big guns from the fire of an advancing ship, which was usually of a very low trajectory, and to relocate these giant guns on a moveable base that would enable them to be turned 270 degrees to protect the dockyard, and any vessels coming downstream on the castle's side of the river.

At the moment the castle's guns had a very narrow degree of maneuverability and could really only fire at ships coming directly down the main channel.

As soon as ships turned to go upriver towards the dockyard, the guns of Upnor Castle became useless.

Red applauded the proposed changes. In the future, they could be used to bombard invaders attacking the dockyard.

Luke countered, "But in the wrong hands they can now be used to attack the dockyard itself."

As they headed back across the Medway towards the dockyard at a speed that amazed Luke, they saw a smaller boat with Charles Franklin heading for his rendezvous with Luke.

To save time, Luke jumped from one small boat to an even smaller one as both continued to move.

Charles could not contain himself regarding Dewhurst's death.

"The old man was murdered in front of us, and nobody saw anything!"

"There is no evidence as yet that Dewhurst was murdered. He was ill and old. We will know more after two o'clock. As bailiff, you do not need to be present."

"But as parish constable, I do."

"It is unusual for an estate bailiff to be a parish constable," commented a surprised Luke.

"Not on the Medway. A dozen or more parishes in the area found difficulty in providing a constable. During the war, they were decrepit old men or scrawny boys. Even lame criminals could outrun them. Sir Arthur, under Lady Mary's direction, as lord of the several manors in which these parishes existed, offered to provide their village constable. His widow Lady Prudence continued the arrangement, and the bailiff of the manor of Holt remains the constable of most of the estuarine parishes."

"An impossible job for one man."

"It is, but I have a team of deputies working with me. I am the nominal constable, but my men do the actual work. Nevertheless, in the case of murder, I investigate and report my investigation to the estuarine magistrate who is now David Harvey."

"Not in this case! Should Dewhurst's death be suspicious, you will work with me. Tomorrow I receive an update of my longstanding authorization to override all existing jurisdictions in pursuit of my investigations. Now, Charles, what can you tell me about the waterways?"

"The Medway is a series of different worlds depending on the level and direction of the tide. At the moment, we have almost reached high tide. At this stage, large boats can sail up most of the creeks, and even very large ships can navigate the Swale and the Medway estuary. At high tide, the estuary is alive with illegal activity. At low tide, the area available to vessels is dramatically reduced. Some creeks disappear altogether and mudflats cover much of the estuary. This is when smugglers move out to pick up illegal goods that were dropped overboard during high tide, and a period when we discover the unfortunate results of criminal activity."

"Such as?"

"Hopefully uncollected casks of brandy, but more often a dead body."

"Can you get me a list of all such finds and any illegal activity, seen or suspected, in the last two months? Assure your sources that they will not suffer from any revelations. Smuggling is not my concern, unless it involves the security of the government."

"Colonel, it is imperative that you understand the give-and-take of local communities."

"I do, but I need your active support in unraveling what is actually happening here. My dragoons arrive tomorrow. They can investigate problems and enforce my decisions, but they cannot elicit information as easily as you can. How did you become bailiff?"

"During the war, I was the senior sergeant in a Medway company of parliamentary infantry. When the first conflict ended, I was appointed one of the assistant bailiffs. When the Royalists rose in revolt in 1648, I was with young Sir Arthur when he died."

"I heard that his death was suspicious."

"His death was straightforward, but how the enemy knew where we were remains a mystery."

"What happened?"

"The Royalists captured Upnor Castle. Sir Arthur led three boatloads of parliamentary troops to recapture it by stealth. We sailed up one of the creeks on the other side of the river well away from the obvious waterways that our opponents had covered. We actually sent boats up these creeks as decoys. It was one of the darkest nights I have known. We were to disembark and attack the fort from the landward side where it was, and still is, poorly defended. I was in the lead boat with Sir Arthur. We rowed up the creek for ten minutes in absolute silence.

Suddenly, without warning from both banks, we were subjected to a hail of musket fire. Sir Arthur gasped, slumped into my arms, and died. I ordered the men to row back down the river but only the Pratt brothers were left alive. As they moved into position to take up the oars, they too were wounded. We three then jumped overboard. The receding tide eventually drew our two leading boats back into the Medway were the bodies of our men were recovered by the occupants of the third boat, which managed to escape without damage."

"Your route was betrayed?"

"Yes."

"Were your three boats close together?"

"Very! They were linked by a thin rope so that none would fall far behind or get lost on such a dark night."

"It is strange that two boats were massacred and the third untouched. If I were laying that ambush I would destroy the last boat first, to prevent an orderly retreat," commented Luke.

# 7

Luke was surprised that so few had gathered to witness the examination of the corpse.

There were only five—the family physician, an apothecary, Matthew Hatch, Charles Franklin, and himself.

The physician made a cursory examination of the body.

His quick investigation concluded with a comment that Dewhurst was old, had had a hard life, and died of natural causes. There was nothing suspicious about the death, and therefore, no coroner was necessary.

He left.

The apothecary had the opposite approach.

He spent so much time with the body that Luke entertained the irreverent thought that he was being paid by the minute.

The apothecary finally reported, "My learned friend may be right, but the finger and toenails of the deceased are striped and brittle."

"Indicating what?" asked Charles.

"High levels of arsenic."

"So this is murder!" exclaimed Luke.

"Not necessarily! This poison entered the major's system over a long period. He may have accidently ingested it, or been taking it as medication. In small amounts, it is beneficial for a range of ailments. If it was deliberately introduced into his body, it was not done last night. Captain Hatch, did the major exhibit any unusual symptoms in recent months?"

"I have been away for some time, but as I told Colonel Tremayne this morning, Alex has complained of headaches and was becoming confused from time to time. His memory was badly affected."

"Both are signs of arsenic poisoning," concluded the apothecary.

"What happens to the body now?" asked Luke.

"My men are waiting outside. Alex had no family. After a funeral service in the chapel at Upnor Castle, he will be interred in the grounds of the fort," replied Matthew.

A servant drew Luke aside to announce that a Captain Williams was waiting in the reception hall.

Luke was delighted to see his friend and deputy, Sir Evan Williams.

Evan reported that Luke's dragoons were now imbedded in a large farm house, Mudhill Farm. There was ample accommodation for all the men and horses, and that Lady Holt's steward had provided an excess of food and fodder.

Luke led Evan to one of the small antechambers and called for food and drink as he updated his deputy on developments.

This repast was curtailed when a breathless cleric, Barnaby Partridge, burst through the door.

"Thank goodness I have found you. Billy Pratt needs to see you urgently. He has been waiting for some time. Someone ignored his initial request."

Luke and Evan met a surprisingly relaxed Billy in the garden.

"Come fishing with us tonight?" he asked.

"Why?" asked Luke.

Billy looked askance at Evan, and his eyes appealed to Luke for an explanation.

Luke answered, "You may speak clearly in front of Sir Evan. He is my deputy and knows all that I know."

The realization that he was talking to a knight of the realm was sufficient for the fisherman to touch his forelock and relax.

"So why must I come fishing?" repeated Luke.

"Strange lights!"

Billy continued. "For the last three nights, members of my family have been fishing downstream from the fort between Hoo Flats and Slede Ooze. From there you can look up river towards the fort, and across the widest part of the Medway estuary towards Gillingham, and further east towards Lower Rainham, Upchurch, and Lower Halstow. On each of these nights they have seen a distant light somewhere east of Gillingham. It was only visible around high tide."

"There must be lots of lights on the estuary at night. What is so unusual about what your family saw?"

"Locals don't need lights. They can sail or row themselves into any creek you wish to name by using landmarks that they know from birth. Lights are only needed to guide strangers to a particular destination—people who would run aground without it."

"So why visible only around high tide?" asked the ignorant Evan.

"At any other time the direct route from a navigable reach in the center of the Medway to any creek along the shoreline from Gillingham to the Swale would be blocked by mudflats and marshes."

"Someone along that shoreline was expecting a boatload of visitors or goods to be delivered to them at high tide by someone who did not know the area well," summarized Luke.

"Exactly," answered Billy.

As high tide approached, Billy rowed Luke and Evan to a vantage point near Hoo Flats.

They waited.

No lights appeared.

Finally, Billy concluded that for some reason the welcoming light would not be displayed that evening.

Luke asked, "Can you pinpoint from here where that light appeared the last few nights?"

"I can take you to the exact spot."

Billy rowed in a zigzag course towards the distant shoreline, avoiding the rapidly emerging mudflats.

With uncanny accuracy, he reached the entrance to a creek, which he said was known as Green Mud.

Luke noticed in the emerging moonlight a stone cairn on which a lantern could have been placed.

Billy confirmed that the mouths of many creeks had such cairns, or used natural rock formations to place warning or welcoming lanterns.

"Thank you, Billy. Can you row us back to the dockyard where we can pick up our horses?" requested Luke.

"No, sir! Collect your horses in the morning. You are almost home. This creek flows past Mud Hill Farm, where Sir Evan is staying, and brings you close to Holt House."

"My god! That's why there was no lantern tonight," exclaimed Luke. "Up until this morning Mud Hill Farm was vacant—an ideal location to hide persons or goods smuggled into the area. It was only yesterday that the Lady Holt overruled her steward, and insisted that my men be located there. All this suggests that someone associated with Holt House is a smuggler which may or may not affect the security of the government," concluded Luke.

Billy responded, "This is something different to our regular smugglers who did use Mud Hill Farm as a warehouse. They were locals who did not need lights to guide them. Either the smuggling network has been taken over by strangers or our smugglers invited outsiders to use their depot."

Luke spent the night in the warmth of a Mud Hill Farm barn rather than walk the twenty minutes to Holt House where he thought entry in the middle of the night might be difficult.

Next morning, a cynical Evan commented, "Billy may be trying to get us involved in some local gang warfare between rival smuggling networks."

"To what end?" asked Luke.

"That we use our military power to crush his enemies."

"A possibility."

Luke briefed Evan and John Martin as to the day's activities for the dragoons and then walked to Holt House to eat with those of the household that were in the dining room.

Prudence was eating alone.

"This is an unexpected opportunity to hear of any developments. I was pleased to see Matthew Hatch yesterday although he does not look well. I gather that fool of an apothecary suggests that old Dewhurst was poisoned. My physician will have none of it."

Luke ignored the remarks and asked pointedly, "Is this estate involved in smuggling?"

Prudence did not react as an offended party and virtually admitted to the charge.

"There have always been smugglers along the north Kentish coast supplying us with French brandy, silks, and ceramics. It augments the income of impoverished fishermen and shepherds. Most of the stately homes of Kent are supplied with their luxury goods in this way."

"So the civil authorities and landowners turn a blind eye?"

"The customs and excise people are encouraged to look elsewhere. Using the levy-free route of the smuggler is a great incentive for the poorer farmers to export their wool. Smuggling is built into our economy and as we pay the government very high taxes there is no guilt in denying it a small amount of income, which usually went no further than the corrupt maws of the custom collectors."

"Which of your staff is involved?"

"None of my staff. Harry Proctor is the person to speak to."

"Prudence, I am not greatly concerned with the day-to-day smuggling of luxury goods and the export of raw wool, but what if the network is being used to smuggle in weapons or foreign troops?"

"Talk to Harry!"

Prudence left, and was passed at the door by the young Alicia Bartram.

The young woman was delighted to find herself alone with Luke.

"Sir, mother tells me that your task is to solve murders and mysteries that might endanger the government. My whole family is beside itself trying to discover exactly what Aunt Prue wants you to investigate. Father is very agitated. He says there are many mysteries on the Medway that are best kept secret."

Luke silently noted the young girl's observation.

She continued. "Would you help me?"

Luke smiled. "If it does not interfere with my mission I would be delighted."

"I am the youngest of my siblings and father will not permit me to have a sweetheart until my other sisters are married. Worse still he declares that he will choose husbands for us all. He is trying to arrange a marriage between my eldest sister Elizabeth and Mr. Harvey, the new magistrate."

"I thought a mere esquire would be beneath the purview of a knight's daughter," Luke commented with tongue in cheek.

"Father is no fool. Mr. Harvey is heir to a distant cousin, the Marquis of Appley. Unless the old man marries a young girl and produces a child before his death, which is imminent, David will become a very rich man and a high-ranking aristocrat."

"So what is the problem you wish me to solve?"

"I have encouraged two lovers because I did not know which was genuine."

"Do they know about each other?"

"No."

"Forgive me, Alicia, but I must ask. How far has your relationship gone with either?"

"I am not an idiot. I would be worth nothing in the marriage market if I had been foolish. Father would never forgive me, and Aunt Prue would exile me to one of her distant properties. I would never disgrace my family—but I will determine my own fate in these matters."

"Who are the two men you have encouraged?"

"There are really three. The third has made no advances towards me, but my sister Elizabeth has been approached indirectly to sound out my interest."

"Who are these gentlemen?"

"Harry and Charles are my open admirers, and Roger is the shy person yet to make a move."

Luke was beginning to feel sorry for these men.

Alicia Bartram had all the physical endowments and personality traits of a very tempting seductress, but she was still a child.

She was playing a dangerous game.

Surely none of these men would encourage such a relationship.

Their alleged interest was probably a figment of her imagination.

He should not get involved.

Nevertheless, as all three men—Charles Franklin, Harry Proctor, and Roger Linton—were persons of interest in more important matters, to be an intimate of Alicia Bartram could be a fruitful source of information.

# 8

Later that morning, Luke and Evan visited The Cottage, a clear misnomer for a medium-sized manor house, which had, with its associated lands, been absorbed into the Holt home estate decades earlier.

John Headley, Prudence's steward, and his wife now lived there.

A valet showed the two soldiers into a large chamber dominated by a desk piled high with papers.

From behind these documents emerged a man with furrowed brow who muttered, "I was expecting you. How can I help?"

"Mr. Headley, this is my deputy Sir Evan Williams. We have a number of questions. Mud Hill Farm! Before our arrival, what was it used for?"

Headley looked anxious. "Is that relevant to your enquiries?"

"It could be central. Until a few days ago I believe it was the transit storehouse for smuggled goods that entered the Medway and were rowed up the creek and left there awaiting distribution," explained Luke.

"That may be so. I have orders not to impede the importation of luxury goods, or upset our tenants who export their wool and fleeces without government levies. The local authorities had a similarly benign attitude to smuggling, although I am not certain that the two new magistrates do."

"If smugglers are accepted by the authorities and Lady Prudence, why did she put our men in their depot? Has she changed her mind? Does she want me to use my authority to destroy a particular operation?"

"She does not oppose smuggling as such. But she worries about what might be smuggled. She had me speak to our man who handles the enterprise on behalf of the estate, and he assures me that nothing contrary to her ladyship's wishes is being imported or exported."

"And what could they be?"

"She would ban anything that competes with what our own tenants produce. And she is probably concerned that weapons and ammunition may be brought in to arm our enemies. Surely that is why she called you in?"

"She discussed that possibility with you?" asked a surprised Luke.

"Not really, but she asked me had I heard any rumor to that effect."

"And had you?"

"Many rumors, but no evidence."

"You are right. I am here to ensure that the Medway is not preparing to assist a Spanish or Royalist invasion," admitted Luke.

"There are superficial advantages for the Royalists if they seize this area as they did in 1648, but there are also many handicaps. Unless their timing is perfect and experienced locals pilot them, their vessels will run aground on the mudflats that emerge when the tide ebbs. Getting their men and weapons ashore is one major difficulty, the other is where to hide them," commented Headley.

"I thought you may be able to answer that last question," said Luke.

"There are numerous empty buildings on our estates that would be an ideal haven for such troops, but Charles checks these regularly, and now with your dragoons this could be done on a daily basis. Consequently, using our buildings in such circumstances would only be a short-term solution—a day or so at the most. I do not know what goes on in the smallholdings of the sheep farmers along the Swale. There would also be many places on the Isle of Sheppey that could be used for such a purpose. These seemingly remote regions are not too far away from key strategic areas."

"Would an invader initially prefer these more isolated areas to a direct assault on the castle and dockyard?" asked Evan.

"Unless they come with overwhelming force, the guns of the fort could destroy any large ships attempting to sail directly to the dockyard, which is now better defended by dragoons sent to reinforce Harry Proctor's infantry."

"So when and where is Proctor placing his next shipment of smuggled goods now that Mud Hill Farm is not available?" asked Luke, attempting to catch Headley off his guard

"I do not comment on Proctor. Despite living on the same estate for decades his exact role in the smuggling ring remains a mystery to me."

"Why does Lady Prudence protect him? He is a worthless soldier and a dubious individual."

"A little harsh! You have only been here a short time and have not had the opportunity of seeing some of the virtues that the lad has. His pampering dates back to the days of Lady Mary who adopted him when his mother, Mary's sister, died. Harry's parents both died of the plague caught on a visit to the continent. As a child Harry was brought up with Sir Arthur and Richard. When he came of age he inherited his family's estate, but within a few years squandered it all on gambling. The Holts took over the estate and Harry returned here to be supported by them. Lady Prudence promised Lady Mary that she would continue to look after Harry."

"What else can you tell me about Proctor?"

"Admittedly he is a useless soldier. That is why he survived the night of Sir Arthur's death."

"How so?

"He captained the third of the three long boats that young Arthur had assembled for the assault. He lost contact with the two front vessels and was so far behind when the shooting started that the insurgents assumed there were only two boats, which allowed his to escape undetected."

"The three boats were tied together by a rope to prevent this happening," probed Luke.

"The rope was cut. Proctor claims it was the result of the shooting. Others have a more sinister explanation."

"Why is Proctor, whom some see as the smuggler in chief and consequently the recipient of loads of money, still dependent on the Holts?"

"He still gambles. He goes up to London for weeks at a time and loses a fortune, but that is not the whole story. He is not the smuggler in chief. He carries out the orders of someone who takes most of the profit. Whoever he is, he has something on Proctor to keep him under the thumb."

"How does Proctor relate to the rest of the household? Lady Prudence's favoritism would not help him," said Evan.

"Detested by all, especially the Bartrams, although just recently Harry and Sir Giles seem a lot friendlier."

"Is Harry courting any of the Bartram girls?"

"No way! Sir Giles would have none of it."

"But young girls have a will of their own. Is Proctor having an illicit relationship with the Bartrams, or any other woman?" asked Evan.

John Headley paled.

"Enough questions, gentlemen, I have work to do."

As they rode away from The Cottage, Evan commented, "That conversation came to a sudden end!"

"Your fault, Evan. We don't have to look far for an explanation. Proctor plays around, and one of his pursuits is Caroline Headley. You raised a very sensitive subject."

Luke suddenly turned his horse around.

"Wait here, Evan! I won't be long."

Luke returned to the cottage.

Evan saw him speak to an out-servant.

On his return, Evan asked, "What was that all about?"

"I enquired as to the whereabouts of the lady of the house, Caroline Headley. She is in Gillingham, eating at The Black Eel. Let us do the same!"

Just as the two officers approached the inn they were nearly knocked over by a red-faced, profanity-uttering Harry Proctor rushing from the building.

He was livid.

So much so that he did not notice the two soldiers.

On entering the inn, they saw Caroline Headley sitting alone on a bench in the far corner of the room.

She too appeared ruffled.

Luke whispered to Evan, "I will join the lady. Follow her when she leaves!"

Luke casually approached Caroline. "Mistress Headley may I join you?"

"Certainly, Colonel. I am a little upset. Given our mutual reputations I was sure you would be throwing stones at my window or waylaying me somewhere on the estate long before this."

"Do not believe all that you hear."

"I hope you take your own advice."

"The Holt household gives me plenty of opportunity to exercise the benefit of the doubt, but can you clarify a number of issues for me?"

"Pleasure before business. My planned eating companion just walked out on me. I need food and drink before I offer you anything—even if it is only information."

Both chose the roasted mutton that had been boiled first, which made it very digestible, if somewhat tasteless.

Luke was surprised that Caroline ignored convention and ordered strong spirits as her drink.

The socially conservative Luke could not resist a comment. "Unusual for a lady to drink whisky! In fact, a woman of your status does not usually eat and drink in a tavern such as this."

"You are a prude and snob, sir! You know nothing of my past, nor of our local traditions."

"Enlighten me!"

"I may be married to her ladyship's steward, but I am a full-time business woman in my own right. For decades I have conducted my business from this and other taverns. It is convenient for myself and my customers."

"And what business is that?" asked Luke, half-suspecting a salacious answer.

"Deep-sea fishing. I own a fleet of North Sea trawlers who supply much of London with its herrings."

"I have not seen such trawlers in the local area."

"No, Queensborough is their home port. It saves a lot of time and all the trouble of navigating the Medway with its tidal idiosyncrasies. I meet my captains there a week today. You and I could meet there and expand our relationship."

She squeezed Luke's hand, but his focus was not diverted. "I would enjoy talking to your captains. How did you become a shipowner, and fish supplier?"

"I was my father's only child. The Dutch killed him. They claimed his boat was trespassing on Dutch herring grounds. I hate those Hollanders. The idiots at Upnor Castle have employed a bunch of them to realign its cannons. Fools! They are only waiting a chance to assist the Spaniards and Royalists invade England."

"That is why I must talk to your captains. They can inform me about current developments along the Dutch and Flemish coasts. A few questions about the Holt household—why did Harry Proctor leave here in such a fury?"

"Harry is a vicious varlet. He has the brains of a frog and like that creature, thinks that if he kisses a number of beautiful women he will turn into a prince. Why Prudence tolerates him I do not know!"

"Today's meeting—dalliance or business?"

"He probably thought both. In the past I have used my feminine wiles to achieve certain ends with Harry, but he is a nuisance, expecting me to comply with his lecherous demands when it suits him. Today's outburst stemmed from two issues. I refused his business proposition, and I warned him that if he continued to pester the Bartram girls and myself, I would inform Sir Giles."

"Would that frighten him?"

"Sir Giles is obsessive about his daughters. He is a violent man. If he thought Proctor had even touched one of his girls, he would kill him."

"Caroline, given your background, why does the moralistic Lady Prudence allow you to grace her table?"

Caroline laughed. "You are the sleuth. Find out why Prue puts up with me, and I will reward you in the way I know best."

She leaned across the table, kissed Luke on the lips, and departed.

Evan followed her.

# 9

Luke returned to Holt House and entered the reception hall where a drunk Sir Giles confronted him.

He shouted at Luke, "Keep away from my daughters, or I'll have you horsewhipped!"

He drew his sword and without warning lunged at Luke.

The momentum of his lunge was sufficient for the unsteady assailant to tumble to the floor.

He hit his head on the slate floor, knocking himself unconscious.

Servants carried Giles to his quarters.

A furious Luke went in search of Prudence who was not happy to have her midafternoon routine disrupted.

"What is it now, Luke?" she asked testily.

"Your ladyship, I have enough problems involving the national interest. I cannot afford to be sidetracked by the oafish behavior of your relatives."

"Meaning what?"

"A drunken Sir Giles just attempted to run me through."

"Why?"

"Apparently I am showing too much interest in his daughters."

"Are you?"

"No! My only recent contact with one of your nieces was at breakfast. We were alone together for some time—apart from half a dozen servants. She asked for my assistance on a personal matter."

"Which of the girls? What is the personal matter you are investigating for her?"

"At this stage, I prefer not to answer as all of it may be unsubstantiated rumor or the result of an overvivid imagination. Second, much of what appears personal may relate to the political and security measures I am looking at and, in that case, needs to be kept confidential."

"I will speak to Giles," replied Prudence calmly.

"You must, or I will take it further. Who does he think he is? Is it true that he is negotiating a marriage of his eldest daughter to David Harvey?"

"Yes, but I have advised against it. David's chances of inheriting the marquisate and the fortune that goes with it rest on the premise that his distant cousin does not remarry and have children. Any aristocrat worth his salt would do everything possible to achieve such an end, even on his deathbed. Without such an inheritance, Harvey is an almost penniless country esquire well below the status required to marry my niece. Incidentally, I am making a new will, and the girls will be well provided for."

"I have another personal question. Why do you tolerate Caroline Headley at your table?"

"Sorry, Luke, there some matters so personal that I cannot answer. This is such a question. Apart from her marital indiscretions, there is a lot to admire in that woman."

Luke was upset by his unexpected confrontation with Giles. He walked towards Mud Hill Farm to get away from Holt House, and to review the work of his troops. He had only ambled a few hundred yards along the tree-lined chalk path towards the farm when he met Charles Franklin walking towards him.

"Afternoon, Charles. This is fortuitous. Can I have a word?"

A felled oak provided a seat for the two men.

Luke was direct. "The fisticuffs I saw between you and Harry Proctor were about you and Caroline Headley. From what I understand Caroline is very free with her favors, so why were you involved?"

"Don't be too hasty in judging Caroline. She is unconventional, but not the wanton seducer of popular gossip. Caroline and I grew up together and before she was forced to marry John, we were very close. We have remained so ever since. We confide in each other continually. John has less and less time for his wife, and in his illness he shuns her company. Do not reveal it to anyone at Holt House, but Caroline is about to leave John and live with me."

"Lady Prudence will be beside herself," noted Luke.

"It is Lady Prudence's potential displeasure and reaction to such a move that prevented us acting up until now."

"Why does Prudence take such an interest in Caroline?"

Charles froze.

"Luke, that is a family secret relating to the late Lady Mary, the details of which even I am ignorant."

"I'll ask you an easier question. Why is Proctor so unpopular within the household?"

"Silly question! You've seen him. He is a lazy do-nothing sponge who thinks every woman is his for the taking."

"That is what worries me. This denigration of Proctor is the common story told to me by everybody except Lady Prudence and John Headley. If I were cynical I would suspect that somebody has orchestrated a campaign to scapegoat Harry for any disasters past, present, and future to divert attention from the real culprits. Who wants to destroy Proctor? I know he is the head of a well-organized smuggling ring that supplies the upper classes of the area with their luxury goods and gives the local farmers a better price for the export of wool to the continent. Does he have enemies within the ring?"

"How would I know?"

"Don't play games, Charles. As bailiff and constable you and your men know the routes, the goods, and costs of the smuggled items. Without your connivance his network could not function. For turning a blind eye, you must receive a sizable reward. Do not worry! Breaches of customs and excise are none of my concern."

"You are right, and Proctor *is* in trouble. He has not paid any sweeteners to local officials, including myself on his last two shipments. We are very unhappy. You are mistaken on one point. Proctor is not the head of the smuggling ring. He is its public face and takes orders from the real leader."

"Do you know who that is?"

"No."

"Are you courting one of the Bartram girls?"

"Don't be stupid! They are little more than children. Giles would kill me if I showed the slightest interest."

"I know. He has just attacked me for having breakfast alone with young Alicia."

"Be careful Luke, once Giles has something in his head it is impossible to dislodge it. Should you suddenly die, I will know who murdered you."

He laughed at Luke's discomfort.

"Is anyone else flirting with those Bartram girls?" Luke asked.

"Apart from Proctor, who claims to have had every woman on the estate, I have heard no rumors, although I have occasionally caught young Linton looking at one of the twins with adoring eyes."

The two men separated, each going in opposite directions.

Luke reached the farm and received John Martin's report on the use of the buildings on the Holt estates.

There were dozens of places where men and arms could be hidden. Daily searching would be essential.

Luke ate supper at the farm to avoid further confrontation with Sir Giles.

Well into the evening, an exhausted Evan arrived.

The three officers immediately adjourned to a small room adjoining Evan's bedroom.

"The delightful Caroline must have led you a merry chase?" teased Luke.

"She did, and her visits raise many a concern."

"Where did she go after The Black Eel?"

"To the dockyard."

"To see Proctor?"

"No, she met with John Neville the naval officer.

Before she left the dockyard, she also visited St. Margaret's and was bid farewell by Barnaby Partridge."

"Both of those visits are a surprise. Why would the puritanical Barnaby entertain Caroline, a reputed scarlet woman?"

"Another surprise is that she does not travel alone. She has a bodyguard, an African who must be well over six feet. He joined her just after she left The Black Eel, disappeared while she was in the dockyard and rejoined her as she headed for Rochester. During her visit to the mayor he was nowhere to be seen. He reappeared again and escorted her down the west bank of the Medway to Upnor Castle."

"Whom did she see there?"

"I don't know, but Matthew Hatch provided a small boat with four oarsmen to take her and her black man back across the river."

An orderly interrupted the discussion.

He announced that there was a man at the door that wished to see Colonel Tremayne urgently.

The man entered the room.

Given his physique and skin color, he was obviously Caroline's discreet bodyguard.

The African addressed Luke. "I am Rollo, servant to Mistress Headley. She would like to see you at The Cottage tomorrow morning. She is concerned by problems at Upnor Castle."

Without waiting for a reply, he turned and left.

"I can see what you mean, Evan. I would much prefer that man on our side rather than against us."

Luke remained silent for some time.

Finally, he spoke. "Gentlemen, maybe our focus is misplaced. We have concentrated on aristocratic and gentry links to the problems we are trying to solve. A clearer picture is emerging of a network of well-placed locals beneath this social level who are all locally born and bred. Charles Franklin, Caroline Headley, and John Neville meet those criteria. We must check on Matthew

Hatch and other garrison members and the Holt household. Was Roger Linton really born and bred in Cambridge as asserted?"

"And the history of Harry Proctor has too many gaps and unanswered questions," added Evan.

"Or rather the opposite! Too many fingers have been pointed at him. I suspect he is being set up to take the blame for whatever might occur," concluded Luke.

"Whatever that might be," mused Evan.

"Proctor's life is in danger," Luke suddenly asserted.

The discussion did not get far as there was another interruption. A well-armed dragoon of Thomas Digges's company had an urgent message for Colonel Tremayne.

The courier had a Welsh accent, and Sir Evan addressed him in his native tongue.

He immediately relaxed.

Evan translated, "Digges would like us to attend the dockyard as soon as we can in the morning. He has Proctor under arrest and confined to a small cell."

"My god, has Digges gone mad? Arresting a fellow officer and confining him in a cell!" exclaimed a horrified Luke.

The dragoon came to his commander's defense and blurted out in English, "Proctor ordered the beating of a soldier. When the sergeant considered the beating had gone far enough, he stopped. Proctor took the whip from him and in a ferocious attack he whipped the soldier to death."

"The soldier died?"

"Yes, sir."

"A master can beat a servant to death if that servant has undermined the master's authority. The same applies in the army. If this soldier went out of his way to humiliate his commanding officer to the extent of undermining his authority, then the death of the soldier, while unfortunate, is not considered a homicide. What did the soldier do?"

"He joked about the officer's failed love life."

"A grey area! In the morning, I will inform Lady Prudence of this development before I see Digges.

"Your orders for tomorrow gentlemen—Evan, go to The Cottage and inform Caroline that I will not be there until around midday, and then join me at the dockyard! Strad, visit the dockyard and mix with the infantry. Get as many stories as you can about the beating! John, repeat the searches that you made today!"

# 10

Prudence refused to see Luke until she had risen for the day.

"Unless it is a matter of life and death, I will not see Colonel Tremayne until ten o'clock."

Luke's reply, repeated by a maid, was blunt.

"It is a matter life or death. Harry Proctor will be executed before the day is out."

Prudence leapt from her bed.

She emerged from her bedchamber heavily draped in one of the bed coverings.

"What madness are you about? Harry executed?" she screamed at Luke.

Luke explained.

Prudence was distraught.

"Luke, delay any decision. There must be an explanation that will save Harry from the death penalty."

"I will do my best, but if Harry is guilty, by the new military code he will be shot."

Tears welled up in her eyes as she turned away and reentered her bedroom.

Luke could hear her sobbing uncontrollably.

Luke and Strad galloped to the dockland.

As they entered that precinct, they felt the tension.

The infantry had been disarmed and stood down from their normal duties.

Digges's dragoons had taken over their responsibilities, and one of his sergeants was drilling the surly foot soldiers.

Strad would have to wait until these men were dismissed from their monotonous drill to mingle among them.

Luke entered Digges's office where he and Matthew Hatch were waiting.

Tom spoke. "Yesterday we had a killing and a potential mutiny. I disarmed Proctor's company, and am keeping them busy with mindless drilling. I imprisoned Proctor for his own safety. As the senior officer in the area, Luke, you have the authority to decide this case. Three local captains who are of senior rank to Proctor, with yourself as presiding officer, would constitute a legitimate court."

Luke replied, "Well done, Tom. I sensed the antagonism of the infantry as we came in, but we must not let their antagonism influence our judgment. Before I convene a formal enquiry, let us hear from Proctor. Then we can decide whether we proceed and on what charge—murder, manslaughter, or neither."

Evan arrived, having completed his assignment for Luke.

Three dragoons escorted Proctor into the room.

He was furious.

"Release me at once. I am an officer who has full authority to discipline my men."

"But not to kill them," commented Evan.

"I do not recognize your authority, gentlemen. I will have you dealt with severely if I am not freed and an apology given—and perhaps some compensation provided for my inconvenience and humiliation."

"Lieutenant Proctor, if I had not arrested you and placed you under the protection of my men, you would be dead. Your own company is seething with resentment and determined to kill the man who murdered one of their number. If I had not disarmed them, they would have stormed this building, taken you from us, and done their worst," explained Tom.

Luke was coldly livid. "Proctor, you were a disgrace to the army before this incident. It is only the good graces of Lady Holt that has protected you from past disciplinary action. You are mistaken about the seriousness of your situation. If I choose, as a senior colonel in the national army with the agreement of my fellow officers, I can have you taken out onto the wharf and executed before the hour is up. Stop your whining and provide us with any evidence that can modify the charge of murder, and the most likely outcome of immediate execution! Why did you take over the whipping of the man from your sergeant, and continue beating beyond reason?"

"The man who died was Corporal Basil Miller. He has been undermining my authority for months."

Luke was further annoyed and momentarily concerned.

Proctor knew his military law.

The only possible justification for his actions, accepted in previous cases, was the need to maintain his legitimate authority.

"So what did Miller do yesterday that justified his arrest and whipping?" asked Matthew.

"He accused me in front of several of my men of neglecting my duties and spending most of my time in the unsuccessful pursuit of several women, including his own wife."

"And were you having an affair with his wife?" continued Matthew.

"That is my business. And what if I had, Miller should have controlled the slut."

Luke glared at Proctor, finding it difficult to believe what he was hearing.

"A wronged soldier tells the truth about a predatory officer and that officer embarks on an act of brutality leading to murder!" exclaimed an equally disgusted Evan.

Harry went bright red and shouted at Evan, "You have no concept of honor, sir! I had to act in the way I did—or appear weak. No one humiliates Harry Proctor and gets away with it."

Luke deliberately needled the accused.

"You returned here yesterday livid at your rejection by Mistress Headley, and Miller's mention of your failed love life triggered something in you that led to this irrational and callous attack on him. Return Proctor to his cell! Bring his sergeant here immediately!"

One of the guards returned with a rather plump but well-built man, who was breathing heavily.

"Sergeant Peter Payne, sir. Forgive my heavy breathing. I am not used to the relentless drilling from which I have just been rescued."

"Relax, Sergeant. You are here as a witness to yesterday's events. We are all aware of Proctor's neglect of duty and poor performance as your commanding officer. That is why Captain Digges was sent here with his dragoons to restore discipline, and why I am here also with dragoons to remedy some of Proctor's failings in the wider community. Tell us what happened!"

"Picking out Miller was a great surprise. All of the men, except Miller, hate Proctor. I spoke to the lieutenant several times that his favoritism towards Miller was undermining my own authority as sergeant and was unpopular with all the other corporals. In essence, Proctor made Miller his deputy, ignoring me and the other noncommissioned officers. We had no commissioned officers in the company other than Proctor."

"In what way was this favoritism manifested?" asked Matthew.

"Proctor chose Miller to carry out several clandestine missions for him and in the lieutenant's absence I have seen Miller in Proctor's room helping himself to the officer's food and drink. They often behaved as partners in some secret operation, rather than lieutenant and corporal."

"Could Miller have been offering his wife's services to Proctor?" asked Luke.

"I know Betsey Miller. She put herself about with Basil's knowledge, but she detested Proctor, who no doubt made advances to her. He claimed to have slept with most women in the dockyard community, but I have not found a single wench who confirms his boasts."

"So what exactly happened yesterday afternoon?" enquired Evan.

"Proctor returned early from lunch in a furious mood. He slammed the door of his room and began hurling furniture around the chamber. By the time I reached him, he was banging his head repeatedly against the wall as if demented. I poured him a drink of strong spirits, which, instead of consuming, he emptied over his head. He then asked me to summon his four corporals. They arrived, and noting his demeanor, they laughed and sniggered among themselves. I heard one of them mumble about 'a pathetic impotent drunken sot.'"

"Was it Miller?" probed Luke.

"No, sir!"

"Please continue, Sergeant," encouraged Evan.

"Proctor, now enraged, grabbed Miller around the throat and demanded he be whipped for comments undermining legitimate authority. I protested that it was not Miller. Proctor replied it did not matter who actually said it, they were all responsible for laughing at him, and one of them must take the punishment for all. He ordered me to take Miller to the whipping post and begin flagellation until he ordered me to stop."

"Why didn't you refuse?" asked Matthew.

"A silly question, sir. Proctor was my commanding officer. He was in a mood in which it would have been dangerous to confront him as by this stage he had drawn and primed his pistol. I feared he would shoot us. I followed orders, but after a certain point I saw Miller was in a bad way. He was not responding well to the punishment. I stopped whipping. Proctor seized the whip from me and continued flagellation until Miller collapsed unconscious. He never recovered."

"Thank you, Sergeant. What can you tell us about Basil Miller? Why was he a favorite of Proctor's, and then singled out for punishment?" asked Evan.

"Basil was a local lad. His family were fishermen. There were rumors that his family did not appreciate him helping himself to their profits. Yet again, I heard that he fell out with his family because he was too close to his elder brother's wife yet again that he was an orphan who learnt very young in life how to look after himself. He escaped his past by joining the army and was delighted when he was posted to the dockyard garrison. He could laud it over his old acquaintances from the protection of his military position."

Evan repeated his question. "Why did Proctor's initial favoritism of Miller come to an abrupt end?"

"I don't know, sir. It may have been that Proctor was initially impressed with Miller but after the corporal revealed his true colors, the lieutenant felt a need to remove him."

Tom changed the direction of the questioning, before Evan could ask what *his true colors* implied.

"Has Proctor been too close to any of the men in a physical sense?"

The sergeant hesitated but finally replied, "Such behavior is not unknown in this company, especially towards the new and younger recruits. Proctor, despite his obsession with women, did not ignore boys."

Tom was shocked by the answer to his question.

The officers interviewed the three remaining corporals, and during an interval to take refreshments, Strad reaffirmed to Luke that the general attitude to Proctor was one of detestation and disgust. They even suggested that the officers should give them the key to Proctor's cell and go off for a meal. When they returned, there would be no problem to discuss.

The officers reassembled after a meal and immediately addressed the problem of whether Proctor should be charged with murder or a lesser offence. All of them felt that Proctor had murdered Miller over a matter that was probably outside military jurisdiction and it would be difficult for a military court to convict for murder.

A consensus was reached that Proctor should be charged by the military for a range of offences that would lead to his dismissal but that the matter of Miller's death be handed over to the civil magistrates.

In the interim, Proctor was to be placed under house arrest at Holt House and responsible to Colonel Tremayne.

It was suggested that the civil authorities immediately look into any connection outside of the military between Proctor and Miller.

Luke offered to initially investigate this matter so that the civil authorities would have something on which to base their charges.

During this discussion, Matthew commented, "Sergeant Payne's evidence regarding Miller being a local related to one of the fishing families in the area is inviting, but it has one weakness. I have been here all my life and know all of the fishing fraternity. I know none named Miller. During our break, I spoke to Red who, like me, is a local. He agrees. There is no Miller fishing dynasty."

"Not necessarily a problem," commented Tom. "Many a man enlisting over the last decade has changed his name. Have your men check on every fishing family and find Basil's real name!"

The group was about to disperse when an orderly announced that there was a man demanding entry who claimed he was Major General Smithers.

He had no identification.

Matthew commented, "I know Smithers. I can identify him."

Luke acted quickly, "I do not like the way this could go. Evan, take Proctor immediately to Holt House! Matthew, after you identify Smithers as genuine, return to the Castle! Tom, you and I will deal with the man claiming to be the general."

The group dispersed with Matthew leaving by the door outside of which Smithers waited.

Matthew nodded positively.

It was Smithers.

Luke greeted the senior officer and introduced himself. "I am Colonel Tremayne of the Lord Protector's special unit investigating subversion and sabotage on the Medway. What can we do for you, General?"

"I believe you are holding a Lieutenant Harry Proctor illegally. I order his immediate release into my custody."

"General, you cannot be serious. You have been criminally misled. If you persist I will have you arrested. I may be a mere colonel, but I act on the authority of the Lord Protector himself. Not only do I act in his name, but also I act as if I am the Lord Protector. This matter in which you must be completely ignorant is far greater than the killing of a soldier by an officer. It could involve a vast plot to subvert the government of the country. Your intervention can only raise doubts in my mind as to your loyalty to His Highness—and it is unnecessary. A decision on Proctor's fate has been delayed. Who has criminally involved you in this matter?"

Bluster had given way to a growing uneasiness.

The general began to perspire profusely.

Luke insisted, "Who has involved you in this possible treacherous conspiracy?"

"Sir Giles Bartram! I was with him in Rochester this morning when he received a message from Lady Prudence Holt that a member of their household had been arrested, and was subjected to a military trial that might lead to his execution. He suggested that I use my authority to have the matter postponed until the family could consult its lawyers."

"Why didn't Sir Giles come himself?"

"He thought that as the trial was being conducted by the military a civilian would have no influence. As a senior army officer, and not a member of the Holt household, I could be considered impartial."

"I will talk to Sir Giles about this. I am also at present a member of the Holt household."

"I am glad, Colonel, that Proctor will live to defend himself at a later date. I am sure that Whitehall does not need to know of my visit here today. I was just helping a friend."

"You were never here, General," said Luke as he winked knowingly at the general, now desperate to leave.

Tom Digges had not uttered a word during the whole discussion between Luke and the general.

After the latter's departure, he could only mutter in awe, "A brilliant demolition of a potentially troublesome senior officer. You make a formidable opponent."

Luke was not displeased with the outcome.

# 11

---

It was midafternoon before Luke finally reached The Cottage to keep his delayed appointment with Caroline.

John Headley met him.

"I am sorry Caroline has not yet returned. After Sir Evan informed us that you would be delayed, she decided to make her regular visit to an aged relative who lives on London Road, a few miles east of Rochester."

"Why did she want to see me so urgently?" asked an impatient Luke.

"I don't know. Most of Caroline's life is hidden from me."

"Why do you stay man and wife given the angst she creates for you?"

"Given the powerful influences that would act to prevent it, divorce is not an option. Despite occasional tensions, for most of the time we happily lead our separate lives. But I am worried at the moment. Caroline is never late. It is one virtue she has retained. She is very punctual."

"While I wait, let me ask you a few questions concerning Harry Proctor. Are there any local families by the name of Miller?"

"Why do you ask?"

"The murdered soldier was a local lad by that name. We are pursuing the possibility that his conflict with Proctor was not related to their military link, but to some local activity."

"I know of no one by that name."

John suddenly smiled. "But I do recall someone mentioning *Miller* a week or so ago. It could only have been Charles, Caroline, or Richard."

Luke and John simultaneously noticed three riders coming down the slope towards them.

"Here's Caroline now, but who is that with her and Rollo. It's a dragoon. Is he one of your men?"

He was.

The leading horseman was Luke's lieutenant, John Martin.

A breathless Martin explained, "Colonel, there has been an attempt to abduct Mistress Headley and then later to kill her."

"How did you get involved? asked Luke.

"Following your orders to investigate all likely hiding places my troop entered a dense wood along the London Road. As we ambled along a narrow path the peace was shattered just ahead of us by a burst of musket fire—three or four shots in quick succession. We galloped towards the noise and saw Mistress Headley and the giant African sheltering behind a fallen tree trunk. He was wounded. I ordered my men to shoot in the direction of the gunfire, and we advanced on that position. The firing stopped. Mistress Headley wanted to return home immediately, and to see to the wounds of her servant. I put him on one of our horses, and escorted them here. I will rejoin my men who are still searching the woods."

"Thanks, Lieutenant, Caroline can tell us the rest," replied Luke.

John Headley called his servants to assist, but both Caroline and Rollo walked into the house unaided.

Luke followed and found Caroline taking a swig of strong spirits. She offered Luke a mug of Dutch schnapps.

"Caroline, can you tell me what happened, or shall I leave my questioning to another day?"

"I am a bit shaken, but I need to tell you what just happened, and what I discovered at the fort. They may be related."

"Let's start with this afternoon," advised Luke.

"After visiting a relative who lives near London Road, I came home by a shortcut which I always take through Wadham Wood. Halfway through the forest, two men wearing black hoods jumped out from behind the trees. They pulled me from my horse and began dragging me into the bushes. I screamed. Rollo appeared and wielded his thick staff to great effect. My assailants ran off. Rollo regathered my horse. I was about to remount when a hail of bullets whistled past me. Rollo placed his body between me and the source of the gunfire. He was hit several times. Fortunately, according to your lieutenant, they are only flesh wounds—nothing serious."

"What happened next?" asked Headley, who up until now had listened in complete silence.

"Rollo and I crawled behind a fallen log as the firing continued. Then Luke's men appeared and the attackers disappeared."

"Have you been attacked before?" asked Luke.

"Yes, from time to time. Periodically highwaymen or demobilized soldiers appear and terrify the locals. Usually a handful of coins satisfy most assailants. However, in recent years in various parts of the estuary and the Downs a number of women have been raped. That is why I have Rollo follow me everywhere."

"How did you come to own an African slave?"

"He is not a slave, and I obtained him as part of our salvage of a sinking Portuguese merchantman just off Whitstable. Now what is the real story of Harry?"

"I hoped you could tell me?"

"Don't play games, Luke! What happened yesterday?"

"After you rejected him he went to the dockyard and killed one of his own men, Basil Miller."

Caroline dropped her glass of schnapps, went as pale as a sheet, and staggered forward.

Luke caught her before she hit the edge of a small wooden table.

Under John's direction he carried her to her bedchamber.

As the two men left Caroline in the care of her servants, John asked pointedly, "What led to her collapse?"

Luke lied.

"The shock of her earlier experience finally caught up with her."

"She is not as tough as she likes to make out. Was it a robbery gone wrong, or an attempted rape?" John asked.

"I have no idea. It could also be a commercial rival, or in a more sinister scenario someone wanting to silence Caroline before she reveals something incriminating about them. My investigation must be creating worries within the household, the garrisons, and the wider community. If Caroline and yourself are having supper at Holt House this evening I will continue my questioning after the meal. She should be completely recovered after an afternoon's sleep."

As Luke walked back to Holt House he reflected on Caroline's dramatic reaction to the news that Harry's victim was Basil Miller.

What was the connection, and was it significant?

At supper that evening, Luke sat next to Giles. He had several questions to ask and he began politely, almost innocently. "How do you know General Smithers?"

"He went to school with me at Rochester Cathedral. Smithers went into law. When our civil wars came, Smithers, always a strong parliamentarian as most lawyers were, joined the forces of the Earl of Essex and rose rapidly through the ranks. He did not join the New Model Army but served in numerous garrisons throughout the country and became an expert in the role of artillery in defending castles."

"It's a wonder he was not consulted about the series of renovations to Upnor Castle?"

"He was, back in 1648, but for the last three years he has relinquished his military roles and returned to the law. I was consulting him about a land transfer when Prue sent a message regarding Harry. I thought your group of officers could do with an extra hand."

"We had reached a consensus before Smithers arrived, but he endorsed our decisions and I have sent them on to the Provost Marshal, and referred other matters to the local magistrates."

"Was that necessary? Couldn't it have been handled in-house?" asked a prickly Giles.

"It could have, but the result would have been the immediate execution of Proctor for murder. Harry is not popular. That is why two of my dragoons are with him day and night. It is not to prevent him escaping, but to stop someone killing him."

"Harry has not come down for supper. That is unusual. He usually likes to put on a display for the women," continued Giles gruffly.

"He is not here because he is under house arrest and that I interpret as confinement to his apartment within the house—with an escorted walk in the garden twice a day. He will eat in his room. If he breaks those conditions, I will transfer him to the Tower of London."

Word had spread of Caroline's misadventure.

Alicia typically ignored the etiquette of the meal table and asked across it, "Mistress Headley, tell us all about your escape!"

Caroline was discreet. "I suffered no harm, thanks to the bravery of my servant and the arrival of Luke's dragoons. It is a warning to all of us in troubled times not to travel without an escort. Alicia, you must stop gallivanting through the woods on your own! Even the coppices near the house are dangerous."

Giles nearly choked on a half-consumed chicken leg. He glared at Alicia.

Roger Linton relieved the tension developing between the Bartrams by asking, "Colonel, is there a connection between the accident to Captain Hatch, the death of Major Dewhurst, the death at the dockyard attributed to Lieutenant Proctor, and this attack on Mistress Headley?"

"Probably some are connected but maybe not all of them," replied Luke diplomatically.

After supper, Luke walked back to The Cottage with the Headleys.

He immediately teased Caroline.

"What were you trying to do with the Bartrams? Giles was about to explode. He will probably hide in every piece of woodland on the estate, heavily armed to deal with any unfortunate male who enters it at the same time as Alicia."

"It was for the girl's good. She is a child playing with fire, and I want Sir Giles to bring her into line before she causes grief to the whole household."

"What was your urgent news regarding Upnor Castle?" he asked.

"The workers repositioning the guns are not Dutch," Caroline replied.

"I know their leader is Dutch but probably an impostor. He did not know the details of the town in Holland from which he claimed to have come. As for his men I don't know."

"I visited the castle yesterday and chatted with the overseer and his workers. I asked the men to show me what they were doing. They are all German."

"How do you know that?"

"When I sailed with my late father, we spent several seasons in the Baltic. I learnt enough German to get by."

"What if they are German?"

"Where is the so called Charles II's current court? Germany. And his courtiers are moving through the hundreds of principalities seeking mercenary troops. What if the pretend workers at the castle are an advance guard of pro-Royalist German troops? If Spain refuses help, the Catholic Germans might come to the party."

"Charles doesn't have the money to pay them," replied Luke coldly.

"But Spain does—if the silver from America gets through. Spain needs her own troops to invade Portugal, and defend Flanders. She cannot waste them on an invasion of England, but she could pay the Germans to do so."

"A possibility, but equally they may be Germans from one of the many principalities that are in alliance with the Lord Protector. Caroline, you amaze me! You have a better grasp of foreign policy than many of the persons who sit around the Protector's council of state. How do you know so much?"

She turned towards her husband. "John, you might like to hear my answer. On the numerous occasions you thought I was having an affair with Roger Linton I was discussing the affairs of the world with him. He has been my unofficial tutor. Given my trading network I need to keep up with political and military developments in the area. In any case even I could not seduce that saint. In return I advised him on affairs of the heart of which he is completely ignorant."

"Matthew can check the details of the gun replacements with Whitehall," commented Luke.

"Strangely not. He tried, but has reached a dead end. Dewhurst apparently signed the documents presented to him by the so-called Pieter Keyjel. They and other appropriate matters cannot be verified as all documents held by the master of ordnance relating to Upnor Castle were burnt in a suspicious fire in his office only three weeks ago."

"This is worrying! Matthew may be in danger. I will send a troop of my dragoons to the castle to protect him," Luke replied.

"The situation is worse than you think. Matthew found Dewhurst's diary. It is very sparse but he does note that a week ago he sent half a company of infantry who should be guarding the guns, and some of the gunners themselves to Sheerness. He thought he was obeying orders which Matthew has not been able to verify," Caroline reported.

"In that case Upnor Castle is not defended," commented a now-alarmed Luke.

"Except for a depleted group of gunners."

"I will act immediately. I will send my dragoons to guard the castle and request an infantry company from London to be sent immediately as the new garrison. The Royalists prisoners must be moved to The Tower, their civilian guards dismissed, and the foreign workmen placed under my supervision."

"No, Luke. Be cautious! The local community has had its fill of military intervention. Your rapid response to that newcomer

Digges's arrest of Harry displeased many local notables, and Matthew will not be happy with your interest in the castle," advised Caroline.

"So what would you do if you were me?" asked a slightly miffed Luke.

"Report your fears, and suggested action to Whitehall, and receive specific authorization for what you wish to do. I suspect that the loyalty of the local landowners to the current government is your basic concern. Do not unnecessarily annoy them, until you have absolute proof that your proposed course of action is necessary."

"Unfortunately waiting for proof is often a fatal error. My approach has always been to act first, and suffer the consequences. Nevertheless, we are so close to London I will have a courier deliver a report with my requests to Mr. Thurloe. I should receive a reply within a day or two at the most."

John entered the cottage and disappeared.

Caroline lingered on the threshold.

Luke embraced her and whispered, "Why did you faint at the naming of Basil Miller as Harry's victim?"

"Basil and I were brought up together. His family were fisherfolk out of somewhere in Essex. His father and brothers were lost at sea, and his mother was unable to cope. My father took the small boy into our family. He was a bad egg and ran away when he was about twelve. I did not know he was back in the area. My father also agreed to support Basil's mother, who was ill for the remainder of her days. Ironically, she was the sick old lady I was visiting on London Road to distribute our monthly charity. Poor John thinks it is another affair that I am having."

"Did she know about Basil?"

"No! Knowledge of her wayward son would have given her too much grief. She thinks he died fighting for his country years ago."

# 12

Two days later, a coach escorted by a small detachment of the Protector's own horse guard arrived in the forecourt of Holt House. An excited servant disturbed the early afternoon meal by announcing that a high official from His Highness wished to speak to Colonel Tremayne.

A small man wearing black emerged from the coach. It was not the Lord Protector, General Desborough, or Mr. Thurloe.

It was Thurloe's senior agent, William Acton, with whom Luke had had some recent dealings. Luke led him into a small antechamber where servants quickly provided refreshments.

Acton spoke quietly. "The government is very concerned with what you may have discovered, but as our emphasis is on winning the loyalty of the civilian elite, it does not want those in the Medway to be diverted from this path by any premature actions of the military. You have no concrete evidence of a locally fostered conspiracy. Already you have aroused considerable consternation among locals who seem to have influence on the council of state. Consequently, you will take no action regarding Upnor Castle. However, a company of infantry will be sent immediately from London to protect the remaining gunners, and as soon as we can, their numbers will be doubled. The prisoners will be removed to the Tower of London and their guards dismissed as you advised.

Everybody within the castle will now be under the direct control of one man—the newly appointed governor, the promoted *Major* Matthew Hatch. An ordnance officer who will command the batteries, and act as Hatch's deputy will directly supervise the artillerymen and the workmen. This new officer, William Neville, will be your eyes and ears within the castle. He is one of Mr. Thurloe's agents. You, personally, are to show no further interest in Upnor Castle."

"Why promote Hatch and give him complete control? He is one of my top suspects."

"If you are right, with enough rope, he will hang himself," Acton lamely replied.

"Have I updated written orders?"

Acton smiled. "You have been close to power long enough to know nothing of importance is committed to writing. That is why I have come in person to give you the government's answer to your questions. On a separate issue, the affairs at Holt House, I do have authorization from His Highness personally empowering you to act as a magistrate in the investigation of any matters that arise out of the affairs related to this household. Both Harvey and Lynne have been advised of this, and requested to cooperate with you."

"Ridiculous! My enquiry into possible insurrection and subversion against the government is stifled, yet I am empowered to continue with a personal concern of the Lord Protector. Has Oliver lost the plot?"

"Who are we to say?"

Acton unexpectedly clasped Luke's hand and whispered, "Be careful, Tremayne! Your very presence here has been designed to provoke somebody, and it appears to be working."

"Thanks for the warning."

"One last thing! I have a warrant to relieve you of Harry Proctor and transfer him to The Tower. That is why I have an escort. His Highness wishes the lieutenant, for his own protection, to be incarcerated well away from Holt House."

"No problem. He is contained on the second floor of the east wing under constant supervision. I will have him brought down."

The two men waited for Proctor's arrival.

The quiet of the antechamber was violently disturbed when a highly agitated Strad burst through the door.

"What is it, Sergeant? Where's Proctor?"

"Missing."

"How can that be? He was guarded day and night. There was even a soldier inside his room."

"I don't know, but I have the current guard detail together awaiting your interrogation," replied a hassled Strad.

Acton was furious. "This is the very development His Highness wished to avoid. I will wait one hour in the hope you will find the missing man. Not up to your usual standard, Tremayne! Or is this a trick to avoid compliance with my orders? I would not be surprised if it were."

Luke left his visitor and questioned Proctor's guards. "When did you last see him?"

"Colonel, my men and I had just relieved the morning detail when Miss Alicia came out of his room," answered their senior corporal.

"Miss Alicia? Are you sure?"

"She was wearing the clothes I have seen her in before, but I did not see her face. I looked into the room and saw whom I thought to be Lieutenant Proctor lying in his bed. I stationed one of my men in the room where he remained until you sent a message to bring Proctor downstairs. The man in the bed proved to be a bunch of rolled-up clothes and some pillows. You will need to speak to the morning detail."

Luke did.

The soldier in charge was aghast.

Luke demanded a detailed account of events during his watch. Towards the end of the narrative, he recalled, "At meal time, Miss Alicia appeared carrying a large bag, accompanied by a servant bringing food. I asked her what was in the bag, and she explained she had brought additional delicacies for Proctor and herself. She and the lieutenant sat at a small table and consumed their meal."

"Was the guard within the room during this period?"

"Yes, but Miss Alicia asked him to inform me that they required more wine. He left the room and, unfortunately, chatted with one of his comrades on the way back. Just as he reached the door, Miss Alicia came out claiming she had changed her mind. Lieutenant Proctor was feeling poorly and was lying on his bed. She left. Proctor was on the bed covered up by a coverlet. Only a few minutes later, the afternoon detail was heard coming up the stairs. I stood down the detail, and our replacements took over."

"Miss Alicia had left the room before the changeover?"

"Yes, we all know Miss Alicia."

"If Alicia left then, who left during the gap in the changeover? Clever Harry Proctor wearing women's clothes!" commented a now-enlightened Strad.

Luke ordered his men and the household servants on a full alert.

Harry and Alicia had to be found.

She was.

Lady Mercy, accompanied by Luke, found a giggling Alicia in her bedchamber.

She could not conceal her grin. "We won. We tricked your soldiers. Harry said it would be easy, and a clever trick to pull on you. You are all stupid. What fun!"

Luke was incandescent. "You scatterbrained milksop! You have been tricked into assisting a prisoner to escape from military custody. You could hang. It is not a game. I will demand that your father punish you severely. You are a disgrace to the family, and have seriously embarrassed the Lord Protector."

Alicia did not comprehend the repercussions of her actions. "Harry said it was a joke. He will be back in his room by now."

"No my girl, Harry Proctor is well gone—and for your sake as well as his, hopefully not to his death."

Luke informed Acton, who remarked as he left, "It is the Lord Protector's view that Proctor is the key to the trouble on the Medway, and the mysteries of Holt House. Concentrate on him!"

Luke expanded the search for Proctor, utilizing not only his own men and most of the household servants but also the still-seething infantry from the dockyard, who were determined to find their hated officer.

A prolonged search proved fruitless.

Luke was very angry. No one had seen Proctor, or rather, no one admitted to any sighting. This was unacceptable.

"The household teems with servants. Either there is a conspiracy of silence to protect Proctor, or he had amazingly disappeared without trace."

"No servants I have met would help Proctor. They detest him," commented Strad.

Next afternoon, a farmhand asked to see Luke. With him was a scruffy unkempt individual who claimed to be a shepherd on the tidal flats of the eastern Medway.

The stranger spoke. "Colonel, a horseman gave me this note and asked that I deliver it to you alone."

The note read, "Colonel, you will find Proctor at The Cottage just after dusk, two days hence. Come alone! John Headley."

Luke asked the shepherd, "Did Mr. Headley give you this message?"

"No, sir. The man was a stranger."

After consulting Roger Linton concerning the authenticity of the writing, Luke and Strad walked across the fields to discuss the situation with Evan and John Martin.

The soldiers agreed.

This was a poorly planned artifice.

Evan summed up its obvious weaknesses.

"Why would Headley who lives only a few hundred yards from Holt House have a message delivered by a shepherd from miles across the county? Why require you to come alone?"

"And according to Linton the note was not written by Headley," added Strad.

"Ignore it, Luke!" advised Evan.

"But why would anyone engage in such a crude machination? It can achieve nothing. But I will not ignore it. Maybe someone is trying to tell us something. Evan, get over to The Cottage now and question the staff!"

Evan and Strad arrived at the cottage and were immediately disconcerted by the lack of activity.

Strad pounded on the main door.

No one responded.

The two soldiers circumnavigated the building, testing all the doors and windows. They were shut fast.

Evan was bemused. "Where is everybody? A whole household with four or five in-servants could not just disappear. Check the stables, Strad!

Strad rejoined his captain a few minutes later.

"Most of the horses are gone, and there is not a groom to be found. Should we break into the house?"

"We may not have to. There is some activity in the barn. One of the out-servants may be able to tell us where the household has gone."

On entering the barn, Evan saw two men stacking bales of hay and asked, "Good fellows, where is your master and the rest of his household? We have an urgent message for him from Colonel Tremayne, but cannot raise anybody up at the house."

"Not surprising, good sir. There is no one there. Mr. Headley left with some of his men before dawn yesterday to visit an estate on the eastern Swale, and the mistress has taken all the servants, except Mr. Headley's valet, with her to Queensborough for several days."

"So where is the valet?"

"He had two days off to visit his sick father. He should be back early tomorrow morning."

"If he is sober," remarked the other hay stacker.

"How long has the house been empty?"

"Only since dawn yesterday."

"Did you see Mr. Headley and his group leave at that time?"

"I saw Mr. Headley's party of about four horsemen amble past the barn. I sleep here. Ten minutes later a lone horseman followed them. I don't know if Mr. Headley was in the first group, or the lone horseman."

"When did the valet leave?"

"He may have left before the group and the lone horse man or he may have been part of either. An hour after they had gone I went up to the house and checked that it had been locked securely."

"Are the Headleys in the habit of deserting The Cottage and leaving it empty for days at a time?"

"Two or three times a year. On most occasions, if the master and mistress are away at the same time, one or two servants are left behind to maintain the place."

"Can you get into the house?"

The hay stacker smiled. "Captain, I have no means of access, but I do know a nimble-fingered gent who may be able to gain you entry. However, the quickest way is to ask up at the big house. Lady Prudence has keys to everything on her vast estates."

"Could Mr. Proctor have been part of your master or mistress's entourage?"

"Quite possibly, but neither the mistress nor any of my fellow servants like him. He has caused tremendous trouble between too many men and their womenfolk. They would have enjoyed turning him over to you."

As Evan turned to leave, the laborer added, "On the other hand, the master has occasionally shown kindness to Harry Proctor. It surprised us all."

# 13

An hour before dusk, Luke and two troops of his dragoons surrounded The Cottage. Evan deployed one troop at all the possible exits, while Luke, Strad, and the other troop entered the building using a gigantic key obtained from Lady Prudence.

Evan concluded that whoever had sent the note either wanted Luke to find evidence of some sort in the house or trap the colonel into a life-threatening situation.

The perpetrator, unless he was completely stupid, would know that Luke would enter the premises before the proposed time and with an ample bodyguard.

The real purpose of what could turn out to be a clumsy charade eluded both senior officers.

The Cottage had been the home of one of the Holt neighbors for half a century. When their estate was taken over by the Holts, it became the home and office for their estate manager, the steward John Headley.

The search of the house was random and haphazard.

No one knew what they were looking for.

Luke's directive *to note anything out of place* was hardly precise.

Strad's keen eye did notice something awry.

He explained to Luke, "Headley is neat and tidy, and his desk is arranged in a very organized fashion. He worked late into the night as his desk reveals clear evidence of candle wax that ran down one stick and another pile of wax a foot away where a second candle must have stood to illuminate whatever Headley was writing or reading. Why is the second candle now yards away behind Headley's chair, and on that small cabinet? If he moved it anywhere, you would expect it to have been onto the small bench near the door where he might have extinguished it as he left the room."

"Very observant, Sergeant, but what does it tell us? asked Luke.

"Look at the base of this relocated candle. That stain could be blood."

"What are you suggesting?"

"Somebody hit Headley, or an unknown person with the candlestick."

"Where's the body? Where's the blood?"

"Perhaps this is the only clue the manipulator is willing to provide," said Evan, joining his companions.

"Is this another stupid game of that irresponsible child, Alicia?" asked Strad.

"Get all of our men into the house and light every candle and taper you can find. We are now looking for bloodstains," ordered Luke.

Luke noted that the Headleys lived well. He had never seen so many expensive candles.

After half an hour of meticulous searching, Luke was disheartened. Then one of his men shouted, "More blood, sir!"

On the kitchen floor, just in front of a cabinet full of pots and pans, were several smears of blood. Even so, being on the kitchen floor, it could be blood from any of the animals that had been prepared for cooking.

Strad noticed another anomaly. "Colonel, there is no dust on the floor at the end of this cabinet. It has been moved very recently."

Luke and Strad pushed the cabinet away from the wall to reveal a door.

They opened it and, armed with a large candle each, descended steps that led into a large cavernous cellar.

Strad noticed more blood at the bottom of the stairs, but as they progressed into the cellar, their anticipation of finding a body, that of Headley or Proctor, rapidly evaporated.

In the middle of the cellar were rows of meat hooks from which hung the carcasses of several sheep.

Beyond the carcasses, along the back and side wall of the cellar, were large barrels. They were full of brine and large portions of meat. The meat was being salted and cured.

At that moment, one of Luke's men escorted a tall thin stranger down the stairs from the kitchen. It was Headley's partly intoxicated valet. He enquired as to what was happening.

Luke explained and then asked, "Why was this cellar door concealed in the kitchen with a cabinet of pots and pans?"

"No problem. The previous owners had the direct link between the kitchen and the meat-curing cellar. When Mr. Headley took over he greatly expanded the curing operation, and made the main entrance to the cellar from outside the building. He closed off the staircase that you used. You will see in the far corner a large double door. That is now the entrance."

"Mr. Headley has a meat-salting business?" asked Luke.

"Yes, and it is very profitable. He has a contract with the navy board to supply all government ships out of the Medway with their salted mutton."

"Did you see Mr. Headley leave two mornings ago?" probed Evan.

"No, I prepared what he needed the previous evening as I left before him. He knew he would be delayed waiting for two of his unreliable deputies and a posse of the bailiff's men, who were to accompany him. They planned to visit one or two troublesome tenants along the Swale."

"When do you expect him back?"

"Sometime late tomorrow."

Luke drew a letter from his pocket and showed it to the valet.

"Is that Mr. Headley's hand?"

The valet looked at it carefully and pronounced, "No, sir! Mr. Headley cannot resist the unnecessary flourish with all his capitals. This is not his signature."

Luke changed the subject. "Did you see Mr. Headley to bed the night before he left?"

"No, sir. He needed to work late to prepare for a difficult confrontation. I left him in his office working on some papers. I brought him a jug of mulled wine just before I retired."

"Can you remember where he had placed his candles?" asked Strad.

"As always, on his desk next to each other."

"How many would he light?"

"Just the two. He would be furious to find any candles lit unnecessarily. He is a miser when it comes to lighting the house. He will have a fit when he sees how many you have used."

Luke was frustrated.

Evan and the dragoons returned to their barracks at Mud Hill Farm, and Luke and Strad walked to Holt House.

Luke brought Lady Prudence up to date on developments—or rather the lack of them.

Prudence suddenly paled and looked as if about to faint.

Luke grabbed her as she began to slide to the floor. Her servants were quickly at her side. After a few minutes slouched semiconscious in a large chair, she recovered and whispered to Luke, "Clear the room!"

Luke obeyed and when they were alone he asked, "What is it, your ladyship? Why did my account of a fruitless search in the Headley's meat curing and salting cellar bring on such a reaction?"

"I hope I am wrong. Lady Mary told me before her death that a young child disappeared on the estate decades ago and was ultimately found, months later, pickled in a vat of Headley's brine. At the time there was some resentment against John Headley for creating a situation where a child could fall into such a vat and drown. Did you search all the vats?"

"No, not thoroughly. My men ascertained what was on the top of several of the vats, but did not empty their contents."

"Your story makes no sense. Why were you led on a wild goose chase with no results? Why was the situation staged as to make you think Headley had been murdered—and then you find nothing? Maybe someone is seeking revenge for that child or has simply remembered the story and used it to dispose of my steward. Empty all those barrels! I pray that my intuition is wrong, and that John is happily fulfilling his duties somewhere along the Swale."

The following day, Luke and his men returned to The Cottage assisted by several of Headley's out-servants who regularly manned the curing cellar and associated storage barns on the estate.

It was a slow process, and as unorthodox pieces of meat surfaced, Luke sent to Rochester for a butcher, and a surgeon.

Between them, the experts concluded that not all of meat was ovine. There was a reasonable amount of horse and some dog—but there was no human.

John Headley had not been disposed of in a vat of his own brine, nor had anybody else.

Luke was in a bad mood.

If Prudence's hunch had been right, he could make sense of the game someone was playing with him. But at the moment, it appeared a nonsense, a complete waste of time.

Then it dawned on him. Perhaps that was the sole purpose of the exercise—to divert him from his immediate priority of finding Proctor.

Maybe he had underestimated Alicia.

Was this part of her plan to assist Proctor's escape—to buy him time to get well away?

Then came Luke's first piece of luck—or was it?

Just as he was about to leave the building, an expensive-looking dagger was found in the grass near the external door of the cellar.

Luke recognized it immediately.

Digges had removed it from Proctor when he was arrested and which, with all his belongings, had been sent back to Holt House.

Either Proctor had been near the cottage or someone had placed the dagger there to create such an impression.

As a dispirited Luke trotted slowly to Holt House, one of his men galloped after him.

The dragoon reined in his horse and shouted for Luke to follow him.

"There's a body," he whispered as Luke followed him into the coppice adjacent to the big house.

The trooper led Luke to a body partly concealed under a bramble.

Luke was stunned.

It was one of the Bartram twins.

The corpse, which revealed a massive wound to the back of the head, was cold.

The girl was covered in a bright red cape that Luke had seen Alicia wearing on several occasions.

Luke had the body taken up to the big house and personally informed Lady Mercy of the tragic discovery.

He stayed with her until she felt strong enough to view the corpse.

On doing so, Mercy collapsed into a torrent of tears.

After some time, she spoke. "Luke, this is not right. This is Frances, not Alicia, yet she is wearing her sister's outer clothes. The bodice and the cape are Alicia's. Frances would never wear such flamboyant outfits in normal circumstances. I need an explanation. Find Alicia for me!"

Luke could not.

Alicia had, similarly to Harry Proctor and John Headley, disappeared without trace.

Luke's own examination of the body revealed the unmistakable signs of strangulation. The rough scour marks indicated the use of a coarse rope—the dockyard was full of such offcuts. Yet there was also a large gash on the back of her head. Could the weapon have been the candlestick found in John Headley's study?

If the body had been Alicia's, it would have made sense. Proctor persuaded Alicia to meet him in or near The Cottage. They argued. He struck her. She was still alive. He then strangled her and took the body into the woods.

Frances Bartram had been murdered, but did the killer know it was Frances?

Why was she wearing her sister's cape?"

Did the sisters have a reputation for confusing their identities to trick their admirers, unbeknown to their mother?

# 14

The next day, Luke continued the coordinated search using his dragoons, the servants of Holt House, and the disgruntled infantry troops from the dockyard. There were now three missing persons—John Headley, Harry Proctor, and Alicia Bartram.

Midafternoon, John Headley returned, completely unaware that the search he encountered as he approached his home was in part directed at him.

Luke outlined the concerns that had been expressed regarding the missing trio.

John agreed that Harry and Alicia may have used his house, but he could not believe they were responsible for a bloodied candlestick.

He emphasized that Harry was genuinely fond of Alicia.

They had grown up in Holt House together for years.

He also felt that from Harry's side it was more of a sibling relationship.

"Harry has always treated Alicia as a young sister. She is still little more than a troublesome child with a wild imagination, which now appears to manifest itself in the belief that one or more men are desperately in love with her. And Harry, if you believe all the foul rumors, already has more than his share of female companions."

Luke was not convinced.

He raised another scenario with John.

"Could Frances have been the intended victim? Was it Frances who rescued Harry? Harry escapes, but their pursuers—possibly dockyard soldiers, murder Frances. Alicia's flirtation with Harry and others may have been sisterly protection of her much quieter sibling."

John disagreed.

"Given a lifetime of observation of these girls it is far more likely that Alicia has run off with Harry. Frances wore Alicia's cloak to give her sister time to escape, by misdirecting the searchers".

Luke commented, "Everybody wants Harry dead!

"Everybody? Not quite. He has alienated members of the smuggling ring of which he is the front man. Most members of this household are angry at his atrocious behavior, and the protection he received from the late Lady Mary, and now from Lady Prudence. Sir Giles is enraged at the very thought of Harry's association with any of his daughters. You know how he reacts. The dockyard infantry sees him as a remorseless murderer of one of their number. If the victim is a local man, some of his relatives may have decided on revenge. Then you cannot rule me out. His attitude to Caroline could be seen as a motive for me to act against him, and for that matter, countless other husbands and fathers whose women folk have been traduced by Harry."

"And where is your wife?" asked Luke feigning ignorance.

"She was required unexpectedly to go to Queensborough by one of her trawler captains who was in a state of panic, according to the seaman who delivered the message. She may have to go on to Whitstable where several of her trawlers were expected to dock. She will be away for several days."

"Given the attempt to abduct her, is it safe for her to be travelling the county?"

"She has her exotic bodyguard who has the knack of being invisible until needed. This time she also took most of our servants with her. That's why the house appeared abandoned to you."

"Where would Harry and Alicia go if they had run off together? You have known both of them for decades. They must have had their secret places on the estate."

"Both know many hidden spots on the estates very well, especially the forests along the slopes of the North Downs. In addition, Harry's smuggling role has made him privy to isolated farmsteads and hidden inlets, as well as the network of caves that follow the northern coast."

"Caves, I would have thought the dominance of chalk in this area would have rendered caves dangerous. Do you know how to access them?"

"One or two minor ones, but it was not wise for me over the decades to have any information about the wider network used by the smugglers. They could become very vicious if crossed, although no one knows who controls them. They are the most likely group anxious to eliminate Harry."

Supper that evening was a somber affair.

From the family, only Prue and Richard attended, and from the household Roger and Barnaby.

The distraught Bartram family chose to eat in their apartment while Caroline and Charles were missing because of business commitments.

Headley's absence was not explained.

Luke was joined by his deputy Sir Evan Williams, Tom Digges from the dockyard, and Matthew Hatch from Upnor Castle.

The remaining guest was the magistrate David Harvey, who with Luke was coordinating both the search for Alicia and Harry and the investigation into the murder of Frances and the death of Dewhurst.

Luke gave Prue and the assembled diners an update on the situation, and others who were involved contributed relevant details.

Prue eventually retired followed by Richard, Roger, and Barnaby, but David Harvey and the soldiers remained to discuss the next day's activities over a continuous intake of wine and spirits.

It was close to midnight when Luke grabbed a small candle to carry a flame to the larger candles in his bedchamber. As he reached the top of the stairs he smelt a pleasant aroma of roses and lemons—a perfume that he had experienced only recently.

He was surprised on reaching the door of his bedroom that it was ajar, and that the pleasing aroma seemed to be emanating from within his room.

He pushed the door open very quietly, but he could see little by the light of his tiny candle.

He transferred the flame to three large candles and immediately noticed that the curtains of his bed had been pulled back.

There under the top cover was a body.

It was a girl.

She was breathing normally.

She was asleep.

Luke half-hoped that it was Caroline.

It was not.

It was Alicia, who had drenched herself in rosewater and lemon juice.

Luke extinguished all the candles except one and, removing only his boots, spent the night in a large chair.

Alicia had obviously been through some traumatic experience, and Luke assumed she would be in a better mood to answer his questions after a long sleep.

Just after dawn Alicia stirred.

Luke carried his chair to the edge of the bed.

Alicia was pleased to see Luke, and was at her ease as she noticed that he had not tried to join her in the bed.

"Sir, forgive me! I hid in your room, and when I heard a servant approaching to light your fire, I concealed myself in your bed. I fell asleep. Please help me—and Harry!"

"Alicia, where is Harry? Is he safe?"

"I don't know."

"What do you know?"

"Harry has been a big brother to me for years. As I became older, I became scandalized by the stories of his many indiscretions and unacceptable behavior and was warned by father, under threat of a beating, never to be alone with him. Then our paths crossed accidently as we took our daily walks in the gardens and coppices near the house. We spent some time talking about intimate matters. Then you had him imprisoned and confined to his rooms. He was very desperate and depressed. I visited him daily, always accompanied by a maid servant, and my dog Clench."

"Where is Clench? I got into the habit of feeding him half my meal under the table every suppertime," Luke remarked.

A tear ran down Alicia's face.

She sobbed gently.

"He is dead, and his killing explains why I helped Harry."

"A dead dog explains why you assisted a murderer to escape, and then put the whole area on an alert when you also disappeared."

Alicia's sobbing increased.

She was at this moment a distraught troubled child, rather than a rational young woman—and she had yet to face another trauma.

Luke realized that she did not know that her sister was dead.

"Alicia, stay here! I will bring your mother to you."

Luke returned with Mercy who was delighted that Alicia had been found.

Luke left mother and daughter alone while Mercy informed Alicia of her twin sister's fate.

He could hear the convulsive sobbing.

After some time, Luke reentered his room.

He gently suggested, "Alicia, although I have to ask you some more questions, this is not the time. Return with your mother and grieve as a family!"

"No, Colonel! I prefer to get your questions out of the way, and then I can mourn my sister."

Mercy looked unhappy at Alicia's response but said nothing.

Luke asked, "How did Clench's death lead you to help Harry?"

She replied, "While I was with Harry in his room a day or so ago, a servant brought him his midday meal. He asked the servant why the regular man who had brought him all his meals since his confinement and whom, I believe, you had specifically authorized, had not brought dinner. He received no reply, and the unrecognized servant scurried from the room.

Harry then playfully grabbed a ribbon from my hair, and as we jostled, I stumbled against a small table and sent the large bowl of stew intended for Harry's meal tumbling to the floor where it spread in all directions. In a flash, Clench lapped up the dispersed mutton pieces at a great rate. Within a few minutes, he began to whine and writhe on the ground, frothing from the mouth and bleeding from the nose. Then he was still. Clench was dead."

"Why didn't you report this to me?"

"Harry was too frightened. Someone had tried to poison him in a most painful manner."

"Who did Harry suspect?"

"He believed it was either a member of the smuggling network who was blaming him for their less than satisfactory recent importations—largely curtailed by your presence in the area, and Caroline Headley's refusal to cooperate. Or the soldiers from the dockyard who were determined to avenge the death of the soldier whom Harry had had to discipline. As both groups had friends and allies among the servants of Holt House, or easy access to it, he knew he had to disappear."

"Where did you go?"

"After he left here, he hid in the disused room in The Cottage. I brought him food and clothing, but he was determined to move on. I expressed my affection for him and my desire to go with him. He seemed shocked but acquiesced. He would make his way south to a forest near London Road, and I would meet him so many paces from a designated rock. He suggested that Frances could wear my cape and be seen in the vicinity of The Cottage and in the coppices to the north to mislead any pursuers."

The reference to her late sister brought on another burst of sobbing.

Mercy implored Luke to bring his questions to an end.

"No, Mother! Let me finish! I spent most of yesterday in that forest. On two occasions, I had to avoid your patrols by climbing a large tree, from which I fell on my second climb. I never found Harry."

"Let us hope that Harry failed to appear because he had your interests at heart and did not want to involve you further in his dubious activities and endanger your life. He may have heard of Frances's death which could have led him to such a noble decision."

Luke did not believe what he had just said. Proctor was incapable of *a noble decision.*

Alicia had the final comment before withdrawing with her mother.

"Or his pursuers caught up with him—and he is dead."

# 15

In the excitement of recent days, Luke had almost forgotten his acceptance of an invitation to spend time at Grey Towers, the ancestral home of the Lynnes, an hour's ride east of Holt House.

Grey Towers was an Elizabethan manor house that ignored the fashion of the period and was built in local rag stone rather than brick. Ragstone and the architectural device of fake defensive towers gave the edifice its name. Ragstone was a hard grey limestone from which most medieval churches of Kent were built.

Luke asked Prudence whether she believed that the Lynnes were genuine converts to the Cromwellian cause.

"The Lynnes would have preferred to stay neutral when the king fell out with parliament. However, given the proximity of London and the strength of parliament in the metropolis, the majority of local families ultimately joined parliament. Only a few remained with the king. Even among these families, there were divided loyalties. But not among the Lynnes. Nicholas, his father, two uncles, and two brothers fought for Charles I. Nicholas's father and two younger brothers took part in the 1648 uprising and were killed by Fairfax as he battled to regain control for parliament. It was only the intervention of my mother-in-law Lady Mary with Cromwell that stopped Grey Towers from being appropriated by the government. This enabled Nicholas to inherit. Arthur believed that Nicholas was an honorable man and that his word could be taken. If Nicholas now accepts that the future of England lies with Cromwell, I, for one, believe him."

"And Lady Matilda?"

"A very different proposition! Be very careful of her. Her family were always opportunists and changed their political and religious alliances depending on what helped them to accumulate wealth. When the war broke out her father fought for the king while his eldest son fought for parliament. He still does, and we both know him well—Matthew Hatch."

"Matthew Hatch is Matilda Lynne's brother? What happened to the family estate he should have inherited?"

"His father spent so much in the king's cause that he was forced to sell his land to his neighbors. Lady Mary bought the western half of the Hatch estates, and the Lynnes bought the eastern half. It was part of this transaction that led to the marriage of Nicholas Lynne and Matilda Hatch."

"Why didn't you tell me this earlier? It could reflect on the loyalty of Hatch to the current government—and his real attitude to you. You own part of what Matthew should have inherited."

"Hatch has been my link with the government for several years. Is he not an accepted and proven loyal member of Cromwell's army?"

Luke decided not to alarm Prudence further.

"Of course, but I must probe his behavior more closely when I return. Why have I been invited to Grey Towers?"

"It fits a pattern. All local Cromwellians have been invited to Grey Towers ostensibly so that the Lynnes can entertain their new political allies."

"You're not so sure of this motivation?"

"Matilda has invited, on separate occasions, Richard, Giles, Harry, old Dewhurst, John Headley, Roger, and Barnaby. On all of those occasions, except for Barnaby's visit, Sir Nicholas was absent on at least one night of their stay, and only in Giles's case did a partner attend. You are one in a long chain. How, with your vast experience of women, would you explain such behavior?"

"Either she is simply a very gregarious and generous neighbor anxious to please her new friends, or she is sounding them out as to their views on a particular matter or enterprise."

"I am surprised that you did not jump to the most obvious. These visits create opportunities for her adulterous proclivities."

"Prudence, I am surprised that you give credence to gossip," replied a teasing Luke.

"It is more than gossip. Two of our servants were previously employed in Grey Towers. In fact, it was Matthew who persuaded me to take them on. They hinted at Matilda's unconventional behavior. I raised the matter with Matthew, who did not deny her amorous activities, but refused to elaborate."

"She is an alluring woman. Perhaps I can turn this to my advantage," said Luke, anticipating an interesting, if not fruitful visit.

"She still maintains a close friendship with several Royalist young men who regularly visit Europe. She could easily continue her contacts with the Royalist Court. She spent much of her childhood at the French Court where her then companions are now powerful women. I feel sorry for Nicholas."

Luke's anticipation of a lascivious couple of days with the allegedly available and alluring Lady Matilda was immediately destroyed.

On arriving at Grey Towers, he was admitted by a servant and led to the great hall where Sir Nicholas greeted him.

"Welcome, Colonel. I am so glad you could accept our invitation. My valet will show you to your rooms. Our main meal will be served here at two o'clock. Matilda likes to keep up with the latest fashion and insists on having dinner later and later. I can remember when it was regularly at eleven. In the meantime, you might like to take a walk in our gardens. Again Matilda has done away with mazes, geometric circles, and knot gardens and introduced a number of colorful flowers and shrubs from Asia and the Americas."

Luke thanked Sir Nicholas and followed the valet up to his room.

He then explored the garden, not to admire Lady Matilda's innovations, but to assess the estate's potential as a hiding place for men and arms.

The magnitude of the house itself and a myriad of outbuildings suggested to Luke that the estate could successfully conceal at least a company of troops.

The large number of horses that Luke could see in a neighboring field were part of Sir Nicholas's racehorse breeding stock, but it would be easy to run a large number of cavalry horses among them. Luke noted that the stables at Grey Towers were two to three times more extensive than the norm.

A hungry Luke arrived in the great hall to dine, and a servant led him to a place at the table.

He was surprised that he knew all of the other guests—Matilda's brother Matthew Hatch; Digges's deputy at the dockyard, Lieutenant Michael Scot; the commander of the refitted frigate, John Neville; and Sir Nicholas's fellow magistrate, David Harvey.

Luke was instantly on his guard.

Could this be a meeting of clandestine Royalists, who might attempt to entrap him into supporting their cause, or at the least discredit him, and have him removed from the scene?

On the arrival of Sir Nicholas and Lady Matilda, the table was filled with a range of dishes of which succulent roast Kentish lamb appealed to Luke.

Luke was astounded when Nicholas came straight to the point.

"Gentlemen, you have been invited here to give us an opportunity to win you over to our cause."

Luke was careful not to ask the obvious.

What was the cause to which the Lynnes were attempting to recruit?

Nicholas turned to Luke. "Colonel, you are central to our scheme. You are more important to the government, and closer to the Lord Protector than your rank suggests. We want you to put certain facts before Oliver Cromwell, which will enhance his position in this region."

Luke was now confused. If this was a potential Royalist plot, why did they want to negotiate with Cromwell?

"What do you wish me to do?" he asked.

Matilda answered.

"Since Lady Mary took over the running of the Holt estate in 1628, and continued by Sir Arthur, and now Lady Prudence, the Holts have been the dominant family in the area. This power has been maintained by the ability of the Holts to side with the dominant group at Whitehall, rather than through a consensus of support from their neighbors. The Holts, as represented by Mary, and now Prudence, promulgate a rigid Puritanism that has an ever-decreasing appeal. Now that the Protector is moving away from the support of religious radicals and the more extreme elements of the army and seeking reconciliation with former Royalists and civilian society in general, this should be reflected in his support and trust in families with similar views to his own changed emphasis.

"That family is not the Holts. It is the Lynnes. Having Nicholas and David appointed to the bench was a good start. But, Luke, we want you to rely on us for accurate information regarding the feelings and views of the landowners of this part of Kent towards Cromwell and his proposed acceptance of the Crown, rather than the outmoded and partisan opinions of the Holt dynasty."

Luke realized that this meeting was not a Royalist plot to displace Cromwell but a Lynne plot to displace the Holts as the dominant gentry family in the Medway.

Luke decided to stir and pretended to adopt the high moral ground.

"I am surprised at this plotting against the Holts by you Sir Nicholas. It was Lady Mary who interceded with the government to prevent Grey Towers being confiscated, and granted to a parliamentarian supporter. It enabled you to maintain you position here. Did not the Holts preserve the Hatch estate for future reestablishment by taking half themselves, and granting the other half to you. It seems to me that you, above all, have benefitted from the generosity and friendship of the Holts—and now you turn on them."

"True, if Sir Arthur had lived the Hatch property would have been reestablished in 1648, and Matthew here would have taken his rightful place as lord of the manor," said Matilda.

"What prevented it?"

"Lady Prudence did not implement her husband's wishes, and probably never fed favorable views of Matthew back to the government. To be fair on this matter she was probably overruled by the dowager Lady Mary, who had little time for the Hatch family."

"You are wrong about Prudence. She has always given Whitehall a very favorable picture of Matthew. His recent promotion is proof of this. You already have a direct input to Cromwell from this family. Prudence accepts Matthew's reports as gospel. He only has to feed Prudence the Lynne-Hatch view of the world, and it flies straight to the heart of government. You don't need me to complicate the situation, but I will mention to Prudence the return of Hatch land."

Matilda smiled. "Thank you, Luke. It is a good start, but if Cromwell wants to be accepted, especially as king, he must win the hearts of the landed gentry, and not rely on your sword."

Matilda giggled as she raised her glass in pretend triumph at each of the four military men present.

He was delighted that this was not a conspiracy of Royalists out to overthrow the government of Oliver Cromwell.

He had initially interpreted the plotting as a battle for local dominance between the Holts and the Lynnes.

But now he was troubled.

Behind this dynastic battle was there a conspiracy of civilian landowners to destroy the power of the military within the government?

# 16

Nicholas organized a horse race to entertain his guests.

Matilda joked, "Are you tempting the Lord Protector's men to break the law which for the last three years has banned such racing?"

"Stop your teasing, dear! The law applies to public race meetings only. Gentlemen may race on their own property if they restrict the participants to immediate locals. Anyhow, as a horse breeder I am exempt from such restrictions. Racing is essential to my breeding program."

Red complained, "Sir Nicholas, I hope that the professional horse soldiers, young Scot and the colonel, start several hundred yards behind us? Their horses have an advantage over our everyday palfreys."

Nicholas smiled. "No need to distress. You shall each ride one of my fine mixed breed fillies that have resulted from putting an imported Arabian stallion to local palfrey mares. These offspring are especially suited to racing. They are sleeker and faster than the average cavalry horse, although they lack endurance. Over short distances they are incredibly fast."

Luke knew of the Lynne stud. Many cavalry horses had been obtained from Grey Towers. In addition to his racing stock,

Nicholas bred heavier animals for the army and ordinary palfreys for the everyday rider.

As they made their way to the stables, Nicholas commented to Luke, "You own a fine black Friesian stallion. Several cavalry regiments have expressed an interest in the breed. I am importing half a dozen Friesian mares from the Netherlands. In fact, I leave for the continent in the morning to finalize their purchase. Would you, at a price, loan your horse to me when I return?"

"If your plans come to pass I will certainly provide the stallion for your mares at no cost, on condition I have first choice of the foals. Both my current Friesians are aging, although they have a few years left of active service."

Nicholas led the group past several empty cubicles and out into a courtyard where the grooms had saddled six almost identical dark chestnut horses ready for the riders.

Luke mounted his allotted steed and was immediately concerned about the saddle. It was lighter and flatter than his cavalry saddle, and he felt much less secure, as both pommel and cantle were almost nonexistent.

Nicholas, who mounted a similar animal, led the group across a large field till they came to a straight area of flat land clearly defined by hedges on both sides, and recently cropped very low by the sheep that now grazed on the other side of the hedges.

Nicholas sent two of his men along the course where about half a mile away they stopped, indicating that this was the finishing line—or so Luke thought.

The point where the two men could be seen was the halfway mark where they would do a sharp 180 degree turn and race back to the starting line.

Matilda arrived and insisted on the starting the race by dropping a large bright yellow handkerchief.

Nicholas, David, Red, Michael, Matthew, and Luke lined up.

Luke was uneasy.

His horse was very unsettled.

He had little time to worry.

Matilda dropped her handkerchief unexpectedly.

Luke was caught napping, perhaps due to his lustful thoughts about the starter.

He was last after the first hundred yards.

He slowly caught David and Nicholas and was soon riding neck and neck with Red, but Matthew and Michael were still well ahead of him as he reached the halfway mark.

He put pressure on the horse as he completed his turn and sensed that it was distressed—and increasingly so.

It broke its stride, suddenly stopped, and then fell to the ground—dead.

Luke did not witness this final act because with its sudden halt, the filly had catapulted him forward.

He hit the ground with a sickening thud and was rendered unconscious —or worse.

Luke was stretchered to the house.

When he regained consciousness early the next morning, he was in a large comfortable bed, and sitting beside it was the alluring Matilda.

"Thank God, you are awake. That fool of a physician said you might stay in a coma forever. You shivered most of the night and appeared incredibly cold. Your head hit the ground so hard I heard the noise from the other end of the course."

"The old head is used to a battering. Twice before I have been seriously concussed—on one occasion losing my memory for months, and on the other regaining it again."

"Last night Nicholas sent an urgent request to Holt House."

"Whatever for? You can nurse me back to perfect health," said Luke, who was becoming attracted to the audacious Matilda, who was now holding his hand.

Matilda, alerted to Luke's fragile condition, stopped and whispered, "Stay here as long as you like, and when you have recovered I will meet your every need, and make your wildest dreams come true."

"Then Holt House can be ignored for weeks," muttered a still-confused Luke.

"Unfortunately not. Nicholas felt that the accident should be investigated by your men, and they could arrive at any time."

"What do you mean?"

"I am leaving by the secret door at the back of the room. David Harvey will explain the situation to you. Nicholas has already left for the continent."

A few minutes later, David arrived.

"Luke, I will not mince words. Someone tried to kill you."

"No, it was an accident. I was not used to the horse nor the saddle. Horses are very temperamental creatures. I pushed her too hard."

"No, your horse was poisoned."

Luke was lost for words.

After a minute or more, he mumbled, "Why would someone want to kill me?"

David laughed. "I'm glad you are able to joke. You are investigating various activities. Dozens of people want you dead before you uncover their criminal or treacherous behavior. That is why Nicholas asked Sir Evan to carry out the investigation into this attempted murder, until you are fit enough to act yourself."

"Are you sure I was the intended victim? How were the horses allocated? It could have been any of us."

"Sleep, Luke! Evan will look into it, and Matilda will look after you. I have to leave. Nicholas and his other guests have already gone."

Luke, exhausted by his fall, fell into a deep sleep.

When he awoke, Matilda was sitting on the end of the bed.

Soon, she was caressing him with immediate effect.

He could not resist commenting on her skill at arousing him. Her abilities were those of a high-class courtesan and not to be expected in an English gentlewoman.

Matilda responded, "As a young girl, I was sent to the French court where women were trained in how to excite men without losing their virginity and, later, how to do so yet avoid pregnancy."

"Prudence told me you spent your childhood at the French court. Do you stay in contact with friends that you made in that period?"

"These are questions of the heart long since put to rest that I do not intend to answer."

"While I am treading on delicate grounds, is it your skill in avoiding pregnancy that has left you childless?"

"You are getting too personal. Nicholas is unable to have children as his numerous childless affairs with the village wenches proved decades ago, although like most men, he blames his wife, as do most physicians. I refuse to accept the solution to the same problem adopted by the Holts over several generations."

"What do you mean?"

"Many of the Holt men have been infertile, and their womenfolk have ensured the succession by being impregnated by family friends. Prudence, because of her strong religious convictions, apparently refused to comply with this tradition, despite Sir Arthur's failings."

"So the succession to the vast Holt estates is uncertain?"

"That is why Prudence persuaded your friend the Lord Protector to give her control until an acceptable solution can be arranged. Her problem is that any settlement struck with the current government could be overturned if the king returns."

"Were the Holt males aware of their cuckolding?"

"Sir Edward apparently ignored his two children carried by Lady Mary. But then he equally disowned his only child by his first wife Lady Katherine who was my Nicholas's elder sister."

"So if the late Sir Edward is to be believed none of the current Holts have any real claim to the estates?"

"All this is but local gossip. Whether Edward's children after Mercy were his, due to some medical miracle, or whether he finally acquiesced in his wife's adulterous solution, who would know?"

"The great aristocrats of England have been doing what you describe for centuries, but I did not realize that the gentry had adopted similar solutions. The tension evident at Holt House might be related to the succession, and not with national security or political and religious loyalties."

"Enough talk, Luke," concluded Matilda as she removed her clothes, other than a transparent chemise, and climbed into his bed.

When Luke awoke, Matilda had gone, and a servant hovering at the end of the bed informed him that he was expected to join Lady Matilda for refreshments.

Luke and Matilda enjoyed several dishes of various cold meats.

Matilda's conversation eventually turned to current politics.

"I was surprised the other week at the Holts that you made favorable comments regarding the young king of the Scots."

"My liking for the lad has nothing to do with my political loyalties. I have served Cromwell for over sixteen years. He has been my platoon officer, company and regimental commander, commanding general of the nation, and now Lord Protector, but hopefully not king. I have never wavered in that loyalty as I believe that only the army under Cromwell's leadership can provide England the reforms, and the government that it needs."

"Surely the current tendency of the government to ignore the army and seek support from the gentry, even former Royalists such as my husband, and the scheme to offer Cromwell the Crown must raise doubts in your mind?"

"I hope to use my influence and these investigations in the Medway to alert Cromwell to the dangers of both those proposed paths. He must not become king, and he must not discard the army. On this issue, you and I are on opposite sides."

"What will you do if the Lord Protector ignores you and persists with the plans that Mr. Thurloe has put before him and which the gentry of this county support? Would you support the new king or not?"

"If I become disillusioned with Cromwell I will transfer to Scotland and serve under General Monk, well away from the intrigues of Whitehall."

A servant delivered a note to Matilda.

She turned to Luke. "Your deputy has been delayed and he will not arrive here until noon. I will keep you entertained until he comes."

# 17

Evan and Strad arrived midafternoon. Luke half-jokingly suggested that it was lucky his life was not hanging in the balance, given the long delay between the initial message to Holt House concerning his accident and their belated arrival.

Evan replied, "I did not get the message until this morning because I have spent the last few days on the Isle of Sheppey looking for Mistress Headley."

"Has she disappeared?" asked a concerned Luke.

"No one knows. She received some bad news in Queensborough about one of her trawlers, and apparently headed for Whitstable immediately. That was about the same time as you came here."

"I'll take over the enquiry into my accident as of now," declared Luke.

"No, you will not," announced Matilda as she entered the room. "He has been seen by a useless physician. He admits his head and neck still ache and his memory comes and goes. I will keep him here for a day or two while you, Sir Evan, look into the incident."

"Well spoken, My Lady! I will ask both of you a few questions and then interrogate your servants, especially the grooms. I gather that the other gentlemen riders have all dispersed?"

Matilda nodded, and she and Luke gave Evan a detailed account of events as they recalled them.

Luke felt dizzy as he rose to accompany Evan and Strad to the stables. Strad grabbed him and, led by Matilda, half-carried, half-supported Luke back to bed.

He slept for most of the day and then had a restless night.

He was a troubled.

How could he properly assess the loyalty of the local army officers and gentry when he was becoming confused as to his own reactions should Cromwell accept the Crown?

He was the most loyal of Cromwell's men; yet could that loyalty be maintained if Cromwell became king?

Whether it was the presence of Evan in the house, or her realization that Luke was not fully recovered, Matilda did not visit him overnight.

When he awoke it was midmorning, and the valet allocated to him was in the room laying out his clothes.

The servant commented, "My Lady invites you to join her and Captain Williams in the dining hall at eleven."

"And where is she at the moment?"

"Riding with Sir Evan."

'Why is Sir Evan not investigating my attempted murder?"

"He concluded that investigation last night."

Luke was astonished.

He dressed quickly, and given Matilda's absence, he pushed open the secret door through which she visited him.

It led directly into Matilda's bedchamber where he immediately went to a small desk and tried to open the drawers.

They were locked.

He heard footsteps approaching.

There were two obvious doors out of the room in addition to the secret panel through which he entered.

He took the door on the left and found himself in an antechamber that was clearly used as an office by Matilda.

The room had long wide windows that gave an uninterrupted view of the drive along which visitors approached the house.

There were several papers and envelopes on a large desk situated under the window.

He was suddenly stopped in his tracks and found he was taking deep breaths.

One of the empty envelopes revealed a broken seal, which he immediately recognized.

It belonged to his old friend and adversary—a senior Catholic peer, and one-time courtier of Charles Stuart at the exile's court, the Welsh peer Simon, Lord Kimball, or rather of his English persona, Lord Stokey.

Stokey had only a few months earlier taken steps to stop Spain landing troops in Wales, which greatly helped Luke suppress the Welsh uprising.

Why was he corresponding with a woman whom Luke suspected of Royalist sympathies, and who lived in an area of vital strategic importance for a potential invasion?

Luke rummaged through the letters on the desk hoping to find the one sent by Stokey without success.

Then through the window he saw Matilda and Evan approaching the house.

Twenty minutes later, Luke, Matilda, and Evan were seated in the dining hall sampling a variety of dishes.

Matilda was apologetic. "I am sorry, gentlemen, but despite my husband's assertion to the contrary, I have not adjusted fully to this new idea of having the main meal in the early afternoon, and then another late in the evening. I become very hungry midmorning. We gentlefolk should follow the field laborers. They have at least a little to eat before they start work at sunrise."

Luke thought of asking Matilda a direct question about Stokey but instead turned his investigative ire on Evan.

"My valet claims ludicrously that you have finished your investigation into the attempt on my life."

"Absolutely correct, Luke! I was about to deliver you my report earlier this morning but you were sound asleep. Lady Matilda invited me to ride with her until you awoke."

"It must be an open-and-shut case to be completed so quickly."

"It was. You were not the targeted victim. The selection of the horse that had been tampered with, was purely random. The grooms did not know in advance who would ride which horse. Neither did Sir Nicholas. He simply allocated the horses as the grooms brought them forward, and the potential jockeys approached."

"So what! All you have proved is that I was not the intended victim but one of us had to be?"

"Not at all. Nicholas had spoken sharply to one of the grooms, and terminated his employment as of the end of the day. This man seethed with rage against Nicholas and according to his fellows was determined to bring disgrace on his master. The death or injury of one of the guests during a race was an ideal form of revenge. The death of a prize horse was an added bonus. The suspect had disappeared, but with some detailed assistance from the other grooms, Strad tracked him down to Rochester, where he is now currently held in the mayor's prison."

Matilda with a cheeky smile yet alluring lips teased, "Oh Luke, you must be *so* disappointed. No one wants to kill you after all."

"I wouldn't be so sure of that," replied a serious Evan.

"What do you mean?" uttered a surprised Luke.

"Sir Giles is threatening to challenge you to a duel. He finally heard that Alicia was found in your bed," explained Evan.

"You have been busy," bantered Matilda.

"The old fool should be detained for his own safety," replied an unhappy Luke.

"He is under house arrest," added Evan.

"What! For threatening to duel with an officer of dragoons?"

"No, for beating his daughter to an inch of her life for sleeping with Proctor and, allegedly, yourself. Lady Holt banished him to an estate near Canterbury, which he has been developing. Four of our men escorted him there. He is not to leave that property until Harvey and Lynne decide the matter."

"Alicia is innocent of any sexual promiscuity," commented Luke.

Matilda could not conceal her look of feigned incredulity using her eyes to flirt with Luke.

"I know!" commented Evan. "Lady Holt brought in three midwives who confirmed the fact. This is what forced her to separate Sir Giles from the rest of his family."

"What does Lady Holt and the magistrates think they are doing? Fathers are permitted to beat their daughters, especially within our class. Given Alicia's behavior, Sir Giles has been sorely provoked," said Luke.

"I am surprised at your attitude," Evan responded in a scarcely concealed reprimand.

"You shouldn't be. If Giles had disciplined Alicia during her childhood and youth, we would not all be in the mess that we are. Alicia aided a murderer to escape, and her behavior caused the death of her twin sister. Where is she now?"

"I don't know. Lady Holt has hidden her away, partly to protect her from her father, and I suspect also to save her from heavy interrogation by yourself."

Luke's desire to spend the rest of the afternoon with Matilda before heading back to Holt House was scuttled by an unexpected arrival.

A servant announced that Charles Franklin urgently needed to speak to Colonel Tremayne.

Charles entered the room and after apologizing to Lady Lynne for the intrusion blurted out. "Luke, you must go to Whitstable immediately. Caroline needs you."

Matilda could not resist teasing Luke. "How many maidens do you need to rescue?"

Charles glared at Matilda. "This is not a joking matter, My Lady. Caroline's life is in danger."

"Evan told me that our men have already spent a day or two searching Sheppey Island for her. What's happened? asked Luke.

"I was working in the parishes on the edge of the Swale. In one hamlet two locals had just returned from a period on one of Caroline's trawlers. They were very unhappy. They had not been paid. Caroline was to meet their captain at Queensborough with the wages for her crew."

"A victim of a robbery!" suggested Luke.

"Caroline is no fool. She would not carry money across the country, and she is usually well protected by her servants, especially Rollo. And that is the most worrying snippet of news. The trawler men I spoke to claim they saw an African bound and gagged in a boat leaving Queensborough harbor."

"Could they have been mistaken?"

"There are not many Africans in Kent," replied an increasingly irritated Charles.

"Why have you wasted time looking for me, instead of continuing the search yourself?"

"My men are continuing the search. Caroline expected trouble. She told me if anything happened I was to contact you, and ask you to go to Whitstable and seek out one of her retired captains, William Maltby."

"Charles, you must come with me. Evan, inform Strad that we leave for Whitstable immediately," declared Luke.

Evan was cautious.

"It might be more useful if we divide our investigation. Strad and I will interview the trawler men that spoke to Charles. Luke, go with Charles to Whitstable, question Maltby and meet us at Queensborough in The Good Shepherd two days hence."

Luke nodded in agreement.

Luke found William Maltby in The Red Herring, an alehouse located well away from the unimposing waterfront.

He was a small rotund man with a head somewhat disproportionately large for his body.

Maltby was entertaining a group of younger men with accounts of his seafaring adventures as they all imbibed a sweet Kentish ale that Luke detested.

William stopped talking immediately he sighted Charles.

"Must be bad news to bring Charlie Franklin this far east. I hope you are looking after my Caroline?"

"Caroline has disappeared," replied a distraught Charles.

Maltby slammed his tankard down on the bench with such force that the contents took to the air.

They were not wasted as the establishment's well-fed black cat jumped silently to the rescue lapping up the spilt liquid.

The old man remained eerily quiet.

Finally, he commented, "I warned her father a decade ago that leaving his fleet to a daughter would cause her trouble down the line. I have been expecting something like this to happen for years, and with the heightened political situation in recent times, attempts to get control of her fleet have increased."

William, Charles, and Luke withdrew into a small antechamber.

Luke asked, "My immediate concern is whether Caroline's disappearance is due to a long-standing desire of someone to gain control of her fleet, or is due to more immediate political and military issues related to a potential invasion—possibly the need for local fishing boats to transport foreign troops from the Netherlands. Tell me about the long-term fishing rivals of Caroline!"

"Ebenezer Fogg, Caroline's father, was a hard and ruthless man. Over the years he forced all the other trawler and drifting fishermen out of business and eventually had a monopoly of all deep-sea fishing out of the North Kentish coast. In the process he ruined, or seriously inconvenienced many traditional fishing families. Young Charlie here was a victim. The Franklins had to find other employment, as did the Nevilles and the Tylers. The civil war came at a convenient time as many of the potentially unemployed young fishermen joined the army, and some now even disport themselves as gentlemen. There would be many offshoots of these families and others who would seek revenge—and there are some in her current fleet who would like to replace her."

# 18

"What is Caroline's relationship with her captains? Do they have any independence?" asked Luke.

"Yes and no. For eight or nine months of the year Caroline employs, and pays her captains and their men for several fishing expeditions into the Baltic, the North Sea, and Atlantic Ocean. She owns their catch and sells it on the London market. For the remainder of the year she leases her boats, usually to her fishing captains, who trade along the Netherlands and French coast over the summer months. During this period, they are completely free to do what they like."

"Such as negotiate with the nation's enemies to transport foreign troops into the Medway?" probed Luke.

"A possibility for a limited few! Most are loyal to Caroline—and to England."

"Bribery can quickly change loyalties," said Charles.

"It would need to be a tidy sum. They already make a fortune as simple smugglers of luxury French, Flemish, and Spanish goods for the gentry. How do you think I enjoy such a comfortable retirement?"

"Maybe Caroline discovered that one or more of her captains were using, or about to use her boats against the national interest?" mused Charles.

"If so would these malcontents attempt to silence her permanently?" asked Luke.

"Yes, one or two would be that ruthless," replied William as a tear rolled down his weather-beaten face.

"What happens to her fleet should she die? Are there any close relatives?"

"No, there was a slightly older boy whom Ebenezer adopted after the lad's father was lost at sea. Ebenezer had high hopes that in time the lad would take over the fleet. But he was a no-hoper, hated the sea, and ran off when he was twelve for a life of crime and debauchery. Ebenezer gradually became reconciled to a girl taking over from him. He was an only child like his father before him, so I doubt whether there are long-lost cousins waiting in the wings. A husband would normally inherit his wife's property on marriage, and certainly on her death. I would check whether John Headley is in such a position. The Holt family has been very successful in twisting the law to suit their own needs. They may have done something similar for Caroline who was a favorite of the old Lady Mary."

"I will check it out," promised Luke.

"Is a Spanish invasion of the Medway using local fishing trawlers a possibility?" asked William.

"Personally I do not believe in a Spanish invasion. Spain is stretched to the limit. Having just raised additional troops, they are all committed to the invasion of Portugal, and those stationed in the Netherlands are in need of reinforcements to combat the imminent Anglo-French advance. No, if Caroline's ships are being used in any invasion it would be from Royalist exiles, perhaps aided by the Dutch and the many German Catholic states," pronounced Luke.

"German mercenaries embarking from the Dutch coast or directly from the German Baltic ports could make use of the expertise of several of Caroline's captains who know this area very well. In fact, one man who for years I have suspected of being a Royalist sympathizer, and who has led recent grumbles against Mistress Headley, has specialized in competing with the Dutch for the coastal trade of the Baltic and their home waters. I would find Captain Thomas Tyler as soon as possible. His boat should have docked at Queensborough a week or so ago!" advised William.

Meanwhile, in a hamlet along the Swale, Evan and Strad found the fishermen who had complained to Charles.

The first fisherman reiterated his grievance.

"I have worked for Mistress Headley for ten years, and never once has she failed to pay me."

Evan asked, "When and where does she pay you?"

"After we deliver our catch to her agent in London and return to Queensborough we are told within a day or two to present ourselves at ten in the morning at The Net and Anchor to be paid. The mistress pays the captain, and then each of the men according to the rates agreed before the journey, with additional rewards if the catch was above that expected—a bonus that made the mistress very popular."

"So what happened this time?" asked Strad.

"Our captain presumably spoke to Mistress Headley on our arrival at Queensborough and told us to meet two days hence to be paid. We arrived at the tavern but she did not appear, nor any of her heavily armed servants, nor that giant African slave who usually carried the coffer containing the money."

"So between talking to your captain and the time allocated for your payment, Mistress Headley disappeared?"

"Yes. Our captain spoke to her while she was paying the men from a trawler that had arrived at Queensborough two days before us. The men working for Tricky Tom got paid, but we didn't."

"Tricky Tom?" asked Evan.

"Captain Thomas Tyler who commands the *Caroline Star,* which concentrates on Baltic fishing."

"Why Tricky?"

"Rumor has it that the records he presents to Mistress Headley grossly underestimates his haul."

"He defrauds his mistress?"

"So it is alleged."

The second fisherman who up to this point had remained silent said, "He also makes secret deals with Dutch and German rivals and merchants during the period in which he is under contract to Mistress Headley—and he is a dastardly Royalist."

Strad and Evan looked at one another.

Luke would be very interested in this information.

Next day Evan, Strad, the Pratt brothers, Charles, and Luke met in an antechamber of The Good Shepherd, just off the Queenborough waterfront.

After a few minutes' discussion, it was agreed that Thomas Tyler was a major suspect in the disappearance of Mistress Headley and her man, Rollo. They would scour the town looking for evidence.

Luke found the harbormaster and introduced himself as an officer on a special mission from the government, which involved an investigation of Captain Thomas Tyler.

The harbormaster, a Ralph Croft was a former officer in the Commonwealth's navy. He had served under the government's hero, Admiral Robert Blake.

He was immediately forthcoming.

"It's about time someone brought that devious fence sitter to account. How can I help?"

"He completed a trawling enterprise, disposed of his catch at the London markets, and returned here a few days ago to be paid by the owner Mistress Headley. Where is he now? Has he left for his freelancing summer trading?"

"Normally you would have missed him. In previous years after Mistress Headley paid off the fishermen Tyler recruited a different crew for his trading adventures, and set sail for Flanders almost immediately."

"So, what has changed?"

"After the previous catch and again just now Tyler waited on high tide and took his boat into the Medway to visit his ageing parents. The boat was left stranded up one of the creeks in low tide, but refloated easily when the waters surged back. Last time he spent two days in the Medway before heading for the open sea. If history repeats itself, he should be passing here at the next high tide in about an hour."

"Do you have any idea why Tyler has changed his routine?"

"His parents are in need of assistance but rumor has it that he has openly entered the smuggling trade, which the gentry of the county encourage. The nearest customs' frigates are in London, another across the Thames mouth in Essex and a third along the southern coast of Kent. Tyler will be long gone by the time any of them, if alerted, arrive."

"No, smuggling does not explain this change of routine. All the fishing captains engage in smuggling and it has been a way of life for them for years. I'm not concerned with that. Tyler, I fear has kidnapped his employer Mistress Headley, and is involved in activities against the security of the state—possibly planning to disembark Royalist and foreign troops in the area. His sudden change in behavior suggests he was testing whether his and other Headley boats could safely navigate the distant reaches of the lower Medway."

"What will you do?" asked Ralph.

"Are there any boats in the harbor I could commandeer to intercept Tyler?"

"There is another of Headley's trawlers, but its captain has gone to the mainland to see if Mr. Headley will pay him and his men. Most of the crew have gone home to take up their summer employment. There might be three or four caretaking the boat until the captain returns."

"I will place it under the control of the government. Harbormaster, how do feel about returning to sea? It may not be a man o' war or even a fast frigate."

"It is not even a ship!" exclaimed the old sailor. "But if Tyler is plotting against the Lord Protector, I can hardly refuse."

Within the hour, Luke had taken over the fishing boat *The Caroline Rose,* installed the harbormaster as captain, and recruited four of the original crew, supplemented by the Pratt brothers, Evan, Strad, and himself.

Charles remained ashore to inform various people of what had happened.

"What are your orders, Colonel?" asked Ralph. "Do you want us to hide around the point so that Tyler will not see us until he is almost upon us?"

"No, let's head up the Medway. That way we will stop him well before he reaches the open sea."

*The Caroline Rose* was soon well into the Medway, drawn along by the incoming tide.

Croft expressed dismay. He turned to Luke.

"There is our quarry, *The Caroline Star,* and it is not coming from the vicinity of the Tyler farm. It is leaving the wharf at Upnor Castle."

"Unfortunately matters are now making sense. How do we stop her?"

"I will cut across her bows and you can order Tyler to return to the castle."

They tried.

Luke shouted, "In the name of the Lord Protector, turn about and dock at the castle!"

The response was unexpected.

"No, sir. I will not divert from my lawful pursuits at the word of a pirate. I doubt that government would confiscate a smelly fishing trawler to exert its dominion when there are two frigates up river. If you continue this charade, I will respond with force."

A musket was discharged in Luke's direction as *The Caroline Star* sailed past *The Caroline Rose,* scraping its side.

Without warning his companions, Luke leapt overboard landing on the deck of the passing boat.

Fortunately, Luke had a soft landing on rolls of netting. Before he could scramble to his feet, a man with a primed pistol towered over him and demanded, "Give me a good reason why I should not blow your brains out for this attempted piracy? You boarded my boat without permission."

Luke slowly rose to his feet. "Because I personally represent the Lord Protector, and of this moment I requisition this vessel in the name of the government."

"On what grounds?" asked Tyler.

"The Medway is targeted for invasion, and any seagoing boats may be part of that invasion. They must be inspected, and if needs be, confiscated."

"How do I know you have such authority? You might belong to one of the many gangs of pirates and smugglers that terrorize this county."

"I am not interested in pirates or smugglers. My concern is with the security of the state. I will search your boat. If all is above board I will return the ship to your command, and disembark at Queensborough. That should not delay your plans, whatever they may be."

# 19

---

Tyler was not convinced.

"I will not be diverted from my activities by a pack of lies. No, sir, I will shoot you now and toss you overboard—or at least confine you to the brig until I can check on your story. You are in no position to argue. You are a single intruder on a hostile ship."

"To kill me would be foolish. If I were whom I claim to be, my death would bring upon you almost immediate execution by the military. Everybody aboard the *Caroline Rose* knows I am here. And if you look astern that boat is not attempting to follow you, but sailing straight to the dockyard. There the newly refitted navy frigate *Valiant* is ready to sail. It will chase you down, and if you do not cooperate it will blow you out of the water."

Suddenly, Luke was taken aback.

He heard a familiar voice.

"Tom, I know this man. He is who he claims to be. Let him search the boat in my company!"

Emerging from behind the main mast was Matthew Hatch.

Luke was temporarily lost for words.

Matthew took advantage of Luke's silence and quickly explained.

"I was coming to join you in Queensborough."

"What are you talking about?" gasped a still stunned Luke.

"Lady Holt told me that Caroline had disappeared and that you, some of your men, and a collection of locals had agreed to meet at Queensborough to try and find her. I went to school with Caroline, and want to help."

"Why are you on *this* vessel?"

"I contracted Tom Tyler to return to the continent the laborers who had been working on the fort. The *Caroline Star* could drop me off at Queensborough as it left the estuary."

Matthew led Luke to the stern. "This hold normally contains the trawler's catch of fish."

Sitting in the open hold were seven or eight men.

Luke had always suspected the nationality of these men. Without warning he asked in Dutch, his single linguistic achievement, "Where will you disembark?"

They looked blankly in his direction and then dropped their heads, except for one man who replied, "Ostend."

Luke swooped. "If you are from republican Holland, why are you going to a Spanish controlled port?"

Matthew intervened, "They don't know where they are going. It depends on Tom Tyler's agenda."

Luke was uneasy, as that was exactly what he feared.

Matthew then took him forward.

This hold was closed.

Matthew ordered the crew to open the hatches.

He explained to Luke, "This forward hold usually contains the provisions for the crew, and the salt required in curing the fish. At the moment it contains the building materials no longer needed at the fort."

Luke peered over the edge and could see nothing but wooden planks and slate tiles.

Luke thought aloud, *Anything could be hidden beneath them. When the frigate catches up and forces the trawler into port this hold can be thoroughly searched.*

He turned to Matthew. "Why choose Tom Tyler to return your laborers to the continent?"

"Caroline's fishing boats in their annual transition to merchant traders have little cargo for their initial trip to the continent. My sister Matilda has used Tom on numerous occasions. Why were you so anxious to inspect this boat to the point of risking your life with that near suicidal jump?"

"Tom Tyler was the last man to see Caroline. She paid him and his crew, and then leased her boat to him. I needed to question him."

"No Luke, you can't fool me. You thought Caroline might be hidden on board."

"It was a strong possibility," admitted Luke.

"Well, I can affirm that she is not here."

"Now Matthew it is my turn to say *you can't fool me.*"

"What do you mean?"

"There are places on board this trawler that you have avoided showing me."

"For example?"

"The trawler's small boat that is covered there on the far side of the deck. And something sinister could be hidden under the planks of wood in the forward hold."

"Let me put your mind at rest regarding the former."

As Luke turned to follow Matthew towards the small boat he noticed that some of the laborers had climbed out of the hold and were gathered around the stern of the trawler.

Emerging from among them was Tyler's boatswain who strode purposefully away from them towards Luke and Matthew.

He brushed past them, intentionally according to Luke's assessment, knocking into Matthew.

The surly boatswain said nothing, and within seconds was confronting his captain in an animated and angry exchange.

Matthew looked apprehensively at Luke and whispered, "I sense trouble. I will go to the captain immediately to discover the boatswain's concern. Be ready to respond to anything I say. You may not have noticed that the pursuing frigate that was quickly overhauling us is taking in sail and tacking. It appears to be stopping."

While Matthew joined the argument between Captain Tyler and his boatswain, Luke looked astern and saw that the frigate was indeed stopping, and attempting to launch one of its boats.

He was jolted out of his reverie by a shout from Matthew. "Luke, for your life, jump overboard!"

Decades of a soldier's reaction to orders had an immediate effect.

Luke jumped, and as he did, he had a fleeting glimpse of Matthew being struck to the ground by the boatswain.

Luke soon surfaced and realized that the boat had been in one of the narrowest channels.

He had only to swim a few yards until his feet touched submerged rocks.

Within five minutes the frigate, which had resumed its chase of the trawler sailed past.

Luke was astonished that it made no attempt to pick him up.

He recognized Evan leaning over the stern railing.

His deputy shouted, "Don't worry, Luke, one of *The Valiant*'s boats is just behind us. It will be with you soon!"

After the passing frigate's wash had subsided Luke could see a longboat heading his way. He recognized Strad controlling the rudder.

Sitting in the middle of the boat with a blanket around him was another familiar figure.

It was Caroline's African servant.

Strad was about to speak to Luke when one of the oarsmen pointed to the disappearing frigate.

Strad realized that someone on board was indicating that there was something in the water that needed to be recovered as quickly as possible.

Strad was blunt. "Colonel, we will return for you. I must recover whatever is in the water further down the channel."

Luke imagined there was a smile on Strad's face as he left his colonel in the water and headed down the estuary.

Ten minutes later, the boat returned, and as Luke was helped aboard, he saw the body of Matthew Hatch lying in the bow.

Luke asked, "Is he dead?"

Strad replied, "He is still breathing—just. He vomited up gallons of water, but it is the nasty gash on the back of his head that is the real problem."

"And what about our African friend?"

"Until a few minutes ago he was alert as well as alive, but he has since lost consciousness."

"I know how Matthew and I finished up in the Medway, but how did Rollo make it into the river?"

"Your hunch regarding the *Caroline Star* and the missing Mistress Headley and her servant was half-right. Rollo was being keel-hauled. He was tied to a line behind the trawler and dragged through the water. Your appearance on board must have panicked them, and they cut the rope. Lieutenant Neville saw what had happened and slowed the ship, while this boat was launched. We did not expect to pick up three half-drowned victims."

"Where are you taking us?"

"Back to the dockyard's infirmary. Major Hatch needs immediate aid, as does Rollo. After we disembark, the sailors will row to Queensborough where they will rejoin *The Valiant*."

"Thick fog is rolling in. It will enable Tyler to lose the frigate," Luke remarked unhappily.

Within the hour, both Matthew and Rollo were accommodated in the large ward of the naval infirmary. A naval surgeon examined Matthew, and both a physician and an apothecary were sent for. News of his situation had been sent to both Lady Holt and Lady Lynne.

Rollo regained consciousness and, after a hearty meal, was anxious to return to his mistress. He became seriously agitated to discover that she was missing.

Luke's questioning of him yielded little useful information.

His mistress had sent him on an errand in Queensborough, just after she had completed her business with Captain Tyler. Rollo was attacked by a group of masked men, blindfolded, fettered, and shackled and kept in a room until with darkness he was transferred to a boat that by its odor he recognized as a fishing trawler. He was kept in the hold until he was unshackled, tied to a rope, and lowered over the stern of the *Caroline Star* and dragged behind the vessel as it left the castle to the jeers and guffaws of crew and passengers. The rope was subsequently cut. He struggled in the water until Strad and the sailors rescued him.

Luke and Strad brought each other up-to-date.

Evan had continued to Queensborough on the frigate.

Luke and his sergeant spent the night in the dockyard barracks, as did Rollo.

Next morning, they joined Ralph aboard *The Caroline Rose* to return to Sheppey Island to continue the search for Caroline.

Before they sailed, Luke looked in on Matthew to ascertain his condition.

He was gone.

Luke was furious.

He sought out the naval surgeon.

"Where is Major Hatch? This may finish up a murder enquiry. He should have been kept here under the best possible care to save his life."

"I had little choice, Colonel. A local magistrate arrived and ordered that Hatch be put into the care of his wife, the patient's sister, Lady Matilda Lynne."

Luke was relieved.

Matilda would probably look after her brother better than institutional doctors.

"Within minutes of Major Hatch's removal Mr. Linton arrived requiring that Hatch be placed in the care of Lady Holt. He was surprised that the Lynnes had acted so quickly."

"Had Matthew's condition improved?" asked Luke.

"We stopped the bleeding and he was breathing normally, but he was still unconscious. His real condition will not be known until he regains consciousness. The wound to his head was quite severe and he had not completely recovered from his earlier injuries. He may never fully recover," concluded the pessimistic surgeon.

Next morning, Luke, Evan, Strad, the Pratt brothers, Charles, Ralph, and Rollo met in The Good Shepherd.

Luke reported that Matthew was near death and that Rollo did not know the whereabouts of his mistress.

Evan noted that in the fog of the previous evening the frigate lost contact with the *Caroline Star.*

"Is there any good news?" asked Strad in feigned frustration.

"Yes," revealed Charles with a slight triumphal tone to his voice. "While you have been playing pirates across the Medway I have found Caroline."

"Great!" replied Luke.

"My totally unreliable source claims she was taken by the Garrison Gang and is being held in the middle of a flooded marsh somewhere in the south west of the island."

"What is this Garrison Gang?" asked Evan.

"For centuries, there was a small garrison here in Queensborough. During the civil war, it surrendered to parliament, its defenders fully expecting, as was the custom, that they would continue to man the fort for their new masters. Unfortunately for them, parliament decided that protecting the westward entrance to the Swale was not important and demolished the fort, leaving a couple of dozen men without employment and full of hatred towards the current government."

"Why did they not seek employment in the new fort we are building further up the island at Sheerness? The last I heard it was still short of men," asked Luke.

"Several years have elapsed between the demolition of the Queensborough fort and the creation of its replacement at Sheerness. During this time, the ex-garrison troops survived by becoming criminals—stand-over men, petty thieves, and small-time smugglers. They were hired by local landlords to coerce rivals or brutalize their workers," continued Charles.

Ralph jumped to his feet. "Half of Tom Tyler's newly recruited crew are members of that gang. Tom's new boatswain, Marsh, is their leader."

"The same man who battered Matthew, perhaps fatally," muttered an avenging Luke.

# 20

"And a man who saw huge profits in taking a large African servant to the continent to sell as a slave. Rollo would bring a fortune," added Ralph.

"Is Tyler complicit in this?" asked Luke.

"He knows these men including Marsh are criminals, although the capture of Rollo was probably a Marsh initiative," Ralph replied.

"Can we trust your informant Charles?" asked Evan.

"Not generally, but on anything to do with the Garrison Gang he is more reliable. He was a petty criminal in Queensborough who took over from his father—pickpocketing, petty theft, hustling, fraud. He was persecuted and badly battered by the Garrison Gang until he relinquished his most profitable activities and scams to them. He now makes money as an informant against them. I use him whenever Garrison Gang activity affects the Holt estates," answered Charles.

"Where do we find Caroline?" asked Luke.

"The Garrison Gang are creatures of habit. Their urban residences are well-known. We could raid them and find nothing. Caroline, with their latest loot, is in one of their many hideouts in the south west of the island. Given the nature of the terrain I suggest that your company of dragoons, as well as those stationed at the dockyard, scour that part of the island. Your men, Luke, could start here at Queensborough, and move south. Given the heavy rain and consistent high tides there are very few negotiable paths. The dockyard dragoons can cross the Swale and land on the south coast and move north. And we should keep this plan secret until all the troops are in position," Charles cautioned.

While Charles spoke, Rollo left the room.

Evan looked apprehensively at Luke, who shrugged his shoulders.

The loyal Rollo would do his own thing.

He would not listen to the soldiers.

Others began to depart.

Luke rose and, in an authoritative voice, asked everyone to resume their seats.

"Gentlemen, I will convert this enterprise to find Mistress Headley and apprehend the Garrison Gang to a higher purpose. I am here because the government anticipates a Royalist invasion assisted or not by Spanish, Dutch, German, or Irish troops. If I were military adviser to Charles Stuart, I would recommend the Medway as the ideal location to disembark his troops. It is close to London and provides a perfect location to blockade the Thames. Consequently, I am declaring martial law in Queensborough and the rest of Sheppey Isle."

"Have you that authority?" asked Ralph.

Luke ignored the question.

He was too busy issuing orders.

"Digges will bring his infantry company here to support his and my company of dragoons. The naval frigate which is still in port will align itself parallel to the coast and initially open all its gun ports on the landward side. It must be ready both to bombard the town, and if necessary demast approaching enemy ships."

"What can we do?" asked Billy Pratt.

"You and your brother can move around the town creating panic and fear! Convince the inhabitants that a Royalist invasion is imminent, and that the Garrison Gang is their ally. Emphasize that martial law has been declared and the island is under the control of

Colonel Tremayne. Three companies of troops, and an armed naval vessel will enforce it. All these developments will soon be evident. Anybody with any useful information should contact Ralph at the waterfront."

An ever-cautious Evan asked, "What do you hope to achieve? This is a bit dramatic."

"Four things! Find Caroline, eradicate the Garrison Gang, and, using the infantry, search every building in the town to uncover useful information, but above all by our precipitate action, I hope we will provoke our opponents to reveal themselves and their precise intentions."

"I hope you are successful. Thurloe and those around the Lord Protector decry the unnecessary provocation of civilians. It could cost you your position, especially as the two members of parliament for Queensborough are regicides, who are very popular with the current regime," remarked the equally prudent Ralph.

Evan nodded in agreement.

Luke's plans were implemented within twenty-four hours.

The Pratt brothers did an excellent job sowing alarm, if not panic, among the population.

Luke's proclamation of martial law was read on the waterfront and posted in the church adding a convincing degree of authenticity to the created situation.

Digges placed his leaderless infantry under the temporary command of dragoon Lieutenant Scot, who began a systematic house-to-house search of Queensborough.

Luke divided his dragoons into four troops.

Ralph had pointed out that Sheppey was really a number of islands divided by hundreds of waterways. The area between Queensborough and the most southern end of the island was essentially marshland, dozens of creeks, some slightly elevated grazing land, a few isolated small farmhouses and a larger number of shepherd huts. Most buildings were elevated to allow flooding watercourses and tidal surges to pass through between the ground and the lowest floor without demolishing the building.

Four barely visible trails headed south. Luke, assisted by Strad, led his troop down the most easterly.

He explained to his men,

"Our aim is to rescue Caroline Headley, and detain any members of the Garrison Gang that we come across. Our task from one aspect is easy. There are not many places to hide. The flat landscape gives us an excellent view of the countryside. The only places to hide would be half-submerged in water, hidden in tall reeds and grasses, or in one of the few buildings that we can see. The last provides our one disadvantage. Anybody hiding in a building will see us coming for miles, and therefore our approach to any building is fraught with danger. We also have nowhere to hide. The Garrison Gang members, former professional musketeers, could very easily pick us off as we approached. Consequently, we must advance along, and to either side of the track in three files, but when we approach any building spread out and surround it from a considerable distance until I decide what to do. Let's go!"

Eventually they came across the first substantial building, which on the mainland would have passed as a shepherd's cottage, but on the island was a small farmhouse.

The dragoons surrounded it from a distance.

Luke and Strad rode towards the building.

An aged man and a young woman came out of the door and walked towards them.

Luke relaxed and dismounted.

The old man spoke. "Welcome, Colonel. Word of your mission has already reached us. We are tenants of the local member of parliament and have opposed the Royalists for decades, but I am afraid I cannot help you other than repeating what you already know—that the Garrison Gang from time to time occupy empty farmlets or shepherd's huts to hide their ill-gotten gain, or abducted victims. We have not seen anything suspicious for weeks."

Luke noticed that the young woman initially appeared terrified. During Luke's conversation with the old man, her demeanor changed. She was clearly troubled by his comments.

She whispered to Luke and at the same time rolled her eyes. "Kind sir, you must leave now, but I would welcome you back once our other guests leave."

The old man grimaced. "Enough, child!"

They both turned their backs and reentered the building.

Luke and Strad returned to the track and ordered the troop to continue ambling south in three files.

After some distance, although still visible from the house, Luke stopped and spoke to his men.

"Our quarry are in that house and have threatened the occupants."

"How do you know?" asked one of the dragoons.

"The woman told us that she had other guests," replied Luke.

"And there were four horses tied up to a rail at the back of the house. Too many for that small household," added Strad.

"We can only approach that house safely after dark. We must progress slowly south until nightfall," declared Luke.

"We don't need to wait that long," said Strad quietly. "A fog is rolling in from the sea. It will be upon us within the hour."

"The gods are with us," muttered a delighted Luke.

Half an hour later, visibility was reduced to twenty yards.

Luke and his men retraced their steps until the outline of the house became visible in the swirling mist.

Luke ordered his men to stay a hundred yards back down the track while Strad and he assessed the situation.

They found a ditch that led in the direction of the house.

It was only few inches deep with brackish water.

They crawled along it towards the house, becoming completely sodden in the process.

Its contours provided their only protection against any alert sentry.

They need not have put themselves through such a wet and uncomfortable experience.

There were no sentries.

They reached the back door of the farm where an adjacent large woodpile, and a small lean-to shed provided places to hide.

Luke was considering his options when the back door burst open and two children, aged about ten or eleven, came out carrying a large pail.

A voice from within the house shouted at them, "Hurry up, we can't wait all day for a drink!"

They headed for a well that lay next to the low shed.

Luke and Strad grabbed a child each.

"Don't be frightened! We are here to help you," said Luke. "What's your name?"

"I am Paul," the boy responded.

"Who is in the house?" asked Strad.

"Grandfather, Father, Mother, and my eldest sister are prisoners of four men who are armed with muskets, swords, and daggers," replied Paul.

"What do they want?"

"They do not want Grandfather to tell you what he saw."

"And what did he see?"

"We don't know. To protect us, he told us nothing."

Luke thought to himself, *Why did they not simply abduct or kill the old man?*

He asked the boy, "Is there any way into the house other than by the front or back doors? The windows are only narrow slits."

"Yes," answered the girl. "There is a trapdoor that leads down a few steps to the area under the house where we keep our sick sheep."

"Does it open from inside, or from under the house?" questioned Strad.

"From inside," said the girl.

Suddenly, the back door opened, and a man shouted, "Come back here at once! If you run away into this fog, we will burn your mother with a hot poker."

Paul shouted back, "We are coming! My sister fell over, and we spilt the water. We are just refilling the pail."

The girl whispered to Luke, "We will loosen the trapdoor from inside. You can then force it from below."

The two children reentered the house.

# 21

---

Luke pondered his options. Night had fallen, completely reducing visibility.

Strad returned to the troop with instructions as to their deployment.

Some surrounded the house from a distance of twenty yards.

The others followed Strad back to Luke, who was hiding behind the wood heap.

The door of the house opened again, and Paul reemerged.

He headed towards the woodheap.

When he was away from the house he whispered, "Soldiers, are you still here?"

Luke answered, "Yes."

Paul continued. "Sir, I can rescue the whole family."

"How can an unarmed boy rescue his family from four armed villains?"

"Easily. I have been sent out to bring in two barrows of wood. Three knaves have settled down in front of the kitchen fire. They have eaten what should have been our meal, stacked their muskets in the corner, and removed their sword belts. They are already dozing in front of the fire. The fourth man ordered all of us into the bedroom and has dragged a bench to its door and placed himself there to ensure that none of us leave the room. He is relying on his sword to keep us in order."

"How can you rescue your family if a guard is posted at the door?" asked Luke.

"The trapdoor! It is in a corner of room into which we have been herded and is hidden from the guard at the door. I can open it and each member of the household can escape, and the guard will not even suspect we have gone."

"An excellent plan, Paul, but if the guard does sense a problem then the trapdoor will be discovered, and all chances of escape will be lost. I have a better plan. Return inside with your wood, and wait near the trapdoor. When you hear my knock open it! My men will enter the room to protect your escape. Well done, lad!"

Paul collected the wood and reentered the house.

Luke organized his men. "Two of you, wait outside the front door and two outside the back. Do not enter until you hear shots. The rest come with me."

It was almost pitch-dark under the house. A faint beam of light filtered through the cracks in the floorboards from the kitchen fire. An even fainter beam from a flickering candle emerged from the bedroom.

Five men including Luke and Strad would enter the bedroom and move quickly around the far walls, obscured from the door. Two men would escort the household down the stairs, where another dragoon waited to lead them away from the house in case a gun battle ensued.

Luke knocked gently.

The trapdoor opened.

Luke's men quickly had the family out of harm's way.

Luke then imitated a child's voice as if in a nightmare.

The guard left his seat and poked his head into the bedroom, shouting at the apparent child to be quiet.

He was smashed behind the ear by the butt of Strad's musket and fell to the floor, unconscious—if not dead.

The dragoons primed their muskets and quietly entered the kitchen.They approached the sleeping men and opened fire at point-blank range.

The dragoons outside both doors entered the house.

To ensure their enemies' demise, Strad put all the victims to the sword.

Luke ordered the bodies be disposed of in a nearby ditch.

The remaining gang member began to stir.

Luke bundled him to the fire where he could clearly see the bodies of his dead comrades being dragged out of the room like carcasses of beef.

"Answer my questions, or suffer the same fate!"

The man was not coerced and asked, "Why kill men simply trying to earn a living to support their families. You will murder me anyhow, so why should I tell you anything?"

Luke was annoyed but continued to question the gang member. "Why take over this household?"

The man spat in Luke's face and proclaimed, "I will tell you nothing. I die knowing that our enemies will be destroyed within the week."

"Who are your enemies?" asked Luke, wiping the saliva from his face.

The man remained silent.

Strad led him outside.

A single shot was heard.

Luke invited the household to reenter their building.

He praised Paul for his part in the enterprise and suggested that the children should retire to the bedroom, while he talked to the adults.

"Old man, why did the gang take over the house? Your grandson said it was because of something you saw."

"A few days ago a large body of horsemen, Garrison Gang members, passed our house heading south. In the midst of the horsemen, closely guarded, was a woman whom I knew—Mistress Headley, the owner of the trawling fleet."

"How did you know it was Mistress Headley?"

"Years ago I worked for her father. I have been on many a trawling expedition with the then young Caroline. It was she."

"What happened next?"

"I was on the track as they passed and I must have looked too intently at the woman. About an hour later four of the gang returned and took over the house to ensure that I did not inform anyone of what I had seen."

"That is something I do not understand. These are ruthless men. If I were in their position, I would have killed you—a certain way of ensuring your silence."

"It was only a temporary occupation. They said I could tell the world what I had seen in three days, as by then, it would all be over."

Paul's father spoke out. "Tell them the full story, Papa!"

The old man went quiet.

The younger man took up the story.

"Colonel, Father was not killed because the leader of the Garrison Gang is his youngest son, my baby brother George. He ordered his men not to harm us."

"Where would the gang take Mistress Headley?" asked Luke.

"Not sure," replied Paul's father. "She would be hidden in one of the many shepherd's huts in the middle of the marshes or taken across the Swale where there are even more isolated edifices."

"Why was she abducted?" continued Luke.

"I don't know, but they said they would release her in a week or so."

"They will not harm her," added the grandfather.

"How can you be sure of that?" asked Strad.

"George is my son."

Luke shrugged his shoulders.

The dragoons spent the night in the kitchen, while the family crammed into the bedroom.

Next morning, the soldiers took up their journey southeast.

Some distance from the house, Luke saw hiding in a patch of tall grass a figure trying to get his attention.

It was Paul.

The boy was anxious. "I don't want them to see me from the house. I can tell you where to find Mistress Headley, and why you must hurry."

"Lad, why would you betray your family, including your uncle?" asked Luke.

"I heard Grandfather tell you that the lady would be in no danger. That's a lie. Uncle George on his last few visits did horrible things to my eldest sister Ruth, his own niece. Father and Mother would not believe us. I heard the gang joke that their leader has his way with every woman they kidnap before he releases her. I want to avenge my sister!"

"You know exactly where Mistress Headley is?"

"Yes. When I was younger, I took messages from Grandfather to Uncle George. He had a base much further to the east than this track would lead you. This leads into the Elmley marshes. Uncle George has a shack halfway along the Capel Fleet, a saltwater canal that once separated the isle of Harty from the rest of Sheppey. The far eastern portion has silted up, but the western half is navigable in high tide by fairly large boats. If he has one of the fishing trawlers, it is probably hiding there in the Fleet."

"Quickest way to get there?"

"Not by land. Return to Queensborough and take a small boat down the Swale and up the Fleet."

"Thanks, lad!"

Luke returned to Queensborough.

Fortunately, he found the *Caroline Rose* had less draft than the frigate.

He commandeered a few extra crew from the frigate and filled the holds with his own men—without their horses.

He sailed into the Swale, with Ralph at the helm carefully keeping to the single deep channel.

On reaching the entrance to the Capel Fleet, Ralph quickly assessed that it was too shallow to enter.

Luke's men disembarked and on foot followed the bank of the fleet inland.

So many other watercourses entered the Fleet that Luke and his horseless dragoons spent their time either wading through deep water or sloshing through mud.

Eventually, they reached drier land, on which several sheep were grazing.

In the far distance, a rather large but ramshackle building was visible—but only just.

The endemic fog was beginning to roll in.

Strad spoke. "Sir, we do not need to wait for the fog to cover our advance. I was a shepherd before the war. We can use the sheep to cover our advance. Hide behind these woolly creatures and direct them towards the building, which, luckily, is on the edge of this pasture field."

Luke, Strad, and three other dragoons were soon on their hands and knees, purporting to be part of the flock. Strad found the lead sheep and carefully manipulated her in the direction of the building. The other sheep—and dragoons—blindly followed.

Strad was so effective that the sheep not only reached the building but also some went through the holes in the wall into the building.

Luke and the dragoons followed.

The building was long and narrow. The nearest end had fallen down. The middle section had damaged walls and a leaking roof, but the far end was well maintained and had clearly been recently lived in by a number of people.

On the small table were a loaf of half-eaten bread and the remnants of a round of cheese.

Strad approached the table and signaled silently to Luke that there was something under the table.

The dragoons surrounded it.

They then together lifted the table out of its position.

On the floor, face down on her stomach, was a woman whose hands were fettered and whose legs were shackled to each other so tightly that she could hardly walk.

Luke lifted her to her feet.

Caroline fell into his arms, sobbing uncontrollably.

An hour later, the combined efforts of the dragoons finally broke the chains that held the fetters and shackles together. Caroline was now free to walk and use her hands, but the separated restraints still clung around her ankles and wrists.

"Where are your captors?" asked Luke.

"They left this morning. They left me food and drink but made it impossible for me to travel far. They said they would return in a few days and release me. By then, my confinement would not be necessary."

"What did they mean? Why were you abducted?"

"It has something to do with my fleet of fishing trawlers. The fishing season is just finishing, and around this time, I lease my boats, usually to my captains, for them to trade throughout the summer along the continental coastline."

"Did your abductors talk about their leader Marsh?"

"Only to terrify me by claiming I was very lucky that Marsh was not here as I would soon learn what a real man was like."

"Did any of them harm you?"

"No, my name and that of my late father commands some respect. These men did not enjoy the role they were forced to play. One of them said that the past week was the worst in his life, but the next fortnight would be the best."

"His best will probably be our worst," bemoaned Luke.

# 22

Luke left three dragoons at the hut to deal with any returning gang members and, in particular, to prevent them from informing anyone that Caroline had escaped.

Luke waited until dark before returning a heavily disguised Caroline to Queensborough.

Her recovery must be kept secret for as long as possible as Luke wanted her abductors to continue their mission, whatever it was, as planned.

Luke and Caroline stayed overnight in the harbormaster's house.

Next morning, he made it his temporary headquarters.

The news now spread quickly that the self-proclaimed military commandant of Sheppey Island had returned.

A crowd, a potentially hostile mob, with grievances against the recently imposed martial law, gathered outside the house.

Luke addressed them as a group, attempting to calm them with a combination of "carrot and stick."

He told them that a Royalist invasion was imminent and he was, therefore, not able to revoke martial law. However, Lieutenant Scott, whose men had implemented the decree on the townsfolk, would carefully consider their complaints.

The Pratt brothers waited patiently at the back of the crowd and, with their hand signals, indicated a need to speak urgently with Luke.

"What's the problem?" Luke asked them as the trio entered the harbormaster's house.

"While you and your dragoons were enjoying a trip across the isle, Tommy and I heard some very disturbing news. We told Mr. Franklin who is in London investigating. He should be back anytime today," Billy explained.

"What did you discover?"

"Tommy and I were drinking in a fishermen's tavern when an old friend arrived. He was very unhappy. He had been forced to walk home from London and had missed out on his usual bonus. He sailed on one of Mistress Headley's trawlers, and having reached London to unload their catch, they were told by her agent that before they were discharged at Queensborough, they were to sail to Ostend, where they would receive cargo for urgent transfer to the Medway. For the fortnight's delay in their discharge, they were to receive several silver coins in recompense. Our friend could not accept the offer as his mother was dying and he had to return here."

"So Franklin has gone to London to see what the agent is up to?" Luke asked Billy to repeat his information to Ralph Croft.

Ralph listened carefully and responded, "I can verify part of the story. My deputy tells me that since Mistress Headley's disappearance, not one of her trawlers has arrived here to be discharged or leased for the summer months. My guess is that Tyler's *Caroline Star* is anywhere between the Swale and Ostend, and the other six trawlers due here over the last week are at or heading to Ostend. The only Headley boat not involved is our *Caroline Rose*."

Charles entered the room.

Luke immediately informed him "Caroline is safe, but we are keeping her recovery a secret."

"Where is she?" he asked.

"Right here," announced a female voice who had heard Charles's entry.

She ran into Charles's outstretched arms.

The other men discreetly turned away as the lovers embraced.

But Luke could not contain his curiosity for long.

He interrupted the lovers. "What did you find out in London, Charles?"

"Caroline's agent received a letter. I read it, and I would swear that Caroline had written it. It directed him to inform her captains to sail to Ostend where they would collect dozens of Protestant refugees fleeing Catholic persecution. They were to bring them back to the Medway. At Ostend, they would receive further orders. To recompense them for the extra two weeks, he was to pay each fisherman a certain number of silver coins and each captain an extra 10 percent on top of his agreed salary. After the mission was over, they would return to Queensborough to be paid."

"Who brought the letter to Caroline's agent?"

"A person purporting to be a protestant clergyman. He emphasized that Caroline, in directing her boats to Ostend, was serving God and the nation. The London agent is an extreme Puritan, who would have readily accepted this direction as part of God's providence."

Luke clapped his hands together in mock appreciation.

"A brilliant plan! Caroline's boats are not being used to bring over a hundred Protestant refugees. They will be filled with a company of Royalist troops. What a masterstroke! No one will suspect a thing. Caroline's fishing trawlers will sail up the Medway unopposed and unload a company or more of seasoned soldiers."

Ralph agreed with Luke's assessment.

"Why would Protestant refugees choose Ostend to embark for England? Ostend is in the Catholic Spanish Netherlands and a port currently controlled by Spain's great maritime ally, the privateers of Dunkirk. Any Protestant refugee would only have to move a few miles north into Protestant Dutch territory—and the Dutch government is more tolerant of the diversity of Protestant opinion than our more rigid English extremists."

"And what have the Dunkirkers done for the last decade apart from attack Dutch and English fishing and trading vessels? They have transported Spanish troops from Spain to their Netherland provinces," added Luke.

"What do we do?" asked Charles.

"Charles, stay here and, with the support of three of my dragoons, protect Caroline. Remember her escape from the Capel Fleet must remain a secret for at least ten days. When all of my troops return from their sweep of the island, which is expected any minute, John Martin will become military commandant for the island. My dragoons and the infantry from the dockyard under Scot will maintain a vigilant surveillance of the island. Digges, with his dragoons, will return to his base and prepare for an imminent invasion.

"Evan, ride to Whitehall and put them in the picture and explain what I am up to!

"Ralph, you will resume you command of the *Caroline Rose* and take Strad and myself and a small number of dragoons to Ostend to join Caroline's other trawlers in our humanitarian mission to rescue the refugees. I will ask Lieutenant Neville to sail his frigate immediately to locate the nearest ships of the English fleet and inform them of the situation and my plan to deal with it."

"And what plan is that?" asked Caroline.

"That's a secret."

"It's a secret, Luke, because you have yet to devise one," joked Charles.

As the *Caroline Rose* approached Ostend, a crew member shouted out, "An armed frigate is bearing down on us!"

Ralph turned to Luke. "A Dutch warship is demanding that we change course away from Ostend."

"Part of our recent treaty with the Dutch was to jointly maintain a blockade of the Dunkirk pirates in Dunkirk, Nieweport, and Ostend, but I doubt that they will risk an international incident by sinking us to achieve their end," said Luke.

"I wouldn't be too sure. Their gun ports have just opened. They will not sink us, but they will demast us and force us to limp back to England," commented Ralph.

As if to prove him right, a shot passed in front of the boat, and a voice from the Dutch ship in broken English was clear. "Englishman, turn away from Ostend, or we will cripple you. The blockade must be upheld."

Suddenly, sustained cannon fire erupted.

It took some time for Luke to realize that it was directed not at the *Caroline Rose* but at the Dutch frigate.

Out of the fog emerged two ships of similar build as the Dutchman. They meant business firing into the frigate's hull.

"Dunkirkers! They fly the black flag with a white ragged cross," explained Ralph.

Outnumbered and in danger of serious damage, the Dutch frigate quickly withdrew.

The Dunkirkers turned and repositioned themselves on either side of the *Caroline Rose.*

A voice echoed across the waters. "We are your escort into harbor. You are very, very late."

On landing, Ralph and Luke were met on the wharf by a tall richly dressed gentleman, who, by his speech, was a well-educated Englishman.

He welcomed them. "I'm a lawyer assisting the refugees flee persecution. Mistress Headley's captains are meeting in Les Trois Enfants at sunset. You must be ready to sail again before dawn."

As Ralph and Luke entered Les Trois Enfants, followed at a discreet distance by Strad, a barmaid asked, "Le Capitaine Anglais?"

Ralph nodded.

They were shown to an antechamber at the back of the main bar.

Ralph was immediately assailed by one of the men present. "Since when has the harbormaster of Queensborough been a trawling captain of Mistress Headley?"

"Since yesterday," lied Ralph. "Old Donald fell ill, and Mistress Headley was anxious to have her whole fleet at the disposal of the refugees. I served in the channel fleet for years and know the area well, so I volunteered."

"And who is your well-armed friend?" asked another captain.

Ralph was about to answer when the lawyer entered the room.

"Gentlemen, I act for the generous but anonymous person who has financed this great act of charity.

"Tell us the plan!" slurred another captain who had obviously spent too much of the day enjoying the refreshments provided by Les Trois Enfants.

"You will load your passengers in time to sail an hour before dawn. You will leave the harbor in darkness to avoid the Dutch blockade. The frigate that was offshore for most of the day will have informed the larger fleet that activity is expected. By dawn, they will have us cut off. However, they never risk their fleet in the dark close inshore."

"Nor should we. I do not sail inshore in the dark," announced the slightly intoxicated captain.

"No worries! Your ship will be perfectly safe. A Dunkirker skiff will lead you out, and you will follow it south along the coast before attempting to cross the channel. It will have only its stern lantern lit, as will you. You leave in line and keep the lantern of the boat ahead, always in view. I have a list of the order in which you sail. The *Spirit of Caroline* will be first, and as she has just arrived, the *Caroline Rose* will be last."

"If we are to leave before dawn, there may not be enough wind to get us moving," suggested Ralph.

"Again, no worries. If needed, we have small boats with lots of rowers, ready to tow you into your correct position and then out to sea."

"How many refugees are we expected to carry?" asked another captain.

"About thirty each. They are accompanied by two or three Englishmen, who will be responsible for their behavior."

Luke nudged Ralph. "The Royalist officers and the so-called refugees are continental mercenaries. It sounds like two companies to me. It is all fitting into place."

Ralph ignored Luke and asked of the lawyer, "Should we lose contact with the rest of the fleet, where are we to disembark our passengers?"

"Enter the Medway and land your passengers east of Gillingham, where they will be reunited with their belongings."

The lawyer left, and the captains indulged in a final pint of bitter Flemish beer.

The captain who had first questioned Ralph commented, "The whole fleet is here, except Tim Tyler and the *Caroline Star.* He is always the first to chase extra money. Why has he missed out on this?"

"Why indeed?" Luke muttered to Ralph.

In the early hours of the morning, the fishing trawlers were loaded with thirty or more passengers each.

Luke's theory received strong support.

All the passengers were male.

A genuine group of refugees would surely include women and children.

Ralph was dismissive. "This can't be an invasion fleet. The men are unarmed. Where are their weapons? Even the designated officers carry only swords. Hardly an offensive force!"

Then Luke saw the light.

"The *Caroline Star* has gone somewhere else to collect arms and ammunition which will be distributed to these troops somewhere east of Gillingham. This whole enterprise reveals the hand of a master strategist. None of my suspects have that ability."

# 23

By the time the sun rose, the English trawlers were well out into the channel. The Dunkirker skiff, having completed its task, turned and disappeared back into the coastal mist.

The breeze was light and progress slow.

As they approached the English coast, Ralph shouted, "Trouble! A large fleet of warships is bearing down on us."

"Great," replied Luke. "My plan is working."

"What plan?"

"I sent Red Nev to inform our channel fleet that several boatloads of Royalist troops would attempt to land on the Kentish coast. They were to be intercepted and taken to Dover where the Royalists could be incarcerated in the castle and their place taken in our trawlers by government soldiers. Evan was to inform Whitehall of this plan and have them send troops to Dover to replace our false refugees."

"A great plan, Luke, but as you can now see for yourself, the ships cutting across our bows and signaling the lead ship to change course are not English—they are Dutch."

Luke erupted, "God's blood! I have been betrayed. Whitehall has ignored me."

Two Dutch warships left the fleet.

They made clear that the English trawlers were to follow one of them into its homeport of Flushing. The second made sure that these orders were followed by firing several shots near the stern of the *Caroline Rose*, which had been slow to change course. The two warships shepherded the English flotilla towards their new destination.

The rest of the Dutch fleet resumed their channel patrol.

Luke was furious that his advice had been ignored.

His mood improved slightly on entering Flushing harbor.

He was impressed by the number of ships it contained.

A dozen large merchantmen of the Dutch East India Company were about to depart, given the configuration of their rigging and general activity surrounding them.

As the *Caroline Rose* tied up, with their bow to the wharf beside their sister trawlers, Ralph commented, "We are in for trouble! There's a company of Dutch soldiers marching towards us."

Within minutes, a Dutch officer boarded and ordered the captain and crew to leave the boat and follow him.

As they complied, they saw as they glanced back at their boat that Dutch troops were storming aboard and roughly manhandling the alleged Protestant refugees.

The English fishermen from all the boats were herded into a small square.

A senior Dutch officer addressed them. "I am sorry for this alteration in your plans. The passengers you were carrying were not refugees but German Catholic troops in the employ of Charles Stuart, the exiled English king, an advance guard of the Royalist invasion of your country. We have assisted your government in their apprehension."

"What will happen to these mercenaries?" asked Ralph.

"They are about to be distributed among our large merchantmen who within the hour will sail for Batavia. Given the demand on our sailors to man our warships, these mercantile vessels are always short of crew. The land-loving Germans will be gone for over a year and will return as very experienced sailors."

As he spoke, another man approached him. They exchanged nods, and the newcomer asked, "Is Colonel Luke Tremayne present?"

Luke raised his hand and moved towards the stranger who explained, "I am the English consul in Flushing. I have sealed orders for you."

The consul gave him a sealed letter and then turned to the assembled throng. "I ask you all to stay here until Colonel Tremayne has spoken to you."

He and the Dutch officer left.

Luke opened his orders.

Eventually, he addressed the anxious fishermen.

"You are to sail immediately for the Medway and anchor off Gillingham. Then when instructed by a government frigate, you will return to Queensborough, where you will be paid off in the usual manner."

Once back aboard the *Caroline Ros*e, a suspicious Ralph asked, "Is that all that was contained in your instructions?"

"Yes, as far as our mission is concerned. There is an addendum that I am to return directly to London and present myself at Whitehall as a matter of urgency."

"Alas, Luke, I warned you. Declaring martial law on Sheppey and issuing orders to the navy went beyond what the government would consider reasonable—despite your ultimate legal authority to do so," commented Ralph.

While the rest of the trawlers entered the Medway, the *Caroline Rose* sailed up the Thames, and soon Luke was in an anteroom awaiting an audience with senior government officials.

He was eventually admitted, and to his dismay, the three most powerful men in England were in the room—General Desborough; the secretary to the council, John Thurloe; and the Lord Protector himself, Oliver Cromwell.

Cromwell spoke. "We are most grateful that you uncovered the plot to land foreign troops on English soil."

Luke interrupted, "If you were that grateful, why did you ignore my solution to the problem?"

"Because while we were grateful for the discovery, we were not happy about your planned solution. To allow enemy troops to land in England was too dangerous. That is why I asked our Dutch friends to prevent this happening," explained Thurloe.

John Desborough spoke. "Colonel, we did not neglect your advice. Captain Williams was sent back to the Medway and, with the assistance of a naval frigate under Lieutenant Neville's command, steps to capture the *Caroline Star*, hopefully full of arms and ammunition have been put in place. In addition, I have sent two additional companies of infantry to the area—one to the castle and the other to the dockyard. The arrival of the trawlers off Gillingham about now, hopefully, will entice the *Caroline Star* out into the open. We adopted all of your recommendations, apart from assisting enemy troops to land in England."

Cromwell intervened, "A year ago, I would have sent you back to the Medway as military governor to control the area. However, given the public outcry against military interference in civil matters, especially so close to the rule of the major generals, I must be circumspect."

"Your declaration of martial law was a mistake. You need the populace to respect and admire the military, not despise it," interjected Thurloe.

Luke gave him a withering glare.

Cromwell continued. "You will return to the Medway as commander of all government forces in the Medway, army and navy. The dockyard, the castle, and all of North Kent between the coast and the London-Canterbury road will be under your control. However, you will exercise this military power in cooperation with and consent of the local civilian leaders, magistrates Lynne and Harvey."

"If that is all, sir, I wish to return to the Medway on the current change of tide."

Cromwell rose from behind the desk and personally escorted Luke to the door.

He stepped outside of the door, shook Luke's hand, and passed him another sealed letter. "Thank you, Luke. This concerns the personal matter you are still investigating. Give my love to Prudence."

Luke did not open the letter until he was aboard the *Caroline Rose,* as it drifted down the Thames with the ebbing tide.

It was not a helpful letter.

Cromwell seemed determined to increase the mystery, rather than offer any meaningful explanation.

The succinct and annoying passage read, "The answer to the tensions and problems besetting Holt House may lie in a fact that has been hidden from all, even Prudence to whom it most concerns. I promised Prudence's grandfather as he lay dying on the field at Marston Moor that I would never reveal the pertinent details to her or anyone else. I must keep that promise."

Luke was angry.

He confided in Ralph.

"A trawler full of arms and ammunition is about to enter the Medway in what might be a signal for an antigovernment uprising, and I am ordered to focus on the personal problems of the Holts."

Ralph read the letter and tried to be positive.

"At least you are now equipped with specific authorization to coordinate and command all military forces in North Kent and, in cooperation with the civil magistrates Lynne and Harvey, to exert absolute authority if necessary."

Mudhill Farm would be his general headquarters as it was close to the dockyard and the residences of the two magistrates.

He would continue to live at Holt House.

On his return there, Sir Evan and Richard Holt welcomed him.

Evan was undiplomatic. "Luke, you missed all the excitement. When the trawler fleet entered the Medway, the *Caroline Star* emerged from hiding up one of the creeks and headed for Gillingham. Our frigate intercepted her, and when she refused to stop, Neville capitalized on his own expertise and, with three cannon shots, demasted the vessel, and young Richard here led a boarding party that soon had the boat under his control."

"Was Tyler in command?"

Richard replied, "No, sir, the boat was controlled by the boatswain Marsh and his cronies."

"I know this boatswain. A nasty piece of work! Is he under guard?"

"No, sir! He resisted arrest, and in a sword fight with me, I pierced his heart."

"Bravo, Richard! I know a young boy on Sheppey who will be delighted to hear the news. Was the ship full of arms and ammunition as we expected?" asked Luke.

"Yes, that's the good news," said Evan.

"And the bad?"

"There was no support for the *Caroline Star*. There was no sign of an uprising, except for a minor riot at the castle."

"What happened there?"

The captain in charge of the newly arrived company of infantry from London assumed they were aiming to fire at the naval base. This assumption stemmed from Whitehall's fear that the castle was in the hands of unreliable troops. The artillerymen were forcibly removed from their cannons. They objected to this treatment, and a physical altercation ensued."

"Damnation, if only the infantry captain had allowed the artillerymen to fire, we would have had proof of their hostile intentions," muttered Luke.

Richard spoke. "Colonel, we did find Captain Tyler. He was bound and gagged and thrown in among the ammunition. He had been badly beaten. One of the crew claimed he had originally been in charge of the operation but fell out with his boatswain after the latter attacked Major Hatch."

"Thanks, Richard. I will interview Tyler when he has recovered," announced Luke.

Evan informed the gathering, "Gentlemen, let's enjoy supper. Lady Prudence, in order to celebrate the freeing of Caroline Headley and the successful forestalling of an invasion and the specific role played in this by her brother-law Richard, has had the cooks prepare a special meal."

The household and the guests were already seated when Prudence entered the dining hall accompanied by a man that Luke knew very well.

Simon, Lord Stokey, was the senior Catholic peer of the realm, a former leading courtier at Charles Stuart's court in exile and an open Royalist. What was he doing at Holt House?

It was only a few months earlier that Stokey had assisted Luke in his Welsh adventures by preventing Spanish assistance coming to the aid of the Welsh insurgents.

Prudence soon answered his question. "My guest is Simon, Lord Stokey, a peer of the realm who had come to see Colonel Tremayne before he visits Sir Nicholas Lynne. Luke, move up here and sit next to his lordship!"

Luke obeyed.

"What are you doing in Kent, Simon? There is not a Catholic for miles," he asked the peer.

"But there are Royalists and former Royalists who, in this time of crisis, need counseling."

"I trust that counsel is, as it was in Wales, for such people to trust the Lord Protector, and not be lured into foolish schemes of subversion and rebellion? Is Sir Nicholas Lynne in need of your help?" probed Luke.

"You will not trick me, Luke, into giving you any personal information. Anyway, this is certainly not the place to discuss such matters."

"So the problem child is Lady Matilda?" suggested a persistent Luke.

"Enough, Colonel! You will find out in due course. All I will say is that Lady Matilda does need your help."

# 24

Luke, using his new authority, devoted the next few weeks to reorganizing the defenses of the Medway.

William Neville was elevated to governor of Upnor Castle in place of the injury-prone Hatch, promoted captain, and given control of all troops associated with Upnor Castle, including the new infantry company.

Thomas Digges's authority was expanded to command all personnel, naval and military, within the dockyard.

Caroline seemed no worse for her experiences but shocked the local community by leaving her husband John and moving in with Charles Franklin. She was no longer welcomed at Holt House.

Charles was also blackballed but only for the pragmatic reason that Prudence did not want a confrontation with John Headley at her table.

Luke was, therefore, surprised to receive a message that Caroline would meet him at The Black Eel in Gillingham.

Caroline's open attachment to Charles did not modify her alluring appearance.

She sat opposite Luke, revealing a considerable cleavage that disconcerted the colonel.

She leaned across the narrow table and squeezed his hand.

"Thanks, Luke, for rescuing me. I asked to meet you urgently because I have now seen the letter I allegedly wrote to my agent authorizing the use of the trawlers to transport the Protestant refugees."

"A clear forgery?"

"No, that's the problem. Charles made me sit down and copy the letter. My copy and the original could not be differentiated. They were identical."

"Were you drugged during your captivity? Maybe you wrote the letter dictated to you while in a trance."

"No."

"Have you the letters with you? I will send them to Whitehall. Thurloe has experts who can determine their authenticity."

Caroline handed over both letters—the suspected forgery and her genuine copy.

"But, Luke, the problem remains. This expert forger could use his skills to damage me further."

"Any suspects?"

"Yes. I do most of my business by word of mouth and in person. Most of the people I deal with may be able to read a little, but they cannot write. The only persons who have access to a reasonable quantity of my letters would be my London agent and, as we shared the same house for years, my estranged husband John Headley."

"You can't jump to conclusions. A single letter could have fallen into the hands of anybody who had an expert copy your hand."

"No. It was John," whispered Caroline.

"Evidence?"

"Our relationship deteriorated dramatically since your arrival. Until I moved in with Charles, I am sure John thought you and I were having an affair. Looking back, I caught him coming out of the chamber where I keep my business files on two occasions about four weeks ago. It was an unwritten rule that certain parts of the house were mine and others his."

"What did he say when you caught him?"

"That he had run out of candles, and he knew I had a couple to spare in that room."

"According to one of your servants, John is obsessed with candles."

"Not with candles—but with their cost."

"What do you want me to do?"

"John is in Rochester till late this afternoon. Visit The Cottage and search it for any evidence that he has copies of my writing!"

Luke and Caroline had a long meal, which ended with a long enduring hug and a peck on the cheek.

Luke went immediately to The Cottage. There were servants everywhere. Prudence had forbidden those that belonged to the estate from joining Caroline.

Luke decided not to alarm them, nor give John any hint of what he was really after.

He asked the servant who answered the door, "Mistress Caroline sent me to recover any letters and files she left behind."

"Too late, sir!" replied the servant.

"What do you mean?"

"All the letters and papers found in Mistress Caroline's part of the house were sent to her days ago. The master was keen to remove every trace of her ever having been here."

"What about letters that may have found their way into your master's part of the house?"

"Strange that you should mention that."

"Why?"

"Only yesterday, the master brought me a bucket full of writings in Mistress Caroline's hand."

"Where are those letters?"

"I burnt them in the great fire that the master ordered to consume everything that belonged to the mistress."

"Take me to the site of the fire!"

Luke followed the servant into the forecourt and found a pile of half-burnt material and a large pile of ashes, among which embers were still glowing. Luke found a small charred portion of a page, which only proved that John had some letters, genuine or forged, in his possession. There was too little to prove that John was or had employed a forger.

On the other hand, there was enough circumstantial evidence to suggest that he may have been behind the forged letter.

If so, to what end?

That afternoon Luke discussed the situation with Evan.

"You don't have to look far for a motive. According to the local males, Caroline has slept with all of them. At the least she has not been faithful to the marriage bed, as her current move to cohabit with Charles seems to verify," commented a prudish Evan.

"But this infidelity has been going on throughout the decade of their marriage. Why would John suddenly act now? The letter may have been part of a personal vendetta to embarrass Caroline, but was it part of a conspiracy to land armed enemies of state in the Medway? Why would John, who has a lifetime of service to an extreme Puritan and parliamentary household, support a Royalist and foreign incursion?"

"Ask him?"

"Eventually. I need to know more about his past as a trusted servant of the Holts. Old Partridge is about the only person of the right vintage to help. We will be at the big house for supper. I will chat with him then."

That evening guests invited by Luke dominated the supper table.

The household was barely represented. Sir Giles had been exiled and his wife and children hidden somewhere in London to protect Alicia from her father and from whomever was trying to kill her. Caroline and Charles were both persona non grata, and John did not attend. Only Lady Prudence, her chaplain Barnaby Partridge, her secretary Roger Linton, and her brother-in-law Richard Holt, were present from the household.

Also attending was his commanding officer John Neville; John's brother William, the new governor of Upnor Castle; Thomas Digges, the commandant of the dockyard; Evan; and Luke.

Supper at Holt House once a week was a convenient meeting place for the senior military officers under Luke's command.

He met his officers before supper for what amounted to a boring administrative routine of reporting. It produced nothing of immediate concern.

After supper, Barnaby and Roger prepared for their nightly game of chess.

Luke asked if the former could spare him a few minutes.

Barnaby seemed relieved to be freed from the intense young man's nightly pursuit of an elusive victory.

Barnaby was a recognized master, Roger a relentless and unsuccessful challenger.

"How can I help?" Barnaby replied.

"You have been associated with Holt House for nearly thirty years. I need to know a little more about its history and the role of certain people over that period."

"That could take a long time. I will tell Roger that there will be no game tonight," replied a delighted Barnaby.

"I'm sorry to upset your routine," apologized Luke.

"To be honest, I need a more skilled opponent. Do you play, Colonel?"

"No," replied Luke a little too quickly.

"Down to family history. There are some secrets, skeletons in the cupboard, that I am not in a position to reveal, but on less delicate matters, I am at your disposal," an eager Barnaby responded.

"John Headley?"

"John was employed by the Holts for some twenty years before I arrived. He had been Sir Edward's valet at the time of the squire's marriage to my sister Mary and had been for a decade or so earlier. Sir Edward went into a decline soon after his marriage to Mary and, for everybody's safety, was exiled to the cottage. John was the only household member in contact with him as he sank into the madness that enveloped him for the last twelve years of his life. He was responsible for Edward's care during this long period of confinement. As a reward for taking on this onerous role, Mary elevated him to steward of the estates, a position he holds to this day, although Lady Prudence has taken away some of his responsibilities and given them to her bailiff and secretary."

"His background? How did he become Sir Edward's trusted valet?"

Barnaby hesitated as if sifting the relevant facts into two baskets—what he could tell and what must remain secret.

"The Headleys were smallholders in the Weald of Kent. John came here as a boy. He was the same age as Edward. They were childhood friends. Gossip alleged that he was an illegitimate son of Edward's father, but there has never been any evidence for this. Jealous servants made up such stories to explain the unprecedented rise of their rivals. On Edward succeeding to the title and the estates, he immediately appointed his friend John as valet."

"So a constant aspect of John Headley's past was his loyalty to Sir Edward?"

"Yes. Why are you suddenly interested in John?" asked Barnaby.

"The Lord Protector hinted that the answers to current problems involving the Holts were to be found in the past."

"Did he give you any details?" probed Barnaby, suddenly appearing agitated.

"No."

A relieved Barnaby commented, "I thought not. The Cromwells were not uninvolved in the more secretive actions of the past. The Protector, like myself, knows that full disclosure would harm innocent people."

"A second reason, for my interest, is Caroline Headley's recent abduction and the involvement of her boats in an abortive Royalist raid. It has been suggested that John may have been involved. Has he shown any Royalist tendencies over the years?"

"John never had a political opinion in his life. Sir Edward was similar. They were the least political of the Holt household over several generations. John may have been converted to the Royalist camp in recent months, but I have no evidence of any earlier commitments to the Stuart cause. If John did become a Royalist, it was probably motivated by problems with his wife. Any political motivation would be inconceivable. He has aged quickly in recent months, and his mind is a little befuddled. Prue has suggested as much on several occasions."

Luke changed the emphasis of his questions. "Has John shown favoritism or particular hostility to any other members of the household in recent years?"

"Hostility is easy. My sister Mary was wrong when she engineered the marriage of the young spirited Caroline to the elderly steward. She believed her wayward ways would not worry him. She was wrong. He hated those she became too close to, especially Charles Franklin."

"Why did John and Caroline consent to this doomed union?"

"Consent is hardly the word. They obeyed the orders of my ruthless sister Mary. She blackmailed John. What particular weapon she used on the then young Caroline, I do not know."

"What did your sister know about John that gave her such power over him?"

"My sister never revealed such things to anybody, especially her brother."

"Anyone else that John disliked?"

"In recent times, he has reversed his view of the Bartrams. For decades, he was very close to Lady Mercy and her daughters and had no time for Sir Giles, but recently, he seems to have turned against them, especially Alicia, and quite strangely is now close to Sir Giles."

"And his other favorites?"

"John never had open favorites, but he was the one member of the household, apart from Mary and Prue, who always saw some redeeming feature in Harry Proctor despite the lad's unrelenting malevolence."

Luke sensed an element of venom in the old vicar's comment and asked, "Given the recent history at Holt House, of all its inhabitants, the person most likely to rescue Harry, yet punish Alicia, would be John?"

"Possibly, but John is a ditherer. He has never acted decisively in his life. What would be his motive? No, it's the dockyard soldiers, determined to avenge the murder of their comrade, that are after Harry. Poor Frances was unlucky as they thought she was his alleged lover Alicia. I hope the army will not cover up their murderous rampage. If the rank and file get away with this murder, none of the superior classes on the Medway will be safe."

Luke thanked Barnaby and made to depart.

Barnaby stopped him. "Luke, I have a confession to make regarding John. He and I have disagreed over the years, but I did not want him to get into deeper and deeper trouble because of any assistance he might give to Harry Proctor. It was I who sent you the message inviting you to The Cottage. I hoped you would find Proctor there without too much involvement of old John."

Luke thanked Barnaby for his frankness.

Luke was pleased with what Barnaby had told him and equally with the areas of the past that he had tried to conceal.

# 25

---

Next morning Luke received a message from Stokey.

They met in Rochester at The Cod and Crab.

Luke was good-humored but blunt.

"My Lord, wherever there is trouble, you appear. Your reputation as a Royalist and effective leader of our Catholic population should terrify me, yet in the end, you act in a way that assists the government I serve without betraying your allies. You are the only man in England who is respected by both Oliver Cromwell and Charles Stuart. You have come to the Medway either to stop a premature insurrection or to assist a benighted Royalist caught up in his own foolishness."

"Flattery will get you nowhere. Your overall assessment is accurate, but the detail is astray. I came to the Medway to counsel my old friend Lady Matilda Lynne, who tells me that, with your arrival, she now feels she has someone to confide in."

"Why did you wish to talk to me?"

"Are you considering a change in political allegiance?"

"Why ask?"

"After years of certainty in our respective political positions, we are both having doubts. You cannot be happy with the thought of Cromwell as king and the curtailment of army influence. I am worried by the divisions within the Royalist ranks and the irrational decisions many of them have and are about to make."

"Come, the Royalist cause is simple—restore Charles Stuart to the throne of England!" uttered Luke.

"Not completely! An increasing number are willing to acquiesce in the return of monarchy in the person of Oliver Cromwell. Many Royalists support the very change that you vehemently oppose."

"Is that your position?"

"Not at all. No, my views are misunderstood. I have opposed Royalist insurrections against Cromwell because they will not succeed and because Cromwell, at the moment, is the only bastion of law and order. Royalists should accept the rule of the Protector only until the time is right to restore the rightful king. There is also a major split among us as to how Charles should be returned. This division is evident within the king's own court, and it explains the recent debacle on the Medway."

"What do you mean?"

"The experienced English advisers tell Charles that he must lead an English army to regain his lands, but advisers closer to the Queen Mother and the Duke of York encourage him to recruit an army of foreigners, mainly French, Spanish, or German Catholics, to invade England. This division is reflected throughout the Royalist community. Some, thankfully very few, support a foreign invasion of England. This I have acted to stop. Most would only support an invasion led by an English king at the head of an English army."

"So the recent incursion—it could hardly be called an invasion—failed because most Royalists refused to support it when they discovered it was made up of foreign mercenaries? Its defeat was not due to brilliant intelligence work and astute tactics and strategy of the Lord Protector's troops and the brilliance of Colonel Tremayne's intelligence work?" Luke teased.

Stokey smiled. "Luke, a warning! You were only dealing with a small advance guard using the fishing trawlers to land unobserved in the Medway. I cannot guarantee that a much larger attack will not happen—and soon. I have sent messages to the king suggesting that he listens to his English advisers. Either invade with an English army with himself at its head or refrain from any such attempts until the time is right. Even if that is the king's view, there are many maverick Royalists who will take matters into their own hands."

"Are any such dangerous gentlemen to be found around the Medway?"

"That, I cannot answer, but others might. Lady Lynne will ask for your help on a delicate matter. She may not tell you all at the beginning, but in the end, her good sense and your charm will lead to a positive result. Look after Matilda! She is a patriotic Englishwoman who may have been betrayed. She may have been led into foolishness. She is confused. Her heart is with the king, but her head with the Protector."

"You seem very fond of Matilda?" commented Luke gently.

Stokey did not answer.

Luke was also silent for a few moments and then blurted out, "Matilda is a clandestine Catholic!"

"Ask her. See her as soon as possible. Unfortunately, I am returning to Wales immediately. I have already left Grey Towers."

Next day, Luke, accompanied by Strad, visited Matilda.

While Strad waited in the reception hall, Luke was shown into an antechamber.

An animated Matilda entered, obviously delighted to see Luke.

"You must have read my mind, Colonel. I was just about to send a servant to Holt House inviting you to dine with me. On the other hand, you may only be here obeying Lord Stokey's directive."

"Matilda, I cannot be diplomatic. Are you a Papist?"

"Definitely not! The Hatch family has been staunch Protestants since Henry VIII broke with Rome. They began their climb up the social ladder through a grant of church lands from the king."

"Then why invite the most powerful Papist peer in the land to visit you? Everyone Stokey visits immediately become a suspect.

Thurloe's men have probably already installed a spy in your household. It was a silly move, Matilda."

"I wanted him to talk to Nicholas."

"Why?"

"I suspect Nicholas is a Papist."

"What do you mean 'suspect'? You have been married to him for decades. You must know."

"It's quite complicated. The Lynne family, throughout last century, was devoutly Catholic. However, in 1610, as part of the marriage agreement between Nicholas's much older sister Katherine and Edward Holt, the family was obliged to renounce Rome and espouse the national church. Nicholas's father and sister adapted to the change without any problems. Everybody assumed that Nicholas had done likewise. He was six years old when the change occurred, so in his very early years, he would have received a thorough Catholic indoctrination."

"When, during your many years of marriage, did you discover that his conversion might not have occurred?"

"Only a month ago. There are parts of this house that Nicholas forbade the servants and myself to enter. One night recently, when Nicholas was abroad, I, after a few too many drinks, ventured into that prohibited area. I found a room that was clearly a Papist chapel—and one that showed signs of recent use by more than one person."

"It doesn't mean Nicholas is a Papist. He may have preserved the chapel from the family's Catholic days to allow Catholics among your servants to worship there. Many Protestant peers in the north of England protect their Catholic servants and their clandestine worship in this way."

"Maybe, but it gets worse. I also discovered not one, but two very large priest holes that took up all of the underground level of that section of the house. Combined, they could conceal a small army. Is that where the recently thwarted invaders were to hide?"

Luke did not answer Matilda's question but asked, "Did Stokey advise you on these matters?"

"No, that is why I need your help. Stokey did not see Nicholas because he has not returned from his last trip to the continent. He left the day after your riding accident. He should have been back a week ago. Stokey could not stay any longer."

"Why did Nicholas go abroad?"

"To sell our wool and buy horses. Rather than go through the merchant companies, he decided to sell directly to the buyers on the continent."

"So where did he go?"

"He was moving up the coast from France through the Spanish and Dutch controlled Netherlands—Dunkirk, Ostend, Antwerp, Flushing, and Amsterdam were mentioned."

"Give Nicholas another two or three weeks before you become alarmed! Several of those towns are in a war zone, and local unrest could make travel difficult. How did he travel to Dunkirk?"

"On one of Caroline Headley's trawlers that was going there to unload some workers and pick up the usual range of luxury goods. After that, he would take local sea transport up the coast."

Luke immediately saw the possibility that Nicholas was taken by the *Caroline Star* to Dunkirk, although he may have been an innocent passenger.

He would not alarm Matilda at this stage.

Matilda was distressed.

She sobbed a little and then pleaded with Luke, "Stay with me! I need comforting, especially with the worry of Nicholas's possible Catholicism and disappearance. I fear the worst."

"What do you mean, *fear the worst*?"

"At this point, I cannot tell you all, although Stokey insisted that if the situation became intolerable, I must confide in you as the only man who could solve my problems."

"Matilda, I cannot stay now, as I have my sergeant with me, and there is much that has to be done today. I will return alone tonight."

The two embraced, and as Matilda pushed her tongue into Luke's mouth, he ran his hands down from her neck to under her clothing until they encompassed her firm and rounded breasts.

His fingers found her nipples.

Two hours later, Luke left Matilda's bedroom as she whispered, "Until tonight, Luke."

A servant girl had taken a fancy to Strad as he patiently waited in the entrance hall.

She plied him with food and drink, which partly relieved his tedious long wait. Eventually, an extremely jealous and angry male servant sent her packing.

As Luke entered the hall, Strad beckoned him to the far wall. He pointed to a portrait that dominated that corner of the room.

"Colonel, who is that man?"

"The master of the house, Sir Nicholas Lynne, probably painted ten years ago."

"I've seen him recently."

"Of course, you have—probably when you and Evan came here to investigate the alleged attempt on my life."

"No, Sir Nicholas had already left for the continent."

"You may have seen him at Holt House. He has been regular visitor."

"No, we are kept in our place at Holt House. I do not often see, let alone mix with, Lady Prudence's guests."

"So where did you see him?"

"I can't remember."

They rode back to Mudhill Farm in silence, where Evan was waiting to report on recent developments.

"I have just interrogated the surviving member of the Garrison Gang who crewed the *Caroline Star.* He jumped overboard before Richard Holt boarded the boat and put everyone to the sword. He was spotted in the water by the Pratt brothers who detained him and brought him to us."

"Did he have anything of interest to say?"

"Yes, he claimed that the *Caroline Star*, on its outward voyage, picked up two gentlemen on the southern shore of the Swale."

"Two gentlemen? I know the identity of one of them. Sir Nicholas Lynne is organizing the illegal export of wool to the continent and using the smuggling contacts of the region to organize a new network. But who was the second? I will press your witness for more detailed descriptions of the two passengers."

"Unfortunately, you can't. He did not survive the interrogation. The only fact about the second man I elicited was that he was a lot younger than the first."

Luke returned to Holt House and, after supper, slipped quietly away to visit Matilda.

When he returned the next morning, Strad was waiting for him.

"Colonel, I remember where I saw Sir Nicholas Lynne. He was leaving Les Trois Enfants in Ostend when we arrived for our briefing. He slipped out of a side door after you had entered the building. I thought, at the time, that this was a shady character."

# 26

Evan commented, "You have probably unearthed the local leader of the failed incursion. It has to be Sir Nicholas. It's too much of a coincidence—Dunkirk to obtain the arms and ammunition, Ostend to oversee the departure of his mercenaries. It fits together."

"He could still be an innocent fellow traveler, simply trying to sell his wool and buy horses," countered Luke.

"The fact that he may be a Papist adds strength to my conclusion that he *is* the Royalist leader on the Medway. You can't believe Lady Lynne's explanation of Stokey's visit? That Papist came here with direct orders from Charles Stuart for Sir Nicholas. It is surely suspicious that a senior Royalist peer is in the Medway at the time of an attempted Royalist uprising and the departure of its local leader to the continent?"

Luke ignored Evan's views.

"The pertinent question at the moment is, *where is Nicholas?*"

"If he was one of the officers aboard the trawlers heading to the Medway with the supposed Protestant refugees, he could be well on his way to the East Indies as crew on a merchantman," concluded Evan.

"The Dutch sent the mercenary soldiers to the Indies as conscripted seamen, but did they do the same to the English officers involved? They would not risk the political fallout over any mistreatment of gentlemen. More likely, they are being held as hostages."

"What will you tell Lady Matilda?" asked Evan.

"Nothing for the moment, but I will get a letter off to our consul in Flushing to ascertain the fate of the English officers. Hopefully, they have been detained for a ransom or for particular services they may be able to perform for the Dutch Republic. I will return to Lady Matilda. I suspect she has a lot more to tell me. I now have to accept the possibility that she may be part of Nicholas's plot," concluded Luke soulfully.

"Or even the instigator of it. She is not the subservient partner in the Lynne relationship. She is the dominating force and probably the brains behind any Lynne project," continued an insensitive Evan.

Luke hoped that this assessment was wrong.

That night he did not allow such doubts to inhibit his physical relationship with Matilda.

As they lay mutually exhausted in each other's arms, Luke whispered, "Tell me the real story of Nicholas's disappearance!"

Luke expected to hear a confession of Nicholas's and maybe Matilda's part in the plot to bring foreign troops into the Medway as a precursor of a rebellion against the government and the reintroduction of the Stuart monarchy.

Her first statement stunned him.

"Nicholas is being blackmailed."

Luke did not have a flexible mind. His prejudices and preconceived ideas determined his response.

"Was he blackmailed because he was organizing a coup against the government or because he was a Papist?"

Matilda looked amazed and confused. "Neither! He would not be involved in any plot, and no one knows about his religious situation—as far as I am aware."

"Then what major indiscretion provides ammunition for a blackmailer?"

"For decades, the Lynnes have exported much of their wool illegally through the local smuggling network and, more recently, their prize horses. Just weeks before he was appointed a magistrate, with the duty to enforce the laws of the land, including those relating to the export of goods, he decided to break with tradition and export our wool ourselves. He was in contact with Caroline Headley with regard to hiring one or more of her boats, and his latest trip abroad was one of many, trying to establish buyers on the continent. He received threats that if he did not continue to use the smuggling network of which Harry Proctor was the public face, information would be passed on to the government that he was not only acting against the law in exporting his wool outside the official channels but also that, indeed, he was no convert to the Protector but a clandestine Royalist plotting to destroy the government."

"What did Nicholas do?"

"He completely ignored the threats and proceeded to establish his own trading connections. Have you received any information blackening Nicholas's name?"

Luke was honest. "No, I have not received any such information, but Nicholas's trip to Dunkirk and Ostend puts him in the middle of an antigovernment plot. He is under suspicion because of this coincidence of events, not from any malicious correspondence. Did Nicholas report this threat to anybody?"

"No! He investigated the situation himself, questioning Harry Proctor at length about it."

"Did he threaten Harry? Did he have any of his men roughen him up?"

"How could you think such a thing? Nicholas is a gentle soul. He lives for his horses. He has always been reactive to political or financial situations. He has never been the instigator or aggressor—unlike myself."

"Did he kidnap Proctor?"

"What makes you ask that?"

"The *Caroline Star* picked up two gentlemen, whom I believe were Nicholas and Harry, and took them to Dunkirk."

"That's true! Nicholas was going to Dunkirk aboard Captain Tyler's boat. I told you that on your last visit."

"It doesn't make sense. Tyler is a captain who participates heavily in the current smuggling network—the very network that Nicholas is challenging by his unilateral activity."

"Exactly, but Nicholas had persuaded Harry Proctor and Tyler to join him and form their own little network. He offered Tyler a lot more than the smugglers had ever paid him, and Harry was about to be dumped by them—or worse. Proctor had become a liability, and elements in the smuggling ring wanted him out of the way permanently."

"That explains why Tyler was relieved of his command by his own men. At some stage, they mutinied against him and took control of the boat. This may have been payback for Tyler's attempt to go out on his own with Nicholas," concluded Luke.

He rode back to Holt House the following day, more confused than ever. If Sir Nicholas Lynne was not behind the local plot, who organized the Garrison Gang to obtain arms at Dunkirk and trick the other boats of Caroline's fleet to sail to Ostend to collect alleged Protestant refugees? And in what capacity and for what purpose was Harry Proctor aboard the *Caroline Star*?

Luke interviewed Tom Tyler who was initially aggressive and threatening. Luke reciprocated in kind.

"If you do not cooperate, you will leave here for the hangman. You were captain of a ship that was importing arms and ammunition for the use of rebels against the state. You were captain of a ship that kidnapped and keel hauled a servant of Mistress Headley, your employer. You did not cooperate with a government official, myself, when I boarded your boat, and you have engaged in smuggling every summer for over a decade. My Puritan masters are not impressed. Need I go on?"

"What do you want?"

"The truth about the aborted plot to land foreign troops in the Medway."

"I know nothing about such a plot. Sir Nicholas and I had planned that after Mistress Headley paid me off and I leased her boat, I would transport his goods and person to the continent and slowly make our way up the coast, negotiating with buyers at Dunkirk, Ostend, Antwerp, Flushing, and Amsterdam. Unfortunately, Sir Nicholas had neither wool nor horses ready for me. Lady Lynne, as compensation, persuaded her brother, Major Hatch, to use me to transport the foreign workers at the castle back to the continent. Sir Nicholas and I would then proceed as planned. He would negotiate future buyers, while I would purchase luxury goods for distribution among the local gentry."

"What went wrong?"

"Trouble began when I was unable to recruit my normal crew and had to employ men who were members of the Garrison Gang. At the last minute, my boatswain was involved in a tavern brawl and severely injured. A man called Marsh, who seemed to have authority among some of the men, volunteered as his replacement. I have since discovered that my normal summer crew had been intimidated by the Garrison Gang to make them unavailable. Their resentment was alleviated by a significant payment to each of them. Someone with money was behind the subversion of my usual crew."

"When did Marsh reveal his true intentions?"

"I never knew what his true intentions were. He annoyed me by keel hauling the African servant whom he and the men had kidnapped without my knowledge, but you need to allow a crew to indulge in some horseplay. I was shocked when Marsh insisted he kill you and throw you overboard and then when he battered Major Hatch for warning you. From that point, Marsh was in command, although they needed my navigation skills. The Garrison Gang were no seamen."

"So you proceeded according to your plan to collect Sir Nicholas and sail to Dunkirk."

"Yes."

"Was Proctor the other gentlemen you picked up?"

"Yes."

"Why did you take him?"

"Proctor was waiting with Sir Nicholas at the pick-up point. I assumed he came as the magistrate's prisoner. I knew he was under arrest for murder."

"What happened at Dunkirk?"

"Sir Nicholas and Proctor went ashore. Marsh ordered me to sail to the opposite side of the harbor without them where a group of men loaded boxes of arms and ammunition. We returned to England immediately. You know the rest."

"What happened to Proctor and Sir Nicholas?"

"No idea!"

"Sir Nicholas made it to Ostend, and there are rumors that he may have inadvertently been arrested by the Dutch and, hopefully, is held for ransom. I sent a letter on Lady Lynne's behalf to our consul in Flushing, seeking advice on this matter. Anything else you can tell me about Proctor? Did he and Sir Nicholas appear friendly?" Luke asked.

"Both men sensed the toxic atmosphere on board the *Caroline Star* and did not want to cross Marsh who clearly also did not want to complicate his mission by having two gentlemen to deal with. There was one fact that may mean nothing, but as we sailed away from the pick-up point on the Swale, I saw a horseman leading a riderless steed. I assumed it was the horse on which Proctor had ridden to the pick-up point."

"What is so important about that?" asked Luke.

"On the blanket of the horse, I could clearly see the arms of the most powerful family on the Medway."

"Which family?"

"The Holts."

Luke leaned back on his chair with such enthusiasm that he nearly tumbled backwards.

He softened his approach to Tyler.

"Go! I will not be pressing any charges against you."

Luke was perplexed.

Harry Proctor had escaped England on the same boat as the magistrate responsible for his detention.

What was the real relationship between the two men, and what happened when they were stranded in Dunkirk?

Where was Proctor?

Why was Nicholas in Ostend? Was he completely innocent of the invasion plot?"

Where was he now?

Luke brought Prudence up to date regarding Harry. She seemed relieved that in his last known situation, Dunkirk, he was alive and well.

Luke was annoyed at her reaction. He was further troubled by Prudence's unexpected rebuke.

"Luke, have you solved the murder of my niece Frances?"

Luke confessed that little had been done so far, but it would now be his first priority, given that other issues were currently on hold, awaiting developments.

Luke took his leave, but as he exited Prudence's chamber, he stopped.

"Prudence, if I am to advance such an investigation, I must speak to Alicia again immediately. Can she return here for a short period?"

"Definitely not! Whoever killed Frances by mistake will try again, and her own father cannot be trusted."

"I must see her," insisted Luke.

"Roger, will take you to them," conceded a reluctant Prudence.

Luke had to smile at Roger's amateurish attempt to conceal the destination by taking a circuitous route that ended at a palatial town house on the banks of the Thames. Even if Luke was confused and unsure of the destination, Strad, who followed at a distance, knew exactly where his colonel had been taken.

Alicia was delighted to see both Roger and Luke.

Luke insisted that he speak to Alicia alone.

"I am trying to discover who murdered Frances and, by deduction, who is trying to kill you. Could Frances have been the intended victim? Had she confided in you regarding any problems she faced or any persons who were troubling her?"

"No, Frances led a very restricted life. She kept her thoughts to herself and rarely left the narrow limits of our part of Holt House. She was terrified of Father and totally cowed by him. But your question is based on a false premise. Frances and I were identical twins. Only the family could tell us apart. In the real world, only our clothing distinguished us from each other. If Frances was wearing my cloak, no one, except Mother, would know it was Frances and not I. No, Colonel, I was the intended victim."

# 27

Luke continued his questioning. “Why would anyone want to kill you? You annoyed us all with your flighty ways and your tendency to see everything as a game, but flippancy is hardly a motive for murder. Did you seriously upset anyone?”

Alicia smiled. “Was I flighty? I had hoped you would have said flirtatious and seductive.” Then she laughed.

Luke responded seriously. “Come, Alicia, this outward appearance of frivolity and sexuality is not the real you. Underneath that facade, there lurks a serious and capable woman who knows much more than she admits.”

“I am not the intended victim because of anything I have actually done to another person. I’m the intended victim because the would-be murderer thinks I know things that he or she does not want revealed.”

“What do you think you know that might fall into that category?”

“I have no idea. There are lots of possible things. I wander the estate daily, hiding in the coppices near the house and in Wadham Wood. I see things, which, at the time, are meaningless but, with hindsight and in the view of others, must be important.”

“Did the people you witnessed in the woodlands see you?”

“Some did, some didn’t.”

"What did you see?"

"Amorous liaisons. The Medway should be overrun with bastards," she joked.

"Just because men and women cuddle in the woods, it does not mean they are about to produce children," intoned a paternal Luke.

"Don't treat me like a child! I know the difference between a flirtatious encounter and frequent and regular intercourse," replied an animated Alicia.

"Surely none of your sightings fitted into the latter category?"

"You are now the innocent. Yes, there were many, but there were two partnerships in recent months that were regular and unbridled."

Luke thought to himself that young Alicia could have no concept of unbridled.

"And who were these couples?"

"Mistress Headley and Mr. Franklin, and Harry Proctor and Goodwife Miller."

"The wife of the man Harry killed?"

"Yes."

"Alicia, if you saw Harry with Goodwife Miller so often, why are you his close friend, claim he was your suitor, and then helped him escape from custody?"

"In the beginning, it was exciting, but it slowly dawned on me that if Harry knew I had seen him, my evidence could reveal a motive for murder. He might see me as a danger and wish to silence me. To be his friend and help him escape seemed the safest option."

"So you became his friend and ally because you were frightened of him?"

"Yes."

"That's not the story you told me before. If you had told the truth then, your sister might still be alive," said Luke harshly.

Alicia began to weep. A gentle sob developed into an emotional, almost hysterical, fit of remorse. She slowly calmed down.

"You didn't need to tell me that. I will never forgive myself."

Luke showed no sympathy, unconvinced by Alicia's explanation of her relationship with Harry.

He bluntly asked, "Did Harry murder Frances, thinking it was you?"

"Why would he want to kill me? Give me a motive and I might be in a better position to answer that question."

Alicia was confused. She had already implied a motive. Harry thought she knew too much about his activities.

Luke did not push the point and asked, "What else did you see on your daily walks?"

"There were dozens of innocent meetings."

"Any of interest to my enquiry?"

"No, although I saw my big sister Elizabeth on several occasions walking with different men—Roger Linton, Harry Proctor, and Major Hatch. And Father never caught her once. She was taking a big risk because Father, in his own mind, has her already married off to Mr. Harvey or, as Father prefers to call him, the Marquis of Appley."

"Did any encounters of a nonromantic nature surprise you?"

"Lots. The most surprising was that, although they live in the same house, Father and Harry met regularly in a secluded part of Wadham Wood. And what makes it even more interesting, they never arrived or left together. They always approached their meeting place from opposite directions. Father came down from London Road, and Harry walked cross-country from Holt House. Why couldn't they meet in one of the isolated and empty rooms in Holt House?"

"Did anything happen at these meetings?"

"A lot of arguments, and Harry handed over letters or sometimes a bag to Father. Mr. Headley was another who met Father well away from the house. Mr. Headley also spent a lot of time walking in the woods with Harry. They seemed to have a lot to say to each other. Harry once told me that, in recent years, Mr. Headley had become like a father to him, although neither revealed a closeness in the presence of Lady Prudence."

"Apart from your father, Harry, and Mr. Headley, did you notice any other unlikely meetings?"

"In the last few months, I have seen Sir Nicholas Lynne on the estate, but he was either going to or coming from a meeting with somebody. He had not made his presence known to Lady Prudence. Perhaps he was simply spying on the Holt horses? The chief groom used to be responsible to Mr. Headley, but in a recent reshaping of responsibilities, he is now supervised by Mr. Franklin. Maybe that was whom Sir Nicholas was meeting."

"Thanks, Alicia. At the moment, your information creates more problems than it solves. Almost everybody on the Medway who carries on an illicit activity on the Holt estate may wish to silence you."

Luke returned to Holt House. Within minutes, Strad arrived. He was very excited.

"Colonel, you won't believe who owns the house you just visited and which family is looking after the Bartrams."

"Tell me!"

"The Lord Protector's son-in-law. It is the home of one of Cromwell's daughters."

Luke was furious.

"This is what annoys me about this case. Cromwell is keeping too much back. I have to solve this case, but I am still not sure what the case is. I am acting with one hand tied behind my back."

"Did Miss Alicia provide any useful information?" asked Strad, tactfully changing the subject.

"Too much. Her father Sir Giles needs to be questioned next. Be ready for an early departure in the morning. We ride towards Dover. I will obtain the exact directions from Prudence."

Prudence was not happy.

"Is it necessary to visit Giles? I have exiled him to a small property that was left in Bartram hands so that they could over the decades, gradually reduce the debt they owe us. His full-time residence on the property may start to improve its financial position, although his fat lambs are too expensive a delicacy, when most local woolgrowers flood the market with cheap mutton. Giles would not have a clue about estate management and relies on a tenant farmer who probably skims off any profit that is made."

"Why did you continue to keep the Bartrams here after Lady Mary's death? Why could they not develop an independent life elsewhere—maybe on the farm you mentioned?"

"I am bound legally to adhere to Giles's marriage agreement with Mercy, in which the Holts guaranteed to provide this opportunity for Giles to slowly redeem his family's financial situation. He never took that provision seriously and was happy to live off our largesse that guaranteed him a home, food, and status."

Prudence reluctantly gave directions to Luke.

Halfway between Canterbury and Dover, Luke and Strad turned north for a few miles. They asked a hedge trimmer the way to Bartram Hall.

Their trip was a waste of time. On approaching the house, they were accosted by a man on horseback that demanded to know why they were trespassing on his land.

Luke responded with a white lie. "We have come with an urgent message for Sir Giles regarding his family."

The man dismounted. "Sir Giles rarely visits. I manage the property for him."

"I understood that he was now here full time."

The man became apprehensive.

"Sir Giles has other interests that require his attention more regularly than Bartram Hall. He is not here."

"Then where is he?"

"I don't know."

"Surely you know what and where his other interests are?"

"Sir, given the Bartram's history over the last few decades, it is best to know as little as possible."

"What are his other interests?"

"He is in trade, probably illegal, but Sir Giles, as a gentleman, never talks about it. Its nature may be a great embarrassment for someone of his status."

"Does this mean he is in London?"

"No idea!"

"When do you expect him back?"

"Not for some months. I have just given him any monies I owed him a week ago when he made a rushed visit."

Luke and Strad rode dejectedly back towards the main road. They passed a group of laborers who were taking a break from working in an adjacent field.

As they trotted past, a voice called out. "Well, if that is not Bevan Stradling!"

Strad pulled up his horse as the man approached. "Well, if it is not my old companion Sam Fernsby."

The man belatedly also recognized Luke. "Greetings, Colonel, I served under you when you were stationed in The Tower and involved in protecting General Cromwell from assassination back in 1653."

The soldiers exchanged greetings, and Fernsby offered his former comrades a share of his meal of the cheese and bread.

Luke declined but saw an opportunity.

"Fernsby, have you lived in this area long?"

"Yes, sir! Apart from my military service, I have been here, as had my father and grandfather before me, all our lives. Years ago, when the Bartrams controlled most of this area, the Fernsby were tenant farmers. My elder brother now leases some land from the Holts, and I work for him."

Luke explained the purpose of their unsuccessful mission.

"I have heard that Sir Giles has more important financial interests than maintaining the remnant of his family lands, but no one will tell us where they are located," asked Luke.

"If you asked at Bartram Hall, they probably do not know. The manager there is a newcomer to the district. When the Bartram wealth declined, their land was taken over by the Holts, and Giles was forced to marry into the family."

"Why did the Bartrams fall on bad times?" asked Strad.

"Sir Giles's father gambled away the family assets progressively during his lifetime. He managed to conceal some capital from the

Holts. This was used by Giles's young brother to set up a general merchant's shop and warehouse in Maidstone. Over the years, it has flourished. As the brother apparently died a decade ago, I guess Giles has had to take over the business."

"Great news, Fernsby! You have made our visit worthwhile."

Luke and Strad stayed at Canterbury overnight and the next day arrived in Maidstone.

They asked around the market for directions to Bartrams the merchant. No one knew of them.

Eventually, Luke went to the local church and confronted the vicar. "I am on government business, and I have urgent news for Mr. Bartram, who, I believe, is a merchant in this town but who appears unknown to the general populace."

"I can only give the same answer as my parishioners. There are no Bartrams in business in this town."

Strad saw a possibility. "Reverend, sir, maybe Mr. Bartram is not the principal in the business. Can you give us the names of all the general merchants in Maidstone?"

"There are many because of the ease of trade down the Medway to London and abroad. Your task will be made easy because they all have premises along the Medway on either side of the river. You don't need the names. You will find them all easily enough side-by-side along the river."

Luke and Strad visited them all. None confessed to having an owner or partner named Bartram.

"We are both known to Giles. Let's return to Holt House and send half a dozen of our men back here who can identify him. They can wait in all of the town's taverns—that should be an incentive—to see if he appears to eat there, in addition to watching each of the merchant firms. Unfortunately, by now, he may be aware of our interest."

# 28

Two days later, six dragoons arrived in Maidstone.

They found their quarry on the first morning of their surveillance but did not inform Luke until the next day. Observation from inside a well-stocked tavern was a chore to be prolonged.

Giles was identified as a man who spent much time in the shop and warehouse of the Mottram Brothers.

Luke and Strad returned to Maidstone and sat in the window of The Three Swans, from which they could see who visited Mottrams.

They were soon rewarded.

Giles appeared and entered the shop

Strad went to the back of the premises to prevent any escape while Luke went through the front door.

The man who greeted him looked like Giles but clearly was not. Giles had been wearing a deep blue doublet and cape. This man wore a large apron over a dull grey habit.

Luke addressed him, “Good, man, may I speak to Giles?”

“Giles who? There is no one by that name here, although we do have a regular customer by that name, Sir Giles Bartram of Holt House.”

"Giles entered this building a few minutes ago. We are not here to punish him. I need to question him on a range of issues. Some may be to his advantage."

The conversation was interrupted by some shouting from the rear of the building and the noise of a brief scuffle.

Giles appeared, followed by Strad who had his sword drawn.

Luke spoke. "Put your sword away, Sergeant! Sir Giles and I need to have a private conversation. Is there a comfortable room where we can have a quiet discussion?"

A ruffled Giles pointed to a distant door. It led to a small reception room.

"Sir Giles, at the moment, I am only interested in trying to solve the murder of your daughter Frances and what I believe is the ongoing threat to her sister Alicia. The problem lies in Alicia's inquisitiveness. She has seen or heard something which another wishes to keep secret. On the other hand, the danger may stem from wider concerns emanating from your relationship with the Holts and other members of the community."

"I am anxious to help solve the murder of my daughter, but I can't see how my position at Holt House and in the wider community is relevant."

"I am surprised that a man of your status and ability has lived with his mother-in-law for twenty-five years and continued at Holt House two years after her death."

"Do you think I want to stay there? A brief history of my family will put you in the picture. My father owned several estates just north of the Canterbury-Dover road. We were a wealthy gentry family. Unfortunately, Father was a gambler, both with cards and dubious investments in overseas adventures. He became so heavily in debt that a debtor's prison seemed a real possibility. He was saved from that fate by the generous Holts."

He spat out *the generous Holts* with some venom.

"You're not thankful that the Holts saved your father and welcomed you into their ranks?"

"The Holts are predatory and none more evil than my late saintly step-mother-in-law, Lady Mary. The Holts took all our land. They transferred the remainder of our outstanding debt to themselves. They would not call in these debts if I married Lady Mercy Holt, whose parentage was in doubt and, therefore, had become a liability on the marriage market. As part of this marriage agreement, I was to live at Holt House until the debt was paid. They leased back to me the home farm of Bartram Hall as the means by which I was to gradually repay the debt."

"But it was too small to provide you with the income needed?"

"Correct. On numerous occasions, I asked Mary to make available to me more of her land so that I could reduce the debt."

"She refused?"

"She was more vindictive than that. She offered me several estates but proposed to increase the debt in terms of what she thought each property was worth—well above their real value. I would have spent my life paying off the new debt without ever reducing that which Father had incurred."

"But you found a way out?"

"Yes, thanks to the work of my young brother over several decades. You have just met him. He took the name of William Mottram. When the Holts moved in and acquired our entire assets, Father and I managed to smuggle some family jewels to William, whom everybody believed had died. He set up a merchant's business in Maidstone, and over the years, I have assisted him with stock and clients. I openly come here as a customer, but no one knows that I am a partner in the enterprise or that William Mottram is my brother."

"It is fortunate I am not a customs and exciseman. I noticed your shelves are filled with luxury items, and by the smell emanating from the warehouse, it is full of fleeces ready for export. Mottram Brothers is the distribution and collection base for the smugglers network. Could your involvement in this trade be a reason that your daughter was attacked?"

"Possibly. The one thing that connects the smuggling and my daughter is that cad Proctor. He is the public face of the ring. Many of us have been very unhappy with his performance over recent months. He has also been paying attention to Alicia. I am not completely ignorant of my daughter's errant behavior. Perhaps a person who hates Proctor is after Alicia, thinking that she is his sweetheart."

"You could be right. What are you going to do concerning Holt House and your banishment from it? By the way, I did not agree with Prudence's decision in this matter. If you had applied more discipline to Alicia as a child, we may not be in this predicament. But I have no children, so I won't lecture you on the matter. Are you going to fight your banishment from Holt House and forced separation from your wife and daughters?"

"In time. According to my marriage agreement, I must reside at Holt House until the debts are paid. Therefore, legally, Prudence cannot exile me, but her actions suit me at the moment. William and I have made so much money as Mottram Brothers that I am almost in a position where I can repay our family debt. I can then move back to Bartram Hall with my family and, in time, increase our lands through the profits of this merchant house."

"You and Proctor lived in the same house for decades, yet you meet secretly with him in the woods to transfer documents and money. Why not meet in the house?"

"Harry pays me for wool, or I pay him for luxury goods. As far as he is concerned, I was acting for my friend William Mottram. He has no idea that I have a stake in the business myself. After all, trade is beneath gentlemen. We could not meet in the house as Prue has her eyes and ears everywhere. Every servant is an instant informer. Linton runs an intelligence network within the house that rivals your master, John Thurloe. Prue continues the regime of fear and intimidation instituted by Lady Mary."

"Lady Mary was a ruthless woman?"

"If I had to define evil, it would be her. She dealt with the family as viciously as she dealt with any outsiders who got in her way. I lived at Holt House for fifteen years when my father-in-law was the nominal head of the family. I never met him. He had been exiled to The Cottage and confined there until his death. Mary claimed that he had gone mad and the family wanted him looked after on the property rather than sending him to an institution.

From a few asides made by John Headley who was the only member of the household who had contact with him, madness was not the reason for his confinement. His confinement caused his madness."

"Why has Prue maintained most of Mary's attitudes? Surely she offered you a better deal when you asked for more land? And why did she continue the favoritism towards Harry Proctor?"

"I never asked Prue for more land, as the merchant house was providing unexpectedly high income. Prue's attitudes seemed to become more rigid just before Mary's death. Just before she died, Mary called in Prudence, her brother Barnaby Partridge, and John Headley. Whatever she revealed, whatever she ordered, has governed the attitudes of those three ever since. Mary probably blackmails Prudence from the grave to continue her regime."

"How are the Cromwell family involved with the affairs at Holt House?" asked Luke unexpectedly.

"Not greatly! Mary spent part of her honeymoon on the Cromwell estate. Linton is also linked in some way with the Cromwell connection."

"What about Prudence?"

"During childhood, she was a friend of Cromwell's daughters."

"Has Harry's failures over recent months provoked others to take over the smuggling network? Was the abduction of Caroline Headley an attempt to win control of boats to carry on the illegal trade?"

"No. The ring can operate quite well as is without Proctor or Headley's trawlers."

"More seriously, some prominent landholders intend to bypass the ring and sell and import directly to and from the continent. Is that likely to lead to conflict in the local community?"

For the first time during the long interrogation, Giles appeared agitated.

"I have not heard of any such development," he replied with a lack of conviction.

"Not true! You have been seen in the woods in animated discussion with Sir Nicholas Lynne, who, at this time, is on the continent organizing such a rival network to the one in which you are involved."

"I came across Nicholas once, walking in the Holt woodlands. It was an accidental encounter."

Luke sensed that he would get very little more out of a now anxious Giles. "Thank you for your cooperation. I will keep your involvement with Mottrams confidential."

As Luke and Strad rode back towards Holt House, the latter asked, "Did that prove useful?"

"Yes, we have solved two of our problems. I am sure that Sir Giles is the head of the smuggling ring and that it is so vital to his chances of escaping the clutches of the Holts that he would do anything to preserve its profitable activities. He may have ordered Proctor's execution."

"Why?"

"Proctor is creating problems within the smuggling network. He may have sold out, encouraging and assisting Lynne to set up a rival group. In addition, he was paying undue attention to Alicia—and we know how Giles reacts to any man who gets near his beloved daughters. Thirdly, Giles lived in the same house as Harry and was in position to poison a meal."

Several days later, Luke received a reply from the English consul in Flushing.

> *The Dutch authorities did not send the English officers to the Indies. I have negotiated the return of seven Englishmen, including Sir Nicholas Lynne and a Harry Proctor. They should arrive in the Medway at the same time as you receive this letter.*

Luke was delighted for Matilda that Sir Nicholas was safe. He was astounded that Harry Proctor was returning. He was concerned that five suspected Royalist officers would enter the country.

They would arrive aboard the mail packet that disembarked its cargo and passengers at Queensborough, Upnor Castle, and then Rochester.

There was still time to meet today's arrival.

Sir Nicholas would probably disembark at Rochester.

Luke, with a troop of dragoons, rode quickly there.

As they entered the town, he was disappointed to see the packet sailing back down the Medway.

He went straight to the wharf and ascertained from the postmaster that no passengers had disembarked.

The official confessed that the ship was a day late, having spent the night at Upnor Castle.

He believed that given this known delay, any passengers anxious to get to their destination would have left the ship at the castle the previous night.

Luke headed downstream to Upnor Castle.

They were warmly welcomed by the governor, William Neville.

"Luke, I am glad you are here. I was just about to send a messenger to alert you that Sir Nicholas Lynne and six men that he claimed were officers returning to serve the Protector disembarked here last night. Given our heightened state of security, the arrival of six officers could be a problem. Five of them, I did not recognize, and a sixth kept his face hidden."

"You would have recognized him. The sixth man was the escapee Harry Proctor."

"What is magistrate Lynne doing covering for an alleged murderer?" asked an appalled William.

"That is what I intend to find out."

"There is another disturbing aspect. Sir Nicholas and the soldiers expected to find Major Hatch here. The men had papers addressed to him. They appeared quite alarmed when I told them that I was now the governor, replacing Major Hatch. When I explained that he was recuperating and was, at the moment, at Sir Nicholas's residence in the care of his sister, everybody relaxed. Sir Nicholas asked to borrow seven horses so that they could move to Grey Towers immediately."

"Anything else strike you as odd?"

"Yes, one of the officers seemed surprised that the castle was defended by so many troops and that we had reinforced its battery of guns with a number of large naval cannons that enabled us to cover all of the river between here and the dockyard. He seemed quite alarmed that they all had a variable trajectory which enabled us to deal with intruders who were close to the shore or well out to sea."

# 29

---

Next day, Luke rode to Grey Towers.

He waited in a reception hall for some time.

Lady Matilda arrived wearing a very low cut bodice.

"Great news, Luke, Nicholas is home!"

"That is why I am here. I need to question him about his traveling companions."

"Not possible at the moment. He was very tired when he returned and has slept for hours. I am reluctant to wake him. But your visit should not be wasted."

She drew Luke to her, and they began to mutually caress. As both became increasingly aroused, Luke pulled away. "Sorry, Matilda, this is not the time."

Matilda feigned major disappointment.

Luke commented, "If I cannot talk to your husband, and it is not appropriate to bed you, may I speak to your recuperating brother, Matthew, to whom I owe my life?"

Matilda laughed.

"You certainly cannot. Matthew has recovered so quickly that, for the last few days, he is across the fields, assisting with the training of our army for Flanders."

A cold shiver went down Luke's spine. He suddenly felt a foreboding. He would not mention that he knew Nicholas had returned with Proctor and five Royalist officers nor that these suspects were intent on reporting to Matthew.

"I'll visit Matthew at the camp."

He gave Matilda a lingering kiss and departed.

Neither he nor Matilda was aware that their closeness had been witnessed through a slightly opened door. The observer was Nicholas.

Luke arrived at Medway Court to be greeted by the camp's commandant, Major General Simon Cobb. Cobb had been Luke's deputy during their service in Ireland almost a decade earlier and an associate in the suppression of the Liffey mutiny only a few weeks earlier.

Cobb was delighted to see Luke, but clearly anxious.

"When the Protector's top agent appears, trouble is not far behind."

Luke responded in like vein. "You always got things back to front, Simon. When a problem arises, you can expect Tremayne to arrive and solve it."

"That is what worries me. You never make a social visit. What dark threat to the security of the state lies within my camp that it warrants your visit?"

"This is a social visit," lied Luke.

"I went to Grey Towers to thank Major Hatch for saving my life and to see how well he was recuperating to be told he was here."

"His offer to help us was exactly what I needed. With changed priorities at the last minute to raise two extra companies, I had no trouble raising the rank and file—our recruiters have conscripted more of the lowlife of London and surrounds. Unfortunately, the supply of officers has failed to keep pace. Hatch said he could help. Today he arrived with five experienced officers who have just left the Dutch service and are ready to train and lead our new companies."

"You say five. Were there not six?"

"No, only five."

"Did you check on their backgrounds? Were they experienced?"

"We have to take their word or that of fellow officers who know them, but all of these men have had recent experience on the continent as mercenaries for the Dutch Republic."

"Their political loyalties and their stance during our civil wars?"

"Impossible to determine effectively! It is more in your field than mine. Two of them were open about their Royalists connections in the past but claimed that they were eager to serve the Protector, though not from any great loyalty or religious conversion. We pay better than the Europeans and the Royalists."

Luke nodded sagely.

"You are devious a bastard, Luke. You have not come here to talk to Hatch. You are here to investigate our new officer recruits."

Luke smiled.

"In that case, I have what could be very bad news for you," said Cobb.

"Tell me the worst!" moaned Luke theatrically.

"Our French allies are very agitated and believe our delay in getting troops to the continent is a sign that we are not serious about our alliance with them against Spain. I have just received orders that, ready or not, we embark for France in three days."

"So in three days, this site will be deserted? That will be a great relief."

"Not quite! The recent recruits and the officers who arrived this morning with Hatch will remain until they have been transformed into two reasonably reliable infantry companies."

"So in three days, this site will be occupied by two unreliable companies of raw infantry under the control of Royalist officers. Our opponents have just failed to land foreign mercenaries in the Medway under the command of these very same officers. They will train a rabble that under their leadership will become two Royalists companies ready to spring into action on a given signal to gain control of the Medway for the king."

"In that case, arrest these men immediately and have them shot as spies," concluded the pragmatic Cobb.

"No! I need to know who is behind them. Who has organized what I consider are excellent plans to subvert the Medway? I do not want to alert them to our knowledge of their latest plan."

"Colonel, you cannot risk the security of the state and allow a pocket of Royalist troops to be developed in such a strategic area," replied an increasingly alarmed general.

"No worries. The Medway has just been reinforced with several companies of troops. Upnor Castle has increased defenses, and the dockyard, in addition to infantry and dragoons, has two units of artillery with large field cannons replacing the temporary ship cannons that previously gave some defense."

"That still risks a bloody confrontation in which some damage could be done to our defenses."

"I have a solution. Depart as planned, leaving behind the new recruits under Major Hatch's command, but in your embarkation for Flanders, take all of the ammunition. Hatch and his men will consider it a typical mistake for which the army has a deplorable record. An army can still train with weapons, but without ammunition, they can pose little threat."

"As recent events proved, the importation of arms and ammunition is very difficult," noted Cobb.

Luke sighed. "I wish I was going with you."

"You can't claim you have missed conflict. You played a major role in suppressing the Welsh uprising only last year and took part in the earlier Medway insurrection only a few weeks ago."

"It's not the same. I'm a cavalryman, but for the past eighteen months, I have headed a company of dragoons. Fighting Welsh peasants is not the same as charging the Spaniards. I had my earliest experience of warfare fighting with the Dutch cavalry against Spanish towns in the Netherlands—the very same centers that your combined French-English army propose to attack."

"If Cromwell would release you, I would be delighted to have you as my cavalry commander. What's wrong with dragoons?"

"Nothing. Unfortunately for my current purposes, they are more appropriate than cavalry."

"This has been an interesting conversation, but you must now find Hatch—if that is the real purpose of your visit."

Luke left the building and found Matthew who was leaving the camp to return home to Grey Towers.

The two men returned there together.

Luke concealed his knowledge of the five Royalist officers but revealed that he knew Harry Proctor was back.

Matthew's face was impassive, revealing no reaction to the news.

He asked, "How do you know?"

"One of the men at Upnor Castle where the Dutch packet docked last night recognized him, although he attempted to hide his face," Luke lied.

"Where is he now?"

"I don't know. Why did he return into such a hostile atmosphere? The smuggling network, the infantry company at the dockyard, and numerous cuckolded husbands are determined to kill him."

Matthew and Luke had a drink in a small antechamber off the reception hall in Grey Towers.

Matthew invited his hosts Sir Nicholas and Lady Matilda to join them. Matilda arrived a few minutes later. "Nicholas is on his way," she remarked.

The three chatted and drank for some time.

Matilda eventually commented, "Where is Nicholas?"

She sent a servant to find him.

The servant returned almost immediately. "Sir Nicholas has ridden out."

Matilda sighed. "Some emergency with the animals, I imagine."

Luke left after several more drinks and cantered down the lane that bordered the Lynne estate.

Suddenly, several musket shots rang out, and the battle-hardened Luke realized they were aimed at him.

He dug his spurs into his Friesian stallion, but as he rounded a sharp corner in the track, he found his escape blocked by a large hay wagon placed at right angles across the road.

In front of the wagon were half a dozen men waving cudgels and staffs.

Luke's horse had been trained to jump battlefield obstacles but not a wagon with such a tall load.

He turned his horse to retrace his path when he intuitively assessed that by doing so, he was reentering a field of fire.

Simultaneously, another group of armed men emerged from behind the hedge, cutting off any further retreat.

Luke dismounted and drew his sword. He was hopelessly outnumbered. He was angry with himself. Having survived so many battlefield situations to die at the hands of a bunch of cutthroats on a lane in North Kent was not the heroic end he had anticipated.

His end would be quick. He could keep the cudgel wielders at a distance as none wanted to get close enough to receive a fatal thrust from Luke's sword.

The staff holders were a different problem. Their staves were long enough to prod Luke continuously while he was unable to reach them.

Finally, one of them knocked the sword from his hand, and the cudgeling mob moved in for the kill.

Luke passed out under the barrage of blows.

When he came to, a familiar face was bending over him. It was John Martin.

His lieutenant was not sympathetic.

"Why do you ride these lanes alone? You are the military commander of the area and as such provoke considerable antagonism from the civilian population. In addition, our current investigations have probably created countless more unknown enemies."

"Thanks for saving me, Lieutenant, but no more sermonizing. It was lucky you were in the area."

"There was no luck to it. After you left this morning without taking Stradling with you, Sir Evan ordered patrols to this area. We have been here all day, and as soon as were heard the musket shots, we galloped to investigate. We passed a hay wagon just down the road and tethered behind it a very flighty and unhappy black stallion, which I immediately recognized as yours. Unfortunately, there was no one driving the wagon, but we have recovered your horse unharmed."

"What about my attackers?"

"They heard us coming and dispersed by the time we rounded that corner and saw your body on the track."

"Anything else?"

"Several of the troop galloped past your body in an effort to catch up with your attackers should they have been foolish enough to stay in the lane."

"Did they find anybody?"

"Yes, he is right here. They ran into Major Hatch who was riding towards them at high speed."

Matthew spoke. "I am glad to see that you are not seriously wounded, but the lump on your head looks a mess. I just missed out on saving your life a second time."

Luke was suspicious. "What were you doing? Following me down the lane?"

"No. As you know, I was comfortably relaxed having drinks with my sister when Nicholas returned. He mentioned that he had heard shooting near the southwest corner of the estate, exactly where I knew your journey home would take you. Matilda gave me a signal, imploring that I investigate. I did. I ran into your dragoons just down the road. What exactly happened?"

Luke and John explained.

The return of Proctor had not unsettled Matthew, but this attack on Luke had greatly upset him.

He was clearly troubled.

# 30

---

Momentarily unaware of his intuitive reaction to what he heard, Matthew was jolted into reality by Luke's question. "Are you all right?"

For a moment, he struggled to reply but then noticeably relaxed. "The batch of new recruits in the camp are the scum of London. They are cutthroats and thieves. I'm afraid this may have been one of their last criminal escapades before they are shipped to Flanders."

Luke saw an opportunity to innocently achieve what in other circumstances may have alerted Matthew and the new officers in the camp.

"Matthew, I understand your worry. In a day or two, you will be responsible for this cauldron of crime. Until you and the officers who remain with you inform me that you have imposed a tight discipline on these men, my dragoons will patrol the perimeters of the camp day and night. The good citizens of Kent must be protected. Inform Nicholas that I will speak to him as a matter of the greatest urgency tomorrow morning at nine sharp."

Matthew departed, and Luke whistled a cheerful tune.

John Martin asked, "What makes a man who has been cudgeled severely appear so happy?"

"I have achieved much without showing my hand. If the camp is soon taken over by Royalist officers who will train a couple of companies of infantry ready to rise against the state, I have ensued that their impact will be reduced. They will not have enough ammunition to wage a full-scale incursion, and our dragoons will patrol the perimeter of their camp. These patrols will be constant and a first line of easily reinforced defense, if necessary. At the first sign of trouble, these troops can be confined to their camp. I will send to Whitehall for even more men. A charging detachment of cavalry will put the fear of God into any raw recruit!" exclaimed the longtime horse soldier.

"When would you expect these Royalists to act?" asked John.

"It will take weeks for the officers to turn that rabble into even a tolerable fighting force. The men will not know they will be acting for Charles Stuart. They will simply be trained to obey their officers whatever happens. After training, they will be waiting for the right moment, which will either be another incursion from the continent or, God forbid, the assassination of the Lord Protector."

Next morning, taking the advice of his officers, Luke returned to Grey Towers at the head of a large troop of dragoons.

Hatch had already left for the camp, and despite Matilda's constant badgering, Nicholas took his time to receive Luke.

Matilda only made fleeting contact at the main door and remarked on the enormous lump that had developed on Luke's forehead. Her reference to a unicorn brought a guffaw from Strad, who then accompanied Luke into the house.

Strad commented, "What have you done to annoy Sir Nicholas? He has avoided you deliberately since his return from the continent. Is it something serious or simply your attentions towards Lady Matilda?"

Strad chuckled again.

The soldiers waited almost an hour in the reception hall before Nicholas finally arrived.

Luke ignored Nicholas's hostile demeanor.

"Nicholas, your recent visit to the continent has cast doubt on your loyalty to the Protector. The visit coincided with an attempted invasion by foreign mercenaries in the pay of Charles Stuart, and you were in the same areas as the conspirators and at the same time. If you were involved, it would not only mean your dismissal as a magistrate but also trial for treason and ultimate execution."

Nicholas seethed. "I can see your evil plan. You have sown false evidence and told lies to incriminate me. You want me out of the way so that you can pursue your adulterous seduction of my wife. I am entirely innocent."

Luke blushed but recovered. "For the moment, let's put aside personal issues. Why did you go to the continent and take the accused murderer Harry Proctor with you?"

"I went to establish a trading group to export wool and horses and import luxury goods without having to go through the existing smuggling network. I took Harry Proctor with me for two reasons. He knew the agents on the continent and could arrange for me to meet them, and I had a request from an old friend to get him out of the country for a while to prevent any further attempts on his life. I always intended to bring him back, which I did. He was in my custody the whole time."

"Where is he now?"

"I have no idea. He disembarked at Upnor Castle and rode to Rochester but did not follow us here. I assumed he returned to Holt House to the protection of Lady Prudence. If that is all, I must get to my horses."

"Not good enough, Nicholas! You have allowed a probable murderer to just fade back into the community. If Proctor kills anybody else, I will hold you personally responsible."

Nicholas had had enough.

He tried to leave the room.

Strad barred his exit.

Luke waved Strad away and called after the retreating Nicholas. "The evidence suggests that you are involved in and maybe the leader of the attempt to introduce foreign mercenaries into the Medway. I will return in a few days with further questions about how you reached Ostend and how you were captured by Dutch warships in the company of known Royalists. If you do not provide acceptable answers, you will be arrested for treason and taken to The Tower."

Two days later, as Luke was eating with Prue, her household and guests that included the magistrate David Harvey, Matthew Hatch burst through the double doors and ran across the extensive hall.

He whispered something to Prudence who went as white as a sheet. She rose and announced, "Sir Nicholas Lynne is dead. Mr. Harvey and Colonel Tremayne, please accompany Major Hatch back to Grey Towers!"

Luke felt a slight of pang of regret. His threat had proved too much for the guilty man who had obviously taken his own life to avoid prosecution—suicide was clear evidence of his guilt.

He turned to David Harvey. "Sir Nicholas was not a soldier. This case is entirely in your hands, and as it involves the death of a magistrate, you may need to involve senior civilian officials from outside the area."

David Harvey was shaken and remained speechless the whole trip to Grey Towers. If this were a deliberate attack on a magistrate, he could be next. Maybe a Royalist fanatic was taking revenge against the turncoats, such as Sir Nicholas Lynne and himself.

As they approached the entrance hall, he commented to Luke, "This may technically be outside your judicial authority, but it does not prevent you taking the lead in the investigation. You find out what happened, I will punish the evildoers."

He then turned to Matthew. "Is the death suspicious? Was he murdered?"

Matthew replied, "That is for you to determine."

Luke asked Matthew, "Before we visit the death scene, tell us all you know."

"Nicholas did not arrive for supper last night. Matilda jokingly said he must have thought you had been invited. Around midnight, Matilda came to my room concerned that according to his valet, Nicholas had not returned to the house. I organized the servants, and we began a thorough search. We found nothing. At first light this morning, a stable hand discovered Nicholas's body under straw in the stall of his favorite racehorse, Lightning Red."

As they approached the stables, Luke asked, "Has the stall or body been disturbed?"

"Unfortunately, yes. Matilda sent for the physician in Rochester who pulled back all the straw from the body and, after a cursory examination, declared Nicholas dead by misadventure—kicked to death by his horse."

"You don't agree?"

"In any other stall, I could believe an agitated horse might kill a person, but Lightning Red had a quiet and lovable disposition, and the relationship between Nicholas and that particular steed was very close. I cannot see Lightning Red killing Nicholas, unless he was strongly provoked, and I cannot see Nicholas provoking him."

"Someone else may have done so while Nicholas was in the stall," said Luke.

"You suspect your brother-in-law was murdered?" asked David.

"Yes."

"It may have been suicide," said Luke. "Earlier today, I made it clear to Sir Nicholas that unless he could explain several events which occurred during his recent visit to the continent, I would return and arrest him for treason."

"So we have three possible explanations. The physician says it's an accident, Matthew thinks it's murder, and Luke thinks that it is suicide," commented David.

"Examine the body Luke!" suggested Matthew.

Luke did and, after some time, turned to Matthew. "Your suspicions are valid. He was murdered. The horse's hooves did not inflict the massive bruise on his head. Also, there are no sharp heavy instruments or edges in this stall against which he could have fallen and suffered such an injury. And there is no blood. Nicholas was clubbed to death elsewhere by a heavy, yet sharp, metal implement, maybe a small axe, and then thrown into this stall and covered in straw. The murderer was not too bright. If he intended us to believe that Lightning Red had kicked Nicholas to death, he was pushing our credulity to the limits by believing the horse had then carefully covered the body with straw. And how could that idiot of a physician miss the axe wound?"

"What's our next move?" asked David.

"Find the murder site! There should be a lot of blood. The house, outbuildings, and grounds need to be searched again for a pool of blood—or what is left of it after last night's heavy rain. As there are no signs of wheeled vehicles outside the stable, the body must have been brought here on horseback."

Matthew suggested, "Last night's rain was heavy and constant. If we trace any hoof prints that are not within the vicinity of the stables, we may find a trail that could lead us to the site of execution."

"An excellent idea!" remarked Luke.

Matilda joined Matthew, David, and Luke.

Luke proffered his condolences, and Matthew brought his sister up to date on their thinking.

She offered advice. "Tracing the horses' tracks may be easier than you think. This stable is only occupied by Nicholas's racehorses, which are all shod with a distinctive shoe that widens at the back. Any print in this area that is different could be suspect."

After several hours of searching, a groom found and traced a suspect print.

A man riding a horse with a ridged shoe had come up the main drive into the area around the stable and then continued on to the fields where the tracks disappear.

Several similar tracks were found leading to the main door of the house and back to the road.

Both Matthew and Luke recognized the prints.

The latter announced, "These tracks are made by an army horse. They all have ridged shoes."

Suddenly, David seemed to take an interest and addressed both Matthew and Luke.

"Both of you have horses shod in this way?"

"Yes," said Luke.

"No," replied Matthew. "Since my return from injury, I have used a local palfrey."

David looked at Luke intensely. "The army tracks in front of the house belong to you. Did you, at any time, ride to the racehorse stables?"

Luke explained that on all visits, he had tied his horse to a hitching rail just to the side of the main door.

David rubbed his hand slowly across his chin.

"Luke, I would be remiss if I did not consider you a possible suspect in this murder."

"What would be my motive?"

"Three possibilities. The army is not happy with the projected return to civilian rule that will occur if Cromwell accepts the Crown and many former Royalists, such as myself and Sir Nicholas, will flood into positions under the new monarch. It would be in the army's interest to remove people like Nicholas and myself to preserve the military's influence over Cromwell."

"I am sure that some of my fellow officers resent being replaced in the country's administration by former Royalists, but murder is going a bit far. And my second motive?"

"Matilda. Your many visits are the talk of the servants."

"And the third?"

"Your belief that Nicholas was a traitor and deserved execution. You have, in the past, acted arbitrarily to remove enemies of the state."

"Are you going to arrest me?"

"No, you may have a perfectly good alibi or, given your rank and power, create one from among your men. However, finding the real murderer is very much in your own interests," suggested an unusually aggressive David.

# 31

Matthew, who seemed miles away as David berated Luke, suddenly clapped his hands against his thighs. "I can help. Come with me!"

Matthew led Luke and David to the hitching rail at the side of the house. He looked closely at the hoof marks, and suddenly, his face broke into a broad smile.

"Luke, your horse never went near the racehorse stables. Look carefully in the mud at the ridged impressions of the army horses. There are two different hoof prints. Yours, the most recent, show the clearly ridged oblong-shaped shoe. Look at the others from several days ago! They are ridged, similar to yours, but the shape is slightly different. These other impressions are more rounded. I recognize these more rounded shoes. The horses I rode at Upnor Castle were identical to these. The blacksmith at the castle obviously shapes his own unique military shoe."

"These marks were made by Nicholas and the five officers who volunteered for service and returned with him the other night. They borrowed horses from the castle," added Luke.

"Yes! This narrows down the identity of the murderer. I have not been completely truthful with you Luke. Nicholas was adamant that Matilda and I must keep a secret to protect the family name. When Nicholas and the five officers arrived the other night, their horses were hitched to these rails overnight, and they returned to

Upnor the next day. The officers received new horses at the camp, but there was a sixth man who came with Nicholas. This was the fact I was asked to conceal."

"And the sixth man?"

"He rode his horse to the domestic stables, which are the furthest away from those of the race horses. As he probably used the paved path beside the house, his tracks would not be visible. As I know all the Upnor Castle horses, except one, were returned to the fort, it is the sixth man who created these fresh tracks to the racehorse stables and is probably the murderer."

"Harry Proctor!" announced Luke.

Matthew looked slightly alarmed. "How did you know?"

"He was recognized as he disembarked at Upnor Castle. He was the main reason I had to question Nicholas. I wanted to know why a respected magistrate assisted a potential murderer to leave the country."

"But he brought him back—perhaps a fatal mistake," commented Matthew.

"Nicholas claimed he did not know where Harry was, having parted company in Rochester."

"A lie, Harry was hidden here for two nights," Matthew confessed.

"Did he organize the attack on me?" asked Luke.

"No, he could not have organized such a well-timed assassination attempt. Where would he find the men? He had no money, and Matilda was so furious that Nicholas had brought him here, that she prevented Nicholas giving Harry any financial assistance. I heard Nicholas advised him to go to his mentor and hide out there until matters regarding his trial were clarified."

"This mentor, who is he? Nicholas said he took Harry with him partly to help establish his smuggling network but also to do an old friend a favor. Would this old friend be the mentor?"

Matthew was silent for some time.

Luke continued. "You spent a lot of time at Holt House and are aware of the undercurrents and personal relationships that developed there. Did anybody show undue concern for Harry?"

"Of course, Lady Prue treated him like a long lost son, but he did not show any special affection in return."

"Anyone else? Someone from Holt House escorted Harry to the *Caroline Star*."

"Over many a meal at Lady Prue's, table I have picked up several nuances. There is no doubt that John Headley treated Harry's regular misdemeanors with more tolerance than the rest and often openly defended him when attacked, which was a regular occurrence."

"By anyone in particular?"

"Yes, Barnaby Partridge displayed an intense dislike of Harry. Apparently, it goes back decades to when Lady Mary basically adopted the boy. Gossip has it that Barnaby bitterly opposed his sister's decision. He thought that on his sister's death, Prue would send Harry away, but the reverse happened. Prue seemed more devoted to Harry than Mary had been."

"Any other comments that may help me regarding attitudes to Harry?"

"I was surprised that the new man Linton put out feelers of friendship towards Harry. Given Harry's lifestyle, it was not compatible with the austere Puritanism that Roger lived by. Anyhow, Harry quite rudely rejected Roger's overtures. For a decade, Harry's other bitterest enemy at Holt House was Sir Giles, but over the last few years, they have become quite close. Then in recent weeks, the antagonism reemerged."

"They probably remained thick as thieves. Harry was the front man for the local smuggling network, and I suspect that Sir Giles was its leader."

Matthew ignored Luke's interruption. "If I were looking for who attempted to poison Harry, my bet would be Giles."

"Why the change of attitude?"

"Harry's interest in Alicia! You know what a temper Giles has, especially where his girls are concerned."

David Harvey and Luke left Grey Towers agreeing that Harry Proctor was the prime suspect. Joint orders were issued requiring his immediate recapture. Before they left, Matthew suggested they could save a lot of time by taking a shortcut across Nicholas's fields and then follow a track along the ridge until they came to the Holt estate. It was much quicker than following the winding lanes.

Luke and David were soon on the ridge from which they had an overview of the Grey Towers estate.

Luke pulled up his horse. He was transfixed by developments in the nearest field. A large wagon was being filled with bundles of hay. What struck Luke was that two men in the field wore striking orange sashes around their waist as had the men who attacked him.

He turned to David. "Sir Nicholas was behind the attack on me. Those men working that field were the assailants."

David looked at him seriously and announced, "Tell no one of your suspicions. It gives you a fourth reason to murder him."

"I thought you had agreed that Proctor was the culprit?"

"I have, but others might use any excuse to blame the military. Your activity in recent weeks has upset many people."

Luke returned to Mud Hall Farm and informed his officers that Proctor was the prime suspect in another murder and must be apprehended immediately. He confided to Evan that it was possible that the fugitive was being harbored by someone at Holt House and that it was most likely Lady Prudence or John Headley or both. He outlined a plan to keep The Cottage under surveillance. With Caroline gone, John now lived alone with a surfeit of in-servants.

Luke sought permission from Lady Prue to search the cottage once again, pretending it was with regard to the murder of Frances Bartram. Luke did not divulge that he was looking for Harry Proctor or evidence that Proctor had recently been there.

Prue revealed that it was a good time, as John was visiting some of her most easterly estates and would be in Canterbury for a day or two.

Luke, Strad, and half a dozen troopers descended on the cottage. During their search weeks earlier, they had concentrated on the section of the house occupied by John. Caroline's part of the building had received only a cursory examination.

Luke, given his experience with old houses, suggested that all the wall panels be tapped. Hidden passages and secret rooms were not uncommon in houses built during the reign of Elizabeth. Luke questioned two of the in-servants—John's valet and a short plump woman who was a good advertisement for her cooking.

"Did your master entertain any visitors before he left for Canterbury?"

"Yes, but we never saw the person. I do not know whether the guest was man or woman," confessed the cook.

"How do you know then that he had a visitor?"

The cook answered, "Because for the last two days, I was instructed to prepare double the usual quantity of food, which the master, normally a spare eater, devoured. There was nothing left."

"Where did this mysterious visitor stay?"

"The cottage once belonged to a Papist family of freeholders who, during persecution at the time of the Armada, had, according to rumor, secret rooms and passages built so that members of the family or visiting priests could escape. I have never found these secret places, but I know the master met the earlier inhabitants and was aware of their location," commented the valet.

"Have you never tapped the wall panels to discover these rooms or passages?"

"Until Mistress Headley left, I was confined to the master's half of the building. The passages and rooms are certainly not in his part of the edifice. I have not had the time in recent days to investigate Mistress Headley's old rooms.

Luke and his men did, but it was to no avail—furniture was moved, wall hangings dismantled, and several panels ripped out.

Luke was frustrated but suddenly beamed.

"The floor! There must be a hidden trapdoor. Let's pull back all the carpets and rugs!"

Still nothing was discovered.

"Part of the flooring are wooden planks. Remove all those lifted in the recent past," ordered an irritated Luke.

Luke was disgruntled. "A house such as this must have secret entries and exits, if not a series of tunnels and priest holes. What have we missed?"

Strad stood in the middle of the reception hall and pointed towards the ceiling. "We have looked everywhere—except up."

Luke was impressed. "Yes, the ornate plasterwork on some of ceilings could conceal a hidden trapdoor."

Strad was jubilant.

"One of the utility rooms in the servant's wing had a ladder lying across the floor where it had fallen, rather than where it was placed," he announced.

Strad raised the ladder and discovered a door in the ceiling that was completely concealed from below by an elaborate square thick plaster creation of fruit, which could be turned aside. Strad climbed through the hole, followed by Luke.

They were amazed. They did not require a torch. The sun streamed in through a slit window, which, from the outside, would be considered part of the legitimate room below. This was a secret mezzanine level, which had, until very recently, been occupied.

"The bowl on the table is still warm. Our visitor has just left," said Luke.

"But where did he go?" asked a perplexed Strad.

"Down the ladder we came up."

"Not likely, Colonel, if I was escaping and came down that ladder, I would have carefully placed it against the wall with other household items, such as the mops and brooms. There must be another way out."

There was.

Strad found a panel that had a candleholder attached. The panel moved inwards when the holder was pulled, revealing a narrow passage way.

It was pitch-dark.

Luke called for candles. Luke, Strad, and two candle-bearing dragoons entered the passage and descended a steep flight of stairs into what proved to be a cave carved out of the chalk, which then narrowed into a tunnel.

After walking for a quarter of an hour, Luke saw a glimmer of light ahead and heard the lapping of water.

Within minutes, they were inches deep in sea water, and after a few more minutes, it was up to their knees.

"It's the Medway, and the tide is coming in. We might as well return to the surface and come back when the tide is fully out. Then we can see where this tunnel leads," declared Luke.

"No, sir. Why waste time? Proctor is just ahead of us. I can see daylight only a hundred yards away. I will walk as far as I can and then swim. I will wait at the entrance until you join me. That way, we may catch Proctor."

"Good thinking, Strad. Off you go! We will return to the surface and search the coastline until we find you."

Strad removed most of his outer clothing and walked further down the tunnel until he was forced to dive forward and swim towards the entrance.

# 32

Half an hour later, Luke and his troop reached the river's edge. They failed to find Strad. Where had he and his quarry gone?

Luke assumed that his sergeant had left the shoreline to follow Proctor, but which way had they gone?

"There is no point in following the estuary either way along the shoreline. It is so low-lying. Proctor could be seen from almost anywhere," argued Luke.

One of the dragoons disputed his colonel's assessment.

"Not necessarily, sir! Proctor may still have gone along the coast. It is riddled with streamlets and ditches. If he crawled into one of these depressions, he could remain hidden until someone stepped on him. He will ultimately find an unattended boat and escape by sea. Most of the creeks are overcrowded with small vessels that their owners leave beached on the banks."

Luke reconsidered his position. "You are right. The southeast of Sheppey Isle had similar low-lying terrain, and it was easy to hide in the depressions."

The discussion was cut short by a shout. "I have found Strad's shirt!" It was placed on a flat rock and with the sleeves arranged to form an arrowhead, indicating the direction Strad had taken.

Proctor and Strad were heading inland—back towards Holt House.

The low mud flats gave way to gently sloping open fields, on which grazed hundreds of sheep.

Some distance up the slope was a small coppice of regenerated small trees and shrubs, an ideal haven for the fugitive.

It was one of several wooded areas between Holt House and the Medway so beloved by the wandering Alicia Bartram.

Luke's men surrounded its coppice and then entered it from all sides.

One of the men put an end to this maneuver.

They found a set of sticks arranged to point towards the flat elevated fields that surrounded Holt House.

It was beginning to get dark.

Luke hoped to overtake Strad before nightfall.

As they approached the expansive wood that bordered Holt House, the dragoons spread out and advanced slowly through the trees.

One of them groaned.

"I've found the sergeant! He's dead."

Luke rushed to Strad's unconscious body. It lay beside a tree, the head resting in a pool of blood.

Luke placed the blade of his dagger across Strad's lips.

"He still breathes," announced a relieved Luke.

They carried Strad to Holt House.

Luke sent to the dockyard for a naval surgeon.

By the following morning, Strad had regained consciousness, and the surgeon had given him the all-clear.

Strad explained, "I entered the wood where I stopped to relieve myself against a tree. I was hit from behind. My next memory is waking up here."

Luke filled in some of the details. "You were hit by a rather large branch from a tree. It was found near your body with a considerable amount of blood on it. You must have a hard head as you were hit more than once."

Luke called Evan to Strad's bedside so that the three of them could review the situation.

"Proctor was clearly heading for Holt House. He must have another friend here apart from Headley," said Evan.

"The obvious person is Lady Prue. Before I confront her, let's interrogate the servants to discover if any of them saw Proctor, around sunset last night, enter the house or skulking in the grounds that surround it. Given the general dislike of the man, they will be more than ready to talk. I will question the person who tried to befriend Proctor, Roger Linton."

Linton was at his desk with a pile of papers in from of him.

Luke went straight to the point. "Roger, I have reason to believe someone in this house is harboring the accused murderer, Harry Proctor. Is it you?"

Linton paled visibly. "No, Colonel. I did try to befriend him when I first arrived, but he spurned my overtures with nasty comments about my lack of masculinity. I quickly joined the rest of the household, apart from Prue, in detesting the creature."

"You were visibly disconcerted by my question. Why?"

"Prue will not hear a bad word against him, despite the overwhelming evidence that he is a cad and a criminal with an abhorrent personality."

"For a secretary, you show a lot of concern for your mistress."

Linton smiled and relaxed. "Colonel, you have not been fully informed on Prue's family history. Before she married Sir Arthur, her family name was Linton. I am her ladyship's youngest brother. Before Father died last year, he called both Prue and her four brothers, including myself, to his bedside. He then saw us all separately. Prue left her last meeting with him in tears and clearly very distraught. When my turn came, Father was quite dictatorial, which was not his normal demeanor. He told me Prue had suffered an immense shock, and he was very concerned about her isolation from friends and family in Holt House. She would appoint me her secretary, and I was to move to the Medway to keep an eye on her and support her in coping with the new burden he had just placed upon her. I asked him what this was. He said that, in time, Prue might feel strong enough to tell me, but until she spoke, it must remain her secret alone. As I left, he was slipping into unconsciousness and mumbled something about lost relatives."

"What did he mean?"

"I asked Prue, but she dismissed it as the ramblings of a partly demented person on the brink of death."

"What did your father tell Prue that so upset her?"

"I've no idea. I asked my eldest brother George, the current lord of Linton Abbey, who would only say it was probably related to something that happened before I was born."

"Could Proctor be your sister's illegitimate child?"

"Impossible, given Proctor's age. Prue would have been a child of ten or eleven when he was conceived."

"That's the most obvious explanation for her obsessive defense of the scoundrel. We could be mistaken about his age. Another possibility is that Proctor is a bastard child of one of your parents—that Proctor is your half brother?"

"Certainly not my mother's child, but as you are aware, the gentry, even of Puritan disposition, have a history of sowing their seed through the community. Father was a normal male. It is a possibility. But if that be the case, why burden Prue with the information and not share it with me?"

"Was your eldest brother old enough to have fathered Proctor?"

"As a rampant older schoolboy, it's a possibility."

"I will speak with Prue," concluded Luke.

"I must insist that I be present. If you pursue this line of sensitive questioning, she may need my support."

Luke and Roger visited Prue the following day. Luke outlined recent developments and told Prue that Harry had been seen heading for Holt House.

Then without warning, he accused her of harboring him.

"I am appalled, Luke, that you should think such a thing!"

"Prue, your behavior towards this thoroughly obnoxious man, who has alienated everybody but yourself, suggests that there is a secret link between the two of you. Are you his mother?"

"How dare you! Harry is related to the Lintons, but as my father indicated on his deathbed, the truth must remain a secret."

"How many people know this secret?" asked a disconcerted Roger.

"There may be many who know parts of the story, but of the three Father said knew it all, two are dead—Father and Lady Mary. The other who may also have died was a member of the Cromwell family, whom father did not identify."

"So that is why the Lord Protector is so interested in what happens in Holt House and sent me here," said Luke.

Roger asked, "Sister, is there any place near the house where Harry might hide?"

"Harry spent most of his life here. He was brought up with Arthur and Richard. Richard might know of hiding places they used as children, but he is currently at sea."

Luke changed the topic.

"Prue, did you know that The Cottage contained secret rooms and a tunnel that ran to the sea?"

"No, Lady Mary warned me that the cottage was an evil place and never to go there, but she did not mention any secret rooms."

"Are there secret rooms or passages in Holt House itself?" asked Luke.

"I don't know. Arthur did tell me if the Royalists surrounded Holt House, I must go to the chapel. Whether that suggests that there was a secret passage from there to the outside world, or simply that the house of God would offer us sanctuary, I'm not sure."

Luke thanked the brother and sister for their assistance and immediately sent his dragoons into the Holt's chapel to search for hidden passages.

Barnaby asked what was happening and admitted that he had searched the chapel decades ago because Lady Mary feared that there was a secret way into the house from the chapel. He found nothing then.

The dragoons had a similar result.

Luke was leaving Holt House when he was stopped by a servant who asked him to return to Lady Prudence immediately.

She welcomed Luke. "You questioning about secret passages reminded me of something young Alicia told me. She said that she had seen people go into the large wood nearest the house and reappear elsewhere on the estate. This troubled her because she had not seen them leave the wood."

"Thanks, Prue. You may have given me the answer to Harry's disappearance. He entered that woodland, clubbed Strad, but was not there when we searched it, and he did not come here. There must be a secret tunnel out of that wood."

Luke's men searched the woods to no avail.

Evan then suggested, "If we accept that there is a tunnel from somewhere in the woods, and it does not go to Holt House, the only other reasonable explanation is that it goes to The Cottage."

"Eureka! Harry Proctor has retraced his steps and is hiding once again in the cottage," cried an elated Luke.

The dragoons galloped to the cottage.

Luke entered the secret room to find discarded wet clothing and the remains of a meal of boiled chickens.

There was a candle that had been allowed to burn out.

Harry had been back but was long gone.

The servants both confided to Luke that they heard noises in the roof, and the cook confessed that two of her chickens had disappeared.

While there, Luke sent Evan and some troopers back into the tunnel to see if it also continued towards the coppice as well as to the Medway estuary.

Later that evening, Evan joined Luke for supper at Holt House.

"Was there a tunnel to the woods?" asked Luke.

"Yes, but no wonder we could not find the entrance, the tunnel began in a hollowed-out oak and the actual entrance was six or seven feet off the ground. We never thought to climb trees and test whether their aged trunks could conceal a passage. Where could Proctor be now?"

"For a man without friends, perhaps his only hope is to waylay John Headley, his possible mentor, on his way home from Canterbury. Where else could he go?" asked Luke.

“I still cannot understand why a man facing a possible charge of murder, and is himself a potential victim, should return to this country. Someone must have offered him an incentive.”

Luke was thoughtful.

“I agree. Harry was offered an incentive that he could not refuse to carry out a major mission, after which, in all likelihood, he would become expendable. He knows too much. We must find him before it’s too late. Otherwise, he will be our next murder victim.”

# 33

---

Luke's immediate focus was changed by a message from Grey Towers. Lady Matilda had to see him urgently.

Her opening remarks killed off his thoughts of an amorous encounter, although her welcoming kiss was passionate and lingering.

"We must put aside our mutual desires until Nicholas is laid to rest and his murderer apprehended. To continue our liaison at this time would be unseemly."

Luke demurred, "Of course! If bedding you is not on the agenda, why am I here?"

"Matthew said I should tell you everything as soon as possible."

"Tell me what?"

"David Harvey has been here three times over the last few days, turning the place upside down."

"Nothing unusual about that. He is the responsible magistrate, and he would be remiss in his duties if he did not conduct a thorough investigation into the death of a fellow magistrate."

"He seemed obsessed with one aspect of Nicholas's recent activities."

"What aspect?"

"His last visit to the continent."

"I am also concerned with that visit, especially why he took Proctor with him and then brought him back. What questions did David ask?"

"Whether Harry revealed details of his contacts on the continent or the names of those Nicholas and he had seen."

"What did you tell David?

"Nothing. I couldn't. I avoided Harry while he was here and could only reply in terms of what Nicholas told me later."

"Which was?"

"That Proctor introduced him to possible agents but Nicholas gave no names."

"Did he explain why he brought Proctor back?"

"He didn't have to. I assumed that as a magistrate, he was doing his duty in returning a potential murderer to custody. I was surprised he took Proctor with him in the first place. In retrospect, Nicholas was probably forced to do it."

"By whom?" asked a very interested Luke.

"David Harvey! If the two magistrates agreed on a certain action, then this helps explain Nicholas's behavior."

"Are you suggesting that both magistrates were agents of Charles Stuart?"

"No, Nicholas had not knowingly done anything to advance the Royalist cause. However, if David is the local Royalist leader, he may have tricked an innocent Nicholas into acting unknowingly for Charles Stuart. Nicholas was a genuine convert to the cause of the Lord Protector more so than myself.

"Nevertheless, if both former Royalists and now magistrates in the area were believed to be behind a conspiracy, it would become a much more viable proposition, which might encourage the ever-cautious Royalist courtiers to act. Nicholas may have been entirely innocent, but it gave a great boost to Royalist morale to depict him as a fellow traveler. David is behind everything."

"There is no evidence against him," countered Luke.

"Matthew also asked me to pass on information I received from your friend Lord Stokey, namely that David Harvey has, for six months, been the Marquis of Appley. His distant relative died some time ago at the royal court, but it has been kept a secret and is not widely known in England."

"Interesting!"

"There is more. Stokey recognized Harvey in the company of fanatical Royalists when he was last in Germany."

"Not necessarily suspicious. As heir to a marquis who was living in exile, it would not be unusual to visit your potential benefactor or pay respects at his passing."

"Stokey also saw Harvey in Royalist company only a few weeks ago in Ostend."

"Again, not unusual for Kent gentry to slip across to the continent on a regular basis."

"Except David told me he had not been abroad for months," replied Matilda.

Despite their initial declarations of restraint and decorum, Luke and Matilda fell into each other's arms.

Next morning, Luke returned from Grey Towers seriously troubled. So much so that he sought out his deputy Evan, and the duo began a day of drinking and contemplation.

Luke updated Evan. The former confided in his friend. "I feel I am being duped by the woman with whom I am falling in love. She is deliberately trying to divert suspicion away from her late husband, herself, and her brother Mathew Hatch. Until she raised several issues yesterday, there had not been a shred of evidence against David Harvey."

"It's not the first time that your attraction to beautiful women has clouded your judgment," remarked Evan philosophically.

"And she probably fabricated the information supposedly provided by Stokey. If it is true, why did he not tell me himself? Stokey has never shirked informing on fellow Royalists, if he believed their thoughtless action would weaken the Royalist cause."

Evan continued. "With your wide experience of women, I was surprised that you have become so close to Lady Lynne. From the very beginning, given her reaction at Lady Holt's dinner table to your comments regarding Charles Stuart, she was at the top of my list as the leading clandestine Royalist in the area. Your seduction by her may be a key part of the Royalist plot. She now knows exactly what her opponents are doing and thinking."

"Don't be silly, Evan, I do not reveal military secrets while making love."

"There is another puzzle to which Lady Lynne may be the answer. You have often remarked on the sophisticated strategy and planning that has gone into the abortive incursion, and now the subversion, of the new recruits into a Royalist army. None of the local gentry—Nicholas, Giles, or David Harvey—have the experience or the ability to create such plans. Lady Matilda is more capable than all the men put together. I'm sorry, Luke, but she is the brains behind the Royalist conspiracy."

Luke was hurting. He did not respond.

Next morning, Luke and David met to discuss their murder investigation.

David confessed, "I've been back to Grey Towers several times. Why Nicholas and Harry went to the continent together, and then returned when it was clearly not in Proctor's interest to do so, lies at the bottom of the murder and maybe of the rumored Royalist uprising, which your actions have only delayed."

"Why did you return to Grey Towers so often?"

"Nicholas was an obsessive diary keeper and letter writer. Your men found no diary in their initial search or any letters relevant to the situation. I thought I might."

Luke, desperately trying to justify the information that Matilda had given him, hoped that there was a diary and letters, which would incriminate David. Then it dawned on Luke. If David was desperate to find and destroy written evidence from Nicholas that would have been harmful, he might have been equally as anxious to silence the spoken word that Nicholas might have directed against him.

Was David Harvey the murderer of Sir Nicholas, his fellow magistrate?

Harvey had visited Grey Towers so often he could have fabricated the evidence against Harry.

Such thoughts were only a little short of fantasy, inspired by his obsessive desire to free Matilda from suspicion.

Her lies were clouding his judgement.

There was still not a shred of evidence against David.

Luke shook his head vigorously and returned to his questioning. "You did not find any letters or diary?"

"No."

"Did you ask Matilda? She may have them and, for family reasons, does not want Nicholas's private thoughts read by outsiders."

"It may be more than protecting the family honor," quipped David.

"What do you mean?"

"Perhaps the Lynnes are the Royalist masterminds on the Medway?"

Luke was beginning to get a familiar feeling.

It was Harvey's turn to divert suspicion away from himself and onto a man who was in no position to defend himself or his family against such accusations.

"Do you suspect both Lynnes are part of this Royalist plot?"

"No! I suspect Nicholas alone. Matilda, despite her upbringing at the French court, is a solid supporter of the Lord Protector," David declared.

Luke's heart sank again.

If Harvey were a Royalist, it would be natural for him to support his possible partner Matilda by trying to direct all Royalist connections onto the dead Sir Nicholas.

Were Harvey and Matilda together the brains behind the Royalist conspiracy on the Medway? Was her brother Matthew also an essential part of the organization? His military experience could explain the sophistication of Royalist strategy.

To Luke, it was, at last, beginning to make sense.

He continued his questioning of David.

"Whom else do you suspect? As a former leading Royalist, you are in a better position than an outsider, such as myself, to pick up on the nuances at social functions that might give you some hint as to the level of disaffection."

"Since I declared for the Protector, and especially since I accepted a position as magistrate, the local Royalists have ignored me. The only links I have with active Royalists are a few friends who are in exile on the continent."

"Are you are often in contact with them?"

"I don't go out of my way to meet them, but if we are in the same area, I try to keep up acquaintances."

"Have you been to the continent recently?"

"Yes, I had several two-day trips to Ostend during the last month. I was copying Nicholas's idea in examining the possibility of trading directly with agents there."

"Won't that upset the existing trading network and bring possible repercussions upon yourself? Proctor may have murdered Nicholas because he was undermining the smuggling ring of which Harry was the front man. You were planning to do the same?"

"Not quite. The smugglers are only interested in wool out and luxury items in. My estate covers acres of mud flats and barely grassed pastoral fields, but these tidal marshes produce the tastiest lamb in the county. I can have my sheep into the butchers' shops in the Spanish Netherlands within hours of leaving the Medway."

"Apart from Nicholas, who else do you suspect?"

"Old Dewhurst. The evidence suggests that he brought in those German laborers to realign the guns at Upnor Castle, which, while making it easier to deal with enemy ships sailing into the Medway, also made it possible for whoever controlled the castle to bombard the dockyard. Your recent addition of guns and men has removed the chances of this eventuality. The new guns brilliantly supplement the realigned cannons, and the influx of troops would make it difficult now for the Royalists to subvert either the castle or the dockyard."

Luke's mind temporarily wandered.

Deprived of a dockyard or castle base, the Royalists would now have to concentrate on the troops at the army camp and march them directly on London.

Luke snapped out of his reverie. "Anything else make you suspect Dewhurst?"

"His death! I initially thought you had isolated him as the traitor and removed him arbitrarily in the manner your reputation had suggested—quietly remove the leader of the conspiracy and give the impression that his death had nothing to do with the security situation."

"Had Dewhurst developed a group of Royalist activists? His own mobility was very limited. He was an old man."

"I have no evidence, but Harry Proctor could have been his right-hand man. Harry's role with the smuggling ring gave him ready access to the continent, and it would be easy to smuggle in people as well as goods. I also think the murder of his corporal at the dockyard was related to this. Proctor used the corporal to act for him on a number of occasions. The corporal may have become aware of antigovernment activity by Proctor and threatened to tell all. That corporal and his wife were living it up in the month before Proctor killed him. Miller could have been blackmailing Proctor."

"An interesting theory, and it does tie up a few loose ends. But as you say, we have no evidence to prove any of it. We must find Proctor before others eliminate him."

Luke had a thought, which he kept to himself. He would visit Corporal Miller's widow.

He did.

Betsey Miller was no shrinking violet nor a weeping widow.

She had made money from her body since she reached puberty.

Her husband had been her pimp, but his demise had not lessened her appeal or her income.

She thought Luke was her latest client.

In the past, he would have been, but his longing for Matilda curtailed his natural proclivity to sleep with this quite attractive and very experienced wench.

She seemed disappointed when the handsome officer declined her offer, but he passed to her in silver coins triple her usual emolument.

"Betsey, I am the officer pursuing Harry Proctor, and I have received information that needs to be verified. I have paid you in advance for any bit of gossip you can give me. For example, did your husband assist Proctor in any way, other than providing your services? According to Proctor's men, your husband and Harry were extremely close."

"Yes, Proctor was foolish enough to use my husband on some of his smuggling enterprises. My Basil came home many a time rubbing his hands and saying that the fool Proctor had given him enough rope to hang him."

"But instead you blackmailed him. I have evidence that you were living it up in the weeks before your husband's death."

"You can't blame a poor woman taking every opportunity that presents itself. Are you sure I cannot satisfy your obvious needs?"

She pulled down her bodice and revealed her very appealing breasts.

Luke found it difficult to control his lust as she moved towards him and put her arms around him. Luke made little attempt to move away as he continued his questioning.

"Did Basil indicate what he had on Proctor that led to his murder? Smuggling is accepted in this region, so it had to be more than that."

"It was. My husband said Proctor was involved in activity that threatened the government and that he was terrified when he heard that you were coming to the area."

"How did he know? My arrival here was a secret. Only Lady Holt knew of it."

"Lady Holt doted on that scoundrel. She must have told him."

"Did he order the shooting at the dockyard when I first arrived?"

"Yes, he went to the Garrison Gang on Sheppey to find someone willing to kill a high-ranking officer, but according to my husband, in his usual incompetent manner, Proctor chose men who did not know one end of a musket from the other and who were almost continually intoxicated. He also returned from the island alarmed that Major Hatch had seen him. If Proctor had used Basil instead, you would not be here. He was the best shot on the Medway and as good as parson Partridge was reputed to be in his youth."

"Thanks, Betsey, you have been very helpful."

"My assistance hasn't finished yet, soldier."

Betsey led him gently to a small bed in the corner of her one room cottage.

After a vigorous and surprisingly lengthy encounter, Luke released his built-up frustrations and left behind a very satisfied Betsey.

# 34

---

Next morning, the intelligence officers met to update the progress of their endeavors.

John Martin reported that the patrols around the army camp were now continuous, even through the night. A few discontents had been caught trying to abscond and were returned to the camp, but nothing unusual had been observed.

The suspected Royalist officers and Major Hatch were training the raw recruits relentlessly from dawn to dusk.

Luke enlightened the others on the information he had garnered from David Harvey and Betsey Miller.

Strad asked, "Did nobody question Betsey at the time of her husband's death?"

"Yes, but she refused to talk. She intended to use the information she had to continue the blackmail of Proctor," replied Luke.

"Our next move?" asked Evan.

"John, continue the patrols, but send a couple of men back into the tunnels. There may be other secret passages that we missed. Evan, Strad, and myself, with a double troop of dragoons, will head for Canterbury and hope to intercept John Headley—with a recalcitrant protégé."

They intercepted the Headley cavalcade much closer to Holt House than anticipated.

"Off on patrol?" queried John cheerfully.

"No, I was coming to see you, as recent developments have raised further questions which you may be able to answer."

John's group consisted of four other horsemen and a packhorse. Evan immediately spotted that one of the riders fell behind the others as the dragoons approached. He was wearing a large hat pulled down over his face.

"I have found Proctor," he whispered to Luke.

Evan rode straight at the trailing rider and flicked his hat off with a dexterous use of his sword.

The man was momentarily surprised but, on recognizing his attacker, shouted, "What are you up to, Evan? It's a bit early in the morning for such larks."

Evan recognized one of John's deputies that he had befriended. He pretended it had been a boyish prank. He also immediately saw the cause of the man's attempt to cover his face. He was terribly sunburnt. Any further exposure would have been painful.

Evan and the deputy fell further behind the others as Luke had turned his troop around, and everybody headed back to Holt House.

Evan chatted with the deputy. "Where did you stay in Canterbury?"

"The Golden Mitre."

"Was your party approached by anybody during your stay there?"

"Many! Our purpose in staying there was so that tenants from the far east of the county could settle their accounts. This allows us to reduce our quarterly trips by almost a week. The tenants come to us, rather than we visiting every tenancy. If John suspects any problems, he will send one of us to investigate the situation later."

"Did any nontenants attempt to see John?"

"Not that I saw, but he may have had a visitor during the night."

"Explain?"

"We had just got to sleep last night, four of us in the same room—only John had a room to himself—when there was repeated knocking on the door. An inebriated guest had mistaken the room and was trying to break down our door. I put him straight, and as he stumbled back along the hallway, I saw a man leave John's room."

Meanwhile, Luke, who was trotting beside John, decided to delay any questioning of the steward until they were in more appropriate surroundings.

"John, will you be having supper at Holt House this evening?"

"Yes."

"Then let us meet after supper, and you can help me clarify a number of points."

Evan, galloping up beside the two leading horsemen, gently interrupted Luke and indicated that he should move out of John's hearing.

When this was accomplished, he blurted out, "I know where to find Proctor."

Evan quickly informed Luke of what he had gleaned from the deputy steward.

Luke reacted, "Take Strad and the double troop and ride post haste to The Golden Mitre."

Luke lied to John that he had just received word of an affray, and he had sent the dragoons to suppress it.

"I'm not surprised that there is trouble. The people are very discontented," replied John undiplomatically.

Much later that day—after supper—Luke and John adjourned to a small antechamber off the dining hall.

Luke asked, "John, you came here as a child in-servant but quickly became Edward's personal valet. Why were you selected ahead of more experienced servants for that role?"

"Edward and I went to school together. There were rumors that I was his illegitimate half brother."

Luke took a deep breath and asked, "True?"

"I honestly don't know. Edward's father, Sir David, sowed his wild oats throughout the Medway villages. Many pregnant brides explained their condition to suspicious bridegrooms in terms of being seduced by the local squire. It caused less trouble than admitting that you had slept with the groom's brother or father. Sir David, and after him Sir Edward, certainly created countless opportunities for such rumors to start. My mother always denied any association with Sir David, although then it would not have been a stain on her character, rather the opposite. Attitudes during the last few decades have become much more puritanical and judgmental."

"I believe that Sir Edward and Lady Mary only had a week or so of normal marriage before Edward became seriously ill. She must have been a remarkable woman to take over and expand the Holt estates."

John frowned. His veins began protrude on his forehead.

Luke realized immediately that he had said the wrong thing.

John took several deep breaths and almost hissed. "Luke, as a soldier you have faced evil in many forms, but I can tell you that Lady Mary was evil incarnate—the most vicious, vindictive, and vengeful person I have known. She was cruel, calculating, and without compassion."

Luke was taken aback. This was the second denunciation of Lady Mary he had heard.

"That is not the image I have received from everybody, except Sir Giles and yourself."

"Lady Mary lied, fabricated evidence, and manipulated family and household through violence and blackmail to do her will and then rewrote history to depict herself as a paragon of virtue."

"Why did a dedicated servant of Edward develop such a bitter hatred of his wife? If she was so evil, why did you continue to serve her for almost thirty years after Edward's incarceration?"

"Her treatment of Edward allowed me to see the real evil, but her threat of blackmail, on the one hand, and reward, on the other, kept me at Holt House."

"Did she not fight to prevent her husband being put in an institution and provided him with relative comfort and freedom on his own estate?"

"It was neither comfortable, nor was he free. He was prisoner in the cottage for seventeen years, and during the last seven or eight, as his condition worsened, he was put into chains."

"What was wrong with him?"

"Until he married Mary, absolutely nothing."

"There was a big age difference between the two. Was he enthusiastic about the marriage?"

"Yes, Edward was besotted with Mary. She was a beautiful young girl, and after the misfortune of his first marriage, he was active in arranging the alliance with the powerful Partridge family who controlled most of neighboring East Sussex. Despite the later lies spread by Mary, Edward had controlled and increased the Holt estates very effectively for fifteen years. Because his first marriage to Katherine was not successful, he threw himself into his role as local magistrate and wealthy landowner."

"What went wrong with his first marriage?"

"Edward was the innocent victim of a deal between his father and Nicholas Lynne's father. Sir David Holt obtained much of the Lynne lands and persuaded them to renounce Roman Catholicism as part of the dowry—an act that brought Sir David the plaudits of King James. The downside was that unknown to Edward but known to his father, his new bride was already pregnant to an unknown."

"What did Edward do?"

"What could he do? He made it known to everybody that the child born soon after his marriage was not his. Edward would have nothing to do with the child, and once he took over Holt House on the death of his father, Lady Katherine, his wife, and the child Mercy were forced to leave. Katherine spent the rest of her life with her child at the home of her father and then her brother at Grey Towers. That is why when Katherine died in 1627, Edward was determined to arrange a second marriage that would give him all he had missed in the first."

"So what went so horribly wrong in the first weeks of his second marriage? Was Mary less interested than Edward believed?"

"No, quite the opposite. Mary was besotted with Edward and, by reports, satisfied his sexual needs on their wedding night beyond all his lustful dreams. He told me as he left for his honeymoon the next day that he had never experienced such a night."

"What went wrong?"

"According to Lady Mary, while progressing through Huntingdonshire, they stayed at the home of the now Lord Protector, then but a simple country squire, Oliver Cromwell, Edward mistook a fellow young female guest for a serving wench and pressed his attention upon her. This infuriated the family of the girl, the family of Lady Mary, and the family of the host."

"What did they do?"

"They believed the honor of all three families had been stained and vengeance was required. A week later, Edward was attacked, beaten severely, and castrated. Lady Mary returned here alone, and several weeks later, Sir Edward came back and was immediately consigned to the cottage where he remained a prisoner for years because of his alleged madness."

"You looked after him through this period?"

"Not really! I was allowed to visit him once a week. I did all I could to make his life better. He was badly treated from time to time by his keepers. The word was put about that he was mad. He was not mad until the treatment he endured progressively turned his mind."

"Who kept him a prisoner? Surely his old servants like yourself took up his case?"

"Mary poisoned their minds with lies about him and gradually replaced them with minions devoted to herself. Supervision of the cottage was taken over by Mary's enforcer, a man who bitterly hated Edward."

"Who was that?"

"Her brother, the apparently gentle vicar Barnaby Partridge. Partridge ensured that, for all practical purposes, Edward was dead."

"What you have told me, if validated, seriously affects the succession to the Holt fortune. Lady Mercy has no Holt blood in her veins, so none of her offspring can inherit. Was Arthur Edward's son?"

"Yes, the product of their marriage night, but Mary, after the incident in Huntington, was determined to stamp out the Holt line."

"Surely she did not contemplate killing her own son?"

"No, she was more vindictive than that. She completely dominated Arthur and married him off to a much older woman whom she knew could not have children. Arthur's early death was a blessing for him and not greatly mourned by his mother."

Luke was bewildered, and his mind was racing. "If Edward was castrated just after his marriage to Mary, then Richard Holt is not Edward's son."

"That is true, and that is why Mary and now Prudence have persuaded the parliament to give them control of the estates. Prudence, on Mary's advice, will probably leave the Holt properties to Richard. His claim, otherwise, could be challenged on the grounds that he could not have been Edward's son."

"The landed gentry would lie, and you would find it impossible to prove that Edward had been castrated. Nevertheless, is there a legitimate heir to such fortune and power?" asked Luke.

"No, but there are numerous bastards carrying some Holt blood."

"That does not count. While a king may legitimize his bastards, the aristocracy and gentry do not. They can never inherit."

"They can never inherit, but an act of parliament could bestow the lands on anybody, including a bastard offspring of a previous owner."

"That offspring would, nevertheless, have to be considered a gentleman. The bastards produced on village women would never make the grade. Did Sir David or Sir Edward impregnate gentry women?"

"Although I do not know who the mother was, there is one bastard whom Mary confirmed to me had been fathered by Edward who was brought up a gentleman."

"Who?"

"Harry Proctor."

Luke took a big breath.

"It does not add up. If Mary was determined to wipe out the Holt bloodline, why did she send one of his bastards to her own sister to bring up and, when those adoptive parents died, took the child under her own wing and obviously instructed Prudence to continue that support?"

"A very simple answer. Pure evil. She kept Harry visible on the estate to torture her husband. She had Barnaby inform Edward that the boy they often paraded around the cottage perimeter, which he could see through the windows, was his son."

# 35

"It is about Harry that I wish to question you. You harbored him after he escaped from his confinement here and then assisted in his escape to the continent. Since his inexplicable return, you hid him in a secret room in The Cottage, and last night, you found him accommodation in Canterbury. Why?"

"Harry's life is in danger from your judicial proceedings, the vendetta of the dockyard troops, and from whomever tried to poison him, killing poor old Clench instead. I owed it to his father."

"Why act now?"

"For most of his life, Harry simply annoyed people. In recent months, that annoyance has escalated to the point where many want him dead."

"Does he know that he is Sir Edward's bastard?"

"Yes. I told him just before he left for the continent. I asked Sir Nicholas to get him to the continent, and in return, Harry would introduce Sir Nicholas to agents and suppliers. I told him to stay abroad—to give Nicholas the slip once they landed at Dunkirk. Nicholas justified his actions on the grounds that Harry had voluntarily surrendered to him and was, technically, in his custody but, as a prisoner, must return with him."

"Why did Harry ignore your advice and give up the relative safety of the continent and come back?"

"He was told by leaders of his smuggling network that all would be forgiven if he returned to England and dealt with Nicholas, whom they suspected had stumbled on information in Dunkirk or Ostend that they did not want made known."

"So when Nicholas gave signs that he might reveal all to me, Harry was ordered to eliminate him?"

"That is your interpretation, Colonel. Harry never confessed to me that he murdered Sir Nicholas."

"He will hang for that alone."

"You have probably already fabricated the evidence against him," muttered a surprisingly embittered John.

"I do not fabricate evidence, but I have had my own doubts whether all the evidence against Harry is genuine. He has become the scapegoat. All the ills of the community are being attributed to him."

"Harry has only belatedly realized that people will do anything to protect themselves, including killing him. God willing, he should, by now, be safely back on the continent. He was at Canterbury last night and this morning was to catch the earliest packet from Dover."

"John, why take these risks personally? You could be hanged for your knowledge about the murder of Nicholas or for assisting Harry to escape lawful custody."

"My days are numbered, Luke. I will be dead within half a year. I am coughing up blood and find it difficult to breathe."

"So you have nothing to lose? Does your newfound foolhardiness extend to treason?"

"There are many Royalist sympathizers among the landed gentry, and the offer of the Crown to Oliver Cromwell has divided the former supporters of parliament. There has been much talk among the tenant farmers on these matters. There is a growing ground swell that if only Charles Stuart could get his invasion plan off the ground, there would be popular support. Because this is an ongoing matter, and you have no evidence that I have acted against the state, I will say no more. It is in your hands what you do about my assistance to Harry."

"I will do nothing until we have Harry Proctor back in custody. Does Prudence know of your illness or of your assistance to Harry?"

"I have been a loyal servant to Sir Arthur and Lady Prue. She is not Lady Mary. I was very surprised but grateful that Lady Prue continued to protect Harry despite his notorious behavior. I will not betray any of her confidences, except to say that I told her after he fled the house that he was safe. Since then, when we have met, I have nodded, indicating that the situation has not changed. She has asked me no questions, and she has played no part in his escape. She is aware that I have difficulty breathing but not how serious the problem is."

Luke changed the focus of his questioning.

"The attempt to poison Harry when he was under house arrest under my protection, who was behind that that? Giles?"

"No, Barnaby."

"You must be joking! Surely an aging and gentle cleric would do no such thing?"

"Look into his past! He was not always a clergyman. He was one of your lot. He fought in the early years of the Thirty Years War and was a brilliant marksman, which I have seen often when he hunted deer. He was a senior officer on the staff of the Duke of Buckingham, planning several operations against Spain that never eventuated. He came to Holt House a month after his sister's marriage to Edward. One of Mary's first acts when she seized control of the estate from the disabled Edward was to send Barnaby to Oxford to study theology and send me to the Inns of Court to pick up the rudiments of a legal training."

Our absences enabled her to impose a personal rule over her family, household, and tenants.

"Why would Barnaby try to kill Harry?"

"He never agreed with Mary in adopting him and was at a loss to understand why Prudence continued Harry's favored treatment. He is determined to remove all traces of the genuine Holt blood.

Mary must have told him that Harry was one of Edward's bastards. And only a member of the household would have known how meals were prepared and delivered. Barnaby has lived here for thirty years."

As Luke left the room, John began a coughing fit, for which Luke could do nothing. He left the room convinced that he had just heard a deathbed confession.

Meanwhile, Evan and his dragoons reached Canterbury where they discreetly guarded the exits of The Golden Mitre.

Evan found the tavern keeper and explained that he was in pursuit of a Royalist spy who had arrived late the previous evening.

"The only guest to arrive late last evening was Mr. Headley's son, Harry. His father paid his accommodation and food. Mr. Headley has stayed here over many a year, but I did not know he had a son," replied the publican.

"He doesn't. Is the man claiming to be Harry Headley still here?"

"No, but you only just missed him. Mr. John Headley told me to wake his son early and have him on the road to Dover before dawn. This Harry abused my servant who tried to waken him and went back to sleep. John Headley tried to get him moving before he returned to Holt House but to no avail. The lazy varlet took his time and then decided he wanted something to eat. I had to cook him some bacon and eggs midmorning. He only left about half an hour ago. I can fully believe he is not John's son. John is a gentleman, but this varlet was arrogant, selfish, and rude."

"Did he reveal anything to you about his activities?"

"Not to me, but he could not help boasting to the servant girl who waited on him. She was so impressed that she immediately told me he was probably the leader of a criminal gang."

"What exactly did she say?" asked Evan.

"Question her directly! Maggie, this officer wants to ask you a few questions about the irritating guest you served this morning."

Evan turned to a plump young girl bedecked in a large brown apron and displaying a broad but beaming face. "Maggie, you are a very observant young girl. That man is a dangerous criminal, so every word he said to you may help us catch him. Did he say where he was going and why?"

"Yes, he was very pleased. He was to be rewarded for a job he had just completed. He was happy because he would be well paid, but above all, his debts to others and serious mistakes he had made would be forgotten. I asked him would he return to England a wealthy man. He said yes because the man he worked for would soon have power and wealth. If I had been a prettier wench, he would have taken me with him. As it was, he tried to take liberties with me."

Evan turned to the innkeeper. "What was this man riding when he left here?"

"A run-of-the mill palfrey. Your soldiers with those fine horses could catch him before he reaches Dover."

Evan thanked him and young Maggie, and the dragoons resumed their pursuit.

Evan confided in Strad. "That pretty much confirms that Proctor was hired to kill Sir Nicholas, and is meeting his employer to be paid before he leaves England."

"Or to be given another mission. It appears that the useless soldier Proctor is turning into a successful assassin," countered Strad.

"Could the next mission be to assassinate Cromwell?" mused Evan.

The soldiers took shortcuts across fields and kept a more than steady pace. They reached the Dover waterfront well ahead of Proctor.

He was later sighted on the edge of town but disappeared from view almost immediately down one of the many side alleys.

Evan was content to wait until he reemerged to board a ship. Evan put three men aboard the packet, which was due to depart within the hour.

The rest of the troop, including Evan, concealed themselves around the pier, ready to block off any escape.

The hour passed, and many passengers joined the ship. Proctor was not among them.

The captain indicated that he was about to sail.

Proctor had not arrived.

Evan was frustrated.

"We saw him enter the town more than an hour ago, but he has not emerged to board the ship."

"He is probably in one of the alehouses that dominate this strip. He prefers to continue drinking rather than board a particular ship," announced a chirpy Strad.

"There are too many shops, taverns, and houses for our small troop to canvass without giving our prey a warning. Proctor may be cleverer than we think. He probably told Maggie a pack of lies. His end destination may not have been Ostend. As we speak, he may be receiving his payment from his unknown employer," declared a disappointed Evan.

"Why not place men at either end of the street containing most of the alehouses and see if Proctor eventually emerges from one?" suggested Strad.

Another dragoon objected, "A waste of time. I know Dover well. Most of the buildings on this street have a back entrance into a myriad of alleys. It would be a waste of time. It would be better if we all adjourned to the nearest inn for refreshment and wait until the next packet is ready to depart."

Evan relaxed. "A much better idea!"

The dragoons stabled their horses around the back of The Sea Eagle and walked up the alley beside the inn.

Evan entered the front door of the establishment. He did a quick turn and pushed the incoming soldiers back into the street.

"God be praised. Sitting in the far corner is Harry Proctor, and facing him with his back to us is his employer. We have them both. Two of you go back down the alley and cover the back door. You two stay out the front in case they get past us. The rest come with me. As we go through the door, one of you move to the right, one to the left, and the rest follow me towards the two suspects. Then surround them."

Given the noise and the general hustle and bustle, the soldiers entered the drinking room of the inn without being noticed. Several of them got behind the suspects before Proctor recognized Evan.

Evan had primed his pistol, while his men had their swords drawn and pointed at the quarry.

"Good god!" shouted Proctor. "The army is here."

His companion rose and turned to leave by the front door. His maneuver put his face right against Evan's pistol.

Evan uttered words of recognition. "Sir Giles Bartram, what are you doing here in the company of an escaped criminal?"

"Sir Evan, as a businessman, I am trying to recoup what Lieutenant Proctor owes me regarding our mutual import and export business. I was trying to get my money back before he escaped to the continent."

"And were you successful?"

"Yes, I have just received a bag of gold coins. I must go and put it in a safe place. You will no doubt return Proctor to gaol to await trial!"

Evan knew he was being tricked. The money that Sir Giles displayed was most likely the payment meant for Proctor.

"Sir Giles, you may go, but you will be questioned later on your dealings with Proctor."

Evan was taking no chances. He escorted Proctor to Dover Castle.

Evan used the name of Colonel Tremayne, a longtime comrade of the castle's governor, to have Proctor taken to the dungeon, shackled, and fettered. He would be picked up within the week.

The dragoons returned to The Sea Eagle.

It had been a very successful day.

Luke would be pleased.

# 36

---

Luke had just risen for the day when a messenger delivered a note from Matilda.

It read simply, “I have evidence regarding Nicholas’s murderer.”

He left instructions at Mud Hill Farm that Evan should join him at Grey Towers, if he returned from Dover before noon.

When Luke arrived at Grey Towers, Matilda was still abed.

A snickering female servant took Luke to the room.

Any expectation of a sensuous greeting was dashed.

Already sitting beside her bed was Matilda’s brother Matthew.

After an exchange of greetings, Luke asked, “What evidence do you have?”

Matilda replied, “Nicholas was an avid letter writer. If he were away for a few days, he would write. Captain Neville brought me a letter late yesterday, which arrived by the latest packet to dock at Upnor Castle, although it was written on the first day he arrived on the continent.”

Matthew intervened, “Unfortunately, Nicholas was not a man for detail. The letter provides a motive for his murder but little detail of individual suspects, except for Harry Proctor.”

He passed the letter across to Luke.

The relevant passage read,

*I hope I am not getting myself into a difficult situation. Everybody that Proctor has introduced me to, I recognize as an active Royalist. People seem to forget that I was one of them and know most of the exiled Kentish cavaliers by sight.*

*I now suspect that the smuggling ring, for which Proctor was a front man for years, may also be a Royalist organization. Its constant illegal trading with the continent keeps open a steady line of communication between the court in exile and clandestine Royalists on the Medway.*

Then followed an addendum, which was attached much later.

*I am now in Ostend. I saw some of our near neighbors from a distance, but Proctor moved me away quickly and denied that they were whom I thought. But later, I saw Proctor talking most suspiciously with these same men whom we both know very well.*

Matthew commented, "You see what I mean? If only Nicholas had mentioned a name. Whoever he saw thought Nicholas recognized him and instructed their minion Proctor to accompany Nicholas home, and if he showed any sign of revealing any of this information, he was to be silenced."

Luke agreed and added, "At this moment, I hope my men have recaptured Proctor and a real interrogation can begin."

Matthew responded, "I must get to the base. The training is progressing very effectively. Are your patrols still active?"

"Yes," replied Luke.

"I will see you, sister, this evening."

Matthew left, and as Luke moved to do the same, Matilda rose from her bed wearing nothing but a transparent chemise.

Two hours later, Luke headed back to Mud Hill Farm.

Evan and his troop returned from Dover a few minutes later.

Luke had seen the depleted troop amble across the field, and his heart sank.

He greeted Evan. "I see your trip was in vain. No Proctor."

Evan smiled.

He whispered, "We did not fail. We have captured Proctor, and he was in the company of Sir Giles Bartram."

"Where is Proctor now?" demanded an excited Luke.

"He is shackled and fettered in a dungeon at Dover Castle watched over by the castle gaolers and two of our men whom I left behind to protect our interests. As it appears, more than one person is out to kill him. It was prudent to leave him in Dover where no one knows the situation. The governor of the castle sends his regards."

"You caught Proctor with Sir Giles? What was Bartram's excuse?"

"Plausible enough to possibly be true! Giles said he was receiving monies from Proctor, which Harry owed the smuggling network. But I think he lied. Giles was about to pay Proctor for killing Sir Nicholas."

"Good work, Evan! Keeping Proctor at Dover is wise. While you were away, John Headley revealed a lot of household secrets and pointed the finger at a senior member of the household as a possible would-be murderer of Proctor. To protect our prisoner, let's spread the word that Proctor has been recaptured and is in the Tower of London."

Remembering John Headley's comment, Luke told Prue that Harry was safe and in custody in London.

Luke could see the immense relief on her ladyship's face.

"Can I see him?"

"Unfortunately not. Apart from his killing of Corporal Miller and absconding from his house arrest here, he is the prime suspect in the murder of Sir Nicholas Lynne and may be implicated in the death of Frances Bartram."

Prue sighed and sighed—almost uncontrollably—and moaned, "Luke, why does the Almighty treat me so?"

Their conversation was interrupted.

A servant announced that there was a courier from the Lord Protector with an urgent message for Colonel Tremayne.

Luke took his leave of Prue and met the messenger—a member of the household cavalry, one of Oliver's lifeguards whom he knew from earlier assignments.

The trooper, Tom Archer, handed him a letter bearing the seal of Secretary Thurloe.

The message was enigmatic.

> *Within the next few days, you will receive alarming news concerning the Lord Protector. It will be false, but you are ordered to act as if it is true and put the whole region under alert for a Royalist uprising. You will await specific instructions from my top agent in the field. This plan will finally flush out the Royalist leaders on the Medway.*

Luke gave Tom Archer a brief verbal reply, querying to himself how he was expected to tell Thurloe's agent from Royalist conspirators.

He immediately sent messages to John Neville commanding the government frigate that had been put on permanent duty to protect the Medway and the two other frigates, which had been sent in the last week, to join it; his brother Captain William Neville, governor of Upnor Castle; and Captain Thomas Digges, commander of all troops associated with the dockyard, to meet at the dockyard the next day.

Luke updated his comrades. "Gentlemen, I have received news to expect a major disturbance at any time, which might foreshadow or even be the long-expected Royalist uprising or foreign invasion."

As if to validate his concern, a messenger arrived. It was the fisherman Billy Pratt.

"Colonel, I have an urgent message from the harbormaster at Queensborough. Just before I left there, he received a report that foreign troops had landed at Sheerness and overrun the partly finished fort, and an even larger party of foreigners had come ashore further along the north coast of the island."

Luke sucked in a deep breath.

As if prearranged, as indeed it was, a horseman galloped into the dockyard and was immediately escorted to the officers' meeting and blurted out, "The mayor of Rochester has just been informed that there has been a major riot in Maidstone with the mob shouting for the return of Charles Stuart. All government officials are leaving the town. He requests, on behalf of the mayor of Maidstone, that you send at least two companies of troops to suppress the revolt."

John Neville commented, "I will send one of the frigates to Sheerness immediately, if my brother can put some of the castle infantry aboard."

Thomas Digges added his response. "I can spare a company of infantry and some dragoons to move on Maidstone."

Luke held up his hand.

"Gentlemen, your response is admirable but exactly as our enemies expect. I do not know whether any of these reports are true. I suspect not. They are designed to divert as many government troops away from the dockyard and the Medway as possible. I would guess that a major event will occur in the next day or so, which will be the signal for all insurgents to move on the Medway, perhaps to enable large foreign ships to land thousands of enemy troops."

"Are we to do nothing?" asked a slightly surprised Thomas.

"Place your establishments on a footing to repel attack. I will send a single dragoon to check out the truth of each of these developments. If they were a ruse to deplete the troops here, our opponents would be well aware that we would check the veracity of the information. That is why I believe the real uprising will begin sooner rather than later, perhaps later today or tomorrow. Our opponents would realize that we would check out the truth of these alleged minor incursions and uprisings. Their time to act is severely limited."

The meeting was again interrupted.

An ashen-faced orderly entered.

"Gentlemen, news has just come through from London. His Highness has been assassinated."

There was a stunned silence.

Luke tried to conceal a knowing grin—a perfect ploy to provoke a premature uprising.

The Royalists must have received news of the Protector's assassination some time earlier, which had led to the series of incidents of which they had only just been informed.

Luke was intrigued.

He asked himself, "Who is Thurloe's secret agent who will instruct me on what to do next?"

He turned to his fellow officers. "Gentlemen, this news makes it imperative that we hold the Medway against any and all opponents. I will send most of my dragoons up the road to hold the bridge at Rochester to control the Dover-London road and passage further up the Medway."

Luke returned to Holt House to find it in complete disarray. The cause to his amazement was not the assassination of Cromwell but the death of the steward John Headley.

Prue was distraught.

Her first words to Luke set him back. "Is this another murder? John knew so much about the past that his death may have eased the worries of several Medway inhabitants."

Luke replied, "Prue, I have not had time to look at the body or examine the situation. I will give you my opinion as soon as I can."

Luke went straight to the cottage where he was greeted eagerly by the valet.

"What happened? Did you find the body?"

"Yes. I awoke this morning and discovered that Mr. Headley was not in his bedchamber. I had seen him undress and go to bed late last night. I found him in his study lying face down on his desk. There was blood everywhere which had effused from his mouth."

"Was it a result of a blow?"

"I don't think so. For the last six months, the master has been coughing up blood more frequently and in increasing amounts. I spent much time these last weeks mopping up after him. In the last few days, he went for minutes without breathing."

"He died of natural causes? Was a physician called?"

"Lady Prudence called her Rochester physician who declared exactly that—death due to blood filling his lungs."

"You don't agree with the diagnosis?"

"I had my doubts until I read this letter. Mr. Headley has not completed it. It was beside the body, and he had just scribbled across it *For Colonel Tremayne's Eyes Only.* I have carried out what I believed was my master's last wish that his letter be concealed from all except yourself."

The valet handed a scribbled note to Luke. It was short.

> *No, I wasn't murdered, although I did help the progress of my disease along the way. I have just heard that Harry has been captured and is in the tower. Perhaps he was an unworthy successor to his much-maligned father. I killed Frances thinking she was Alicia to save Harry from further trouble. Alicia was a curious girl who discovered matters that needed to be concealed. Take note of what I told you and unravel what has really been going on at Holt House since the marriage of Lady Mary and Sir Edward thirty years ago.*

Luke believed only part of the letter.

John was dying, but he may have speeded up the process with poison or taking too much of the prescribed medication.

Luke doubted his admission that he had murdered Frances Bartram. It was completely out of character.

More likely, he thought that Harry had done the deed and was covering for him. But to what end? Harry was already the suspect in two killings. A third would not matter.

Perhaps he was covering for someone else.

Luke reported to Prudence that John had not been murdered and that her physician had been right. He died from his breathing problems.

He was still with Prudence when an agitated Matilda burst into the room.

# 37

"Luke! The time has come. Save the Lord Protector and England," said Matilda.

"But he's already dead!" uttered a confused Prudence.

"He might as well be unless Luke acts now. Ride immediately to the army camp with five men capable of replacing the treacherous officers now training the recruits. You also need to surround the camp with as many men as you can muster to prevent any of them escaping should things go awry. These troops need to be concealed from any travelers using the lanes around the camp."

Luke was delighted.

His new love was Thurloe's secret agent.

"What's the plan?" he asked.

"The assassination of Cromwell was announced to trigger the Royalist insurrection. The Royalist officers now have two companies of soldiers who will obey their orders, without knowing they are partaking in a Royalist plot. Already, one officer suggested to the men that a mock attack on the dockyard would be good preparation for what they would have to do in Flanders."

"What exactly has the false announcement triggered?" asked Luke.

"Matthew has received orders from the Royalist high command that the local leaders will arrive around midnight tonight to take charge of the insurrection."

"Matthew is a Royalist?"

"No, he will explain when you arrest the real Royalist leaders whose identity still remains a mystery. He wants you and a small troop to remain in the camp to place these treacherous leaders, whomever they turn out to be, under arrest."

Prue was on her knees, praying either for the repose of John Headley or the sparing of Oliver Cromwell.

Luke had no time to enquire which. He was amazed that the usually cautious Thurloe had spread false news of Cromwell's assassination. It could easily backfire and provoke wholesale rebellion across the land.

Luke quickly organized his men and sent a warning to other officers in the region of expected trouble in the training camp and sought troops from them to augment his dragoons around the camp's perimeter.

As soon as it was dark, Luke's small group quietly entered Medway Court where Major Hatch was entertaining his fellow officers at dinner.

Luke could hear from his initial hiding place in an adjoining chamber the raucous behavior and the drinking of several toasts of loyalty to Charles Stuart.

Luke and his men entered the dining room.

Faced with overwhelming firepower, the six officers, including Matthew, surrendered without any resistance. Five were quickly dispatched under armed escort to the Tower of London.

As soon as they had gone, Luke, Evan, Strad, and two other sergeants from Luke's dragoons replaced them at the dinner table.

Luke asked Matthew, who was now released and had resumed his role as commandant of the camp, what was going on.

"I will explain all when this is over. Suffice to say I am Thurloe's agent, you must hide once again in the next room, and when my new Royalist masters arrive, give them enough time to convict themselves then move in and arrest us all, myself included. At this point, I do not want my cover blown."

Luke did not have to wait long.

About an hour after the junior Royalist officers had been removed, a sentry knocked on Matthew's door. "Major, there are two gentlemen claiming to be senior officers who demand entry."

"Show them in!"

Luke could hear the door open. The visitors entered the room.

Luke sensed the surprise in Matthew's voice.

"Gentlemen, I would never have suspected either of you. You have fooled everybody."

"Everything ready to go?" asked one of the men.

To Luke, the voice was familiar, but he could not immediately identify it.

Matthew replied, "The officers are with their men who, at this moment, are being woken quietly. The patrolling dragoons must not become aware of any undue activity. I imagine that you would want to move at first light?"

"Yes, a job well done, Major. You too have fooled the government agents, especially the all-knowing Tremayne," replied the second of the senior officers.

Matthew then surprised his guests. "Your mention of Tremayne reminds me of the need for security. Throughout this operation, I have been concerned that Thurloe had placed a government agent among us. How do I know that you really are senior Royalist officers designated to lead the insurrection in Kent triggered by Cromwell's death?"

The two men produced documents.

Matthew commented aloud for Luke's benefit. "I see you are not David Harvey, magistrate of the Lower Medway, but David, Marquis of Appley, major general in the king's army, and you, Sir Giles, are his deputy as a colonel of infantry."

"And you, Major, have been promoted to colonel to command the second unit of foot."

Luke almost snickered aloud.

Neither man had any military experience. They were incompetents.

Harvey's newfound aristocratic status probably accounted for his elevated position.

Matthew was heard to say, "Gentlemen, it is an honor to serve the king, but why did my brother-in-law Sir Nicholas Lynne have to die?"

"The fool Proctor! He agreed to help Nicholas establish his own trading network by introducing him to continental business agents. The idiot introduced him to people who were to a man part of our network—all of them active Royalists. Nicholas recognized most of them and myself, when I inadvertently crossed his path," answered Harvey.

"Did you not try to persuade Nicholas that he was mistaken?"

Sir Giles answered, "The whole plan was almost destroyed by Proctor. He blackmailed Nicholas, threatening to swear that your brother-in-law was a Royalist spy. He demanded from Nicholas a regular stipend to make up for the money he lost when I sacked him from the smuggling network. Nicholas had seen a lot more than he revealed, and with Proctor's inane pressure, I thought he would reveal all to Tremayne. I am sure that he would have but for his jealousy over the colonel's affair with his wife. But I could not rely on his long-term silence. I had to act. I offered Proctor a fortune to kill Nicholas and then intended, when he arrived for payment at Dover, to have him killed. Unfortunately, Tremayne's dragoons arrived before that little toad could be dispatched. I understand he is in the tower."

"And that is where you two gentlemen are going," Luke quietly announced as he and his men entered the room with pistols primed and swords drawn.

An astonished Harvey and Giles were disarmed and stripped to their underwear.

Luke then turned to Matthew and, for the benefit of the two traitors, denounced him. "And you are the greatest scoundrel of them all. You befriended me and betrayed all those close to you. As you are an army officer currently in the service of the Lord

Protector, I have the authority to deal with you on the spot. For you, no long wait for trial and ultimate execution. Sergeant, take this man out, and have him shot!"

Harvey and Giles paled visibly when Evan insisted, "But surely we can do the same for these two? They have documents confirming they are soldiers in the employ of Charles Stuart, and given the clandestine nature of this enterprise, they can be deemed as spies. You have the authority to execute spies on the spot."

A few minutes later, several shots were heard.

"That double-dealing Hatch is no more," Luke triumphantly proclaimed.

Evan repeated his earlier comments. "Colonel, it will be all over in five minutes. Let me dispatch these two. Their wealth will buy them freedom in these troubled times. I do not trust the judges and lawyers."

"There will be no such lawlessness," said a man who had quietly entered the room, followed by a troop of Cromwell's own lifeguard.

It was John Thurloe, secretary of state and head of the government's intelligence network.

"The Protector's own bodyguard will escort these men to the tower. I will be staying at Holt House for a day to conclude this matter and to explain a few things. Congratulations, Colonel!"

"Before you take these men away, may I question Sir Giles alone?" asked Luke.

"Yes, we will wait in the antechamber. Don't be long!"

Luke asked Giles, "I can understand Harvey's position. I assume he was always a Royalist, and when he inherited his title, he discovered that, in England, under the current regime, his succession could be challenged. He went to the Stuart court in exile, and Charles confirmed that when he became king, Harvey's title would be validated beyond any legal challenge. In return, he was asked to lead this insurrection. But, Giles, you have come from a long line of parliamentarians. You lived for decades in the most anti-Royalist establishment in the county. Why support this insurrection?"

"Power and money! Under the current government, despite my increasing wealth from trading and the gradual accumulation of land, it would take generations to reestablish the Bartrams as the most powerful family in the county. The Holts would provide a permanent obstacle to my rehabilitation."

"What exactly were you promised?"

"The Holt lands and the marriage of my daughter Elizabeth to my fellow conspirator, the Marquis of Appley. If you want a simple explanation of my change of loyalty, blame the mean and humiliating existence I suffered under Lady Mary. It was an emasculating and stifling experience."

Next evening supper at Holt House was limited to a select few: guest of honor, John Thurloe, Cromwell's chief minister; the widowed Lady Matilda Lynne; and the local military establishment—the Neville brothers, Richard Holt, a resurrected Matthew Hatch, Thomas Digges, Sir Evan Williams, and Luke.

During an excellent supper of cold meats of every variety, John Thurloe rose to his feet.

"I rise to toast two of England's most effective agents. One has a brilliant record of service to Oliver Cromwell both when His Highness was an army officer and, for the last four years, as Protector. His Highness has asked me once again to offer you, Luke, the rank of major general.

"Our second hero played an even more dangerous game. He was a double agent. Lady Prudence was aware that Matthew Hatch was especially close to the government, and she used him to pass on any information she thought potentially dangerous to her friend the Lord Protector. When the government became alerted to a potential Royalist invasion or uprising, I asked Hatch to play a double game. He convinced enough people that he was a clandestine Royalist, and he was soon included in their plans. He almost gave the game away when he saved Luke's life, but he managed to find a suitable explanation for his Royalist masters who, until the last minute, namely last night, remained a mystery. For some time, Sir Nicholas Lynne was suspect because of his possible dormant Catholicism, but Lady Matilda has since discovered that the chapel was maintained for his Papist servants and tenants and that he never attended any Catholic service."

"Ladies and gentlemen, raise your glasses to Colonel Tremayne and Major Hatch."

Luke thanked the gathering on behalf of Matthew and himself but also pointed out the dedicated service of all the army and naval personnel in the defense of the Medway.

Prudence changed the subject.

"Mr. Thurloe, I understand that David Harvey, now Marquis of Appley, Sir Giles Bartram, and Harry Proctor are all in the tower. Could I receive a pass to visit Harry? He has lived with me for most of his life."

Thurloe replied, "Lady Prudence, for security reasons, Harry Proctor is not yet in the tower."

He looked anxiously at Luke. "Colonel Tremayne, could you personally escort Proctor from his current place of detention to the tower as a matter of urgency but bring him through this estate on your way to London?"

He then turned to Lady Prudence. "Luke will then give you time with Proctor."

Luke glared at Thurloe—a not uncommon occurrence.

It was a nice gesture, but to have Proctor back at Holt House was a security nightmare. His would-be killers had yet to be identified.

Luke turned to the gathered throng. "Harry is a vital witness in our prosecution of Harvey and Bartram. There are so many groups out to kill him—including unknown assailants close to home, let alone smugglers, Royalists, cuckolded husbands, and the infantry at the dockyard. His visit here must be kept secret. Digges, none of your men must know of it."

Three days later, Luke took his whole company to Dover to recover Harry Proctor.

Every precaution was taken. Proctor had his feet shackled underneath the belly of the horse, and his hands were tied together with only enough slack to give him control of his steed.

He was forced to wear a large grey wig and dress in clerical garb.

Luke was on edge the whole journey.

At last, they reached the forecourt of Holt House, and Luke relaxed.

Harry was helped to dismount. His feet were now even more tightly shackled together so that he could only just hobble towards the main door.

Luke sighed with relief.

# 38

It was premature. A single shot rang out.

Harry fell to the ground.

Luke raced to the body.

It was a brilliant shot.

Harry was dead—a musket ball through the heart.

The shot came from the wood that bordered the house.

Luke led several mounted dragoons to the area.

No one was there.

Luke then ordered the whole troop to ride as fast as they could to The Cottage.

The shooter had probably disappeared into the secret tunnel from its entrance up an old oak.

Luke arrived at the cottage just as Barnaby Partridge emerged.

"What are you doing here, Mr. Partridge?" he asked.

"I am paying my respects to John Headley. He and I have lived on the Holt estate for thirty years. He was an old friend."

Luke was perplexed. The cleric's excuse was reasonable.

Barnaby returned to Holt House while Luke sent his men up the hidden passages to see if they could find a musket or any evidence of very recent use of the tunnel.

Later, Luke questioned Barnaby. "Before you visited the cottage, where were you?"

"I took my daily walk to the riverbank a little earlier than usual. I did not want to be around to see Prue fawn over that pathetic creature."

"Did you see anybody as you walked back to the cottage?"

"Yes, one of the soldiers from dockyard ran out of the wood. It was that rather rotund sergeant fellow. Did he shoot Proctor? Prue is hysterical. I cannot comfort her. I have sent for a cunning woman to give her a calming mixture of herbs."

Over the next few days, Luke and the other military officials on the Medway stood down their men.

The two companies of partly trained troops from Medway Court were immediately dispatched to Flanders to be integrated into the more experienced units.

Luke discussed the situation with Evan. "The attack on Strad and myself and the murders of Basil Miller and Sir Nicholas Lynne were the work of Harry Proctor. Although John Headley confessed to the murder of Frances Bartram, I suspect that she too was Harry's victim. If old Dewhurst was murdered, it may also have been his work."

"To what end?"

"They all thought Matthew was a Royalist agent. Removing Dewhurst would enable Hatch to take over Upnor Castle.

"What about the attempts on Caroline Headley? She has dropped out of sight since she went off with Charles Franklin."

"The Garrison Gang and others were probably ordered by Harvey and Bartram to put pressure on Caroline to make her boats available for their importation of arms, ammunition, and foreign officers."

"What about the murder of Proctor?"

"Barnaby Partridge did it, but I will never be able to prove it" was Luke's surprising comment.

"Why would a kindly old cleric shoot a man who has lived with him for decades? And could such an elderly man be such an accurate shooter? Strad is the only man I know who could have shot a man through the heart at that distance," said Evan.

"I discovered from his nephew Richard and John Headley, just before his death, that Barnaby was not only a brilliant marksman, which we knew, but also a senior member of the English army during the early years of the Thirty Years War. He served the late king as a staff officer to the Duke of Buckingham."

"What happens to us now?" asked Evan.

"You will lead our company back to Whitehall to await future assignment. As there are deep-seated divisions in this household, the Protector has given me a few more weeks to find the answers and perhaps bring peace to Holt House and to Lady Prudence."

Luke stood in the forecourt of Holt House as his company of dragoons led by Sir Evan trotted past heading for Rochester and eventually Whitehall.

Only Strad remained to assist Luke.

Holt House was now a mausoleum. It was semi-deserted.

Partridge, Linton, and Luke were Lady Holt's only companions. She was not seen by any of them. She took to her bed on Harry Proctor's death.

For a week, she would see no one, except the wise woman that Barnaby had arranged to bring her herbal calmatives.

Luke tried daily to speak with her but in vain.

He escaped this depressive atmosphere and went to Grey Towers, where his reception was rapturous.

He and Matilda made love undisturbed for days, and Luke, for only the third time in his life, professed undying love.

Towards the end of the week, this lovemaking was put on hold. The couple was joined by Matthew for the reading of Nicholas's will.

The male Lynne line was exhausted. Research by the attorney had failed to find any distant cousins. Therefore, the details of the will would take precedence over the traditional rules of hereditary succession. Nicholas Lynne left his estate to his brother-in-law, Matthew Hatch.

Matthew immediately made clear that his sister could stay there during her lifetime. She would manage the estate as he wished to continue his work for John Thurloe, which could involve prolonged absences.

"In fact, I leave for Whitehall in the morning," he informed them.

Matthew then turned to Luke.

"I am aware of the feelings between Matilda and yourself. If Matilda wants to formalize your relationship, you are welcome to make Grey Towers your home."

The two men hugged each other.

On the eighth day of her self-imposed isolation, Luke was summoned to Prue's bedchamber.

She looked very ill. The medication was not having its desired effect.

Also present was her brother Roger Linton.

Prue turned to him. "Roger, there are family secrets that you must be told. Luke, I want you to report to Oliver what I am about to say and to thank him for his protection over the years."

"Not you too, Prue! This sounds like a deathbed confession. I already had one from John Headley."

"It may well be," Prudence retorted haughtily. "Each of you know parts of my story, but to recount it in detail may help you understand what has been happening at Holt House these last thirty years."

"Something happened to you as a child!" Roger exclaimed.

"At the age of ten or eleven, I moved into the Cromwell household as a companion to Oliver's much younger daughters. One night another guest mistook me for a serving girl and raped me."

"Good god, no wonder the details were kept from me!" exclaimed the pious Roger.

"It became even worse for me. By a fluke of nature, even though still a child, I became pregnant as a result of this attack. As my delivery drew nigh, I was taken into Wales where my child was born. I never saw the baby. Father arranged for its adoption."

"Your problems did not end with you giving birth, did they?" whispered Luke.

"No, when I approached marriageable age, my mother explained to me that I could never marry. No one of the right status would marry a woman who had not only lost her virginity but also who, because of the difficult childbirth and incompetence of the midwife, was unable to bear children. The whole purpose of marriage at our level of society is to bear children and continue the family line."

"Why then the marriage to Sir Arthur Holt?" questioned Roger.

"Father and Lady Mary had become friends as a result of my rape. Father told me at the time of my marriage that it was Lady Mary's husband who had raped me and that Mary wished to make amends and marry me to her son."

"Didn't Arthur object?" asked Luke.

"Arthur obeyed his mother."

"But she was deliberately preventing the Holt line from procreating through Arthur."

"Yes. On her deathbed, she confessed that apart from helping me find a partner, and ultimately a respectable place in society as a wealthy widow, she was determined to snuff out any and every trace of Holt blood within the landed gentry."

"Where did Harry Proctor fit into this?" Luke asked.

"Mary told me that Harry was one of Edward's bastards which she had had adopted by her own sister. When her sister and husband died, Harry was brought to Holt House."

"If Mary was determined to snuff out Holt blood, why did she pamper one of Edward's bastards?" asked a perplexed Roger.

"She wanted to torment Edward while he was alive by having Harry paraded around the cottage where Edward could see but not communicate with his son. Secondly, she feared that Harry might marry into a gentry family and unbeknownst to that family, the Holt blood, *the tainted blood* as Mary called it, would continue. She would keep an eye on him. Barnaby told me that Mary had a third reason. She had become close to Harry's mother and hoped, for her sake, under Mary's tight supervision, he might mature in personality and character more like his mother than father."

"Why did you continue to pamper him after her death?" Roger gently asked.

"On her deathbed, Mary asked me for Harry's mother's sake to continue to keep an eye on him, with the hope of his moral rehabilitation. She also hinted that if this was not forthcoming, then Barnaby, who was present at the time, would deal with the problem."

"So Cromwell kept an eye on you because your rape was a breach of the rules of hospitality. He must have felt very guilty. I now understand why he sent me here. He did not want you involved in any more heartbreaking events."

"He sent you here following the even more shattering news I received just before my father's death. Father told me that Harry Proctor was my son, the product of my rape."

Roger was aghast. "Are there any other secrets that you wish to divulge?" he asked.

"Yes, perhaps the most important of all. The Linton, Partridge, and Cromwell families took action, which led to Sir Edward's castration, confinement, and ultimate lunacy. While Arthur was Edward and Mary's son, Richard is not. Mary was indeed his mother. On his deathbed, our father revealed to me that he was Richard's father and that he and Mary maintained a very close relationship for a long period. They were lovers."

Roger seemed in a trance.

"Harry Proctor was my nephew, and Richard Holt is our half brother," he mumbled.

"I am about to renounce my claims to the Holt estates as enshrined in an act of parliament and allow the properties to be transferred to the rightful heir, as he must remain to the outside world, Richard Holt. The secret of his true paternity must remain hidden forever."

Prudence started to yawn uncontrollably and struggled to keep her eyes open.

"You have more relatives here than Harry and Richard," added a sleepy Prudence.

"Our father must have begun his adulterous relationship with Mary soon after I was raped. The first child of their affair was a girl and not officially recognized by Mary as her own. That child is Caroline Headley. That is why Mary put up with her wayward behavior for so long and married her off to old Headley, whom, rumor had it, preferred boys to girls. Maybe that was the weapon Mary used to bully him and keep him acting in her interests."

She sighed and fell back onto the pillow.

"Please leave. I must rest."

Luke was apprehensive.

"I was right, Prue. This is a deathbed confession. What have you taken?"

"It is too late, Luke. I took the herbs in triple the quantity recommended, which I was warned would send me into a deep sleep, from which I would not recover. I took the mixture several hours ago, and I can feel it working. Give my thanks to Oliver."

Roger moved to the bed and kissed his sister.

He said to Luke, "I will stay with her until the end. Is there nothing to be done?"

He whispered to his sister, "Why did you do this, Prue?"

"Harry's death was the last straw. I felt there was nothing for me. God has not looked kindly upon me—raped as a child, mislead, if not lied to by Lady Mary whom I treated as a mother, and treated as a pawn in an adulterous romance between Mary and our father. In the end, despite all my help, Harry's evil streak increased with time. He was truly his father's child."

Luke had left the room and quickly found the cunning woman who worked as a scullion in the Holt kitchen.

"Woman, Lady Prudence has taken triple the amount of mixture that you prescribed. She is slipping out of consciousness. Is there an antidote?"

"If she has just taken the medicine, it can be reversed easily, but if it has been in her body for over an hour, nothing can be done."

"But with God's help, we can at least try," declared Luke.

Luke and the woman entered Prudence's bedroom armed with other herbs and slightly warmed milk.

Prudence was now unconscious.

Luke forced open her mouth as the wise woman introduced spoons of herb-infused milk down her throat. It was to no avail.

Prudence had a convulsive fit and vomited up most of the milk. Subsequent attempts met with the same result.

Within the hour, she was dead.

# EPILOGUE

Her body lay in state for four weeks in the family chapel to enable friends, neighbors, and, above all, tenants to pay their respect.

It was not the death of a woman that was on display—it was family wealth and power.

The new squire, Sir Richard Holt, guided by his uncle Barnaby, made sure that this Holt wealth and influence was evident in a most ostentatious display at Prue's funeral a month after her death.

It took place in the one church big enough for the occasion, Canterbury Cathedral.

Leading the mourners was the Lord Protector himself, accompanied by one of his daughters.

Luke was put out.

The Protector arrived in a coach surrounded by his bodyguard in shiny silver breastplates and striking plumage in their helmets.

He had protected Oliver for over ten years without this unnecessary pomp.

Representatives of the Linton and Partridge families followed the Protector then followed the aristocratic and gentry families of Kent.

Luke escorted Lady Matilda Lynne as part of this cohort.

Coming last among the gentry mourners was the new lord of all he surveyed, Sir Richard Holt.

Last of all was the Reverend Roger Linton who would conduct the service in honor of his sister.

Lady Holt's servants and tenants, including the Pratts, congregated at the back of the cathedral.

After the funeral, her coffin was loaded onto an ornate black draped wagon pulled by four magnificent black horses.

The Lord Protector provided a troop of his lifeguards to escort the wagon.

Prue would be buried on her family's Linton estates, well away from the Medway lands that had caused her so much grief.

Two days later, Barnaby Partridge was on his knees in prayer before the communion table in the Holt family chapel.

In the deserted chapel, he spoke aloud to himself.

"Lord, forgive me my sins in the service of my sister's solemn promise to eradicate all trace of Holt blood. The rape, which dishonored her marriage, turned a kind and lively woman into an evil monster, whom I willingly served. I kept my solemn promise to Mary to eliminate the last of the Holt blood should there appear no hope of redemption. I hesitated for several years, hoping, for Prue's sake, that the boy would reform. Thank you, God, that my aim was true. Mary has been avenged, but at what cost?"

He then left the chapel and took his daily walk to river's edge.

It was high tide.

He kept walking.

The Pratt brothers, who had been fishing some distance away from where they saw a figure enter the water, reached the location too late to save him.

The body of the Reverend Barnaby Partridge was floating on the surface.

Luke paid his respects to the body, dressed in military and not clerical garb, as it lay in the chapel.

He suddenly had an intuitive flash of enlightenment.

David Harvey and Sir Giles Bartram were the local leaders of the aborted Royalist rebellion, but they did not have the ability to plan it.

Barnaby Partridge did.

Printed in the United States
By Bookmasters